Paul Scott was born in London in 1920 and educated at Winchmore Hill Collegiate School. He served in the army from 1940 to 1946, mainly in India and Malaya. After demobilization he worked for a publishing company for four years before joining a firm of literary agents. In 1960 he resigned his directorship with the agency in order to concentrate on his own writing. He reviewed books for *The Times*, the *Guardian*, the *Daily Telegraph* and *Country Life* and devoted himself to the writing of thirteen distinguished novels including his famous 'The Raj Quartet'.

In 1963 Paul Scott was elected a Fellow of the Royal Society of Literature and in 1972 he was the winner of the *Yorkshire Post* Fiction Award for *The Towers of Silence*, the third novel in 'The Raj Quartet'. In 1977, *Staying On* won the Booker Prize. He went to the University of Tulsa, Oklahoma, as a visiting Lecturer in 1976.

Several of his novels were adapted for radio and television, in particular *Staying On* and *The Raj Quartet*, which was turned into a highly-acclaimed television series under the title *The Jewel in the Crown*.

Paul Scott died in 1978.

D1004493

PAUL SCOTT

THE CORRIDA AT SAN FELÍU

Carroll & Graf Publishers, Inc.
New York

Published by arrangement with William Morrow & Co., Inc.

First Carroll & Graf edition 1986

Carroll & Graf Publishers, Inc.
260 Fifth Avenue
New York, NY 10001

ISBN: 0-88184-274-5

Manufactured in the United States of America

Contents

¡Oh blanco muro de España!
¡Oh negro toro de pena!
¡Oh sangre dura de Ignacio!
¡Oh ruiseñor de sus venas!

Oh white wall of Spain –
Oh black bull of anguish –
Oh Ignacio's strong blood –
Oh nightingale of his veins –

From the Lament for Ignacio Sánchez Mejias
(matador), by Federico García Lorca:
translated by Arturo and Ilsa Barea

Part One

Edward Thornhill

Edward Thornhill died on the night of October 20th, 1962, when the car he was driving was carried away with the bridge near the village of Toroella de Sta Barbara during the floods that devastated many parts of Catalonia in that month. With him in the car was his wife, Myra. They had been spending a few days in Barcelona and were trying to get back to the villa in a small resort on the Costa Brava where they had been living since the previous April. The villa belonged to Señor Enrique García, the Spanish publisher, whom Thornhill had gone to Barcelona to see.

Señor García strongly advised them not to attempt the journey back to Playa de Faro because reports were coming in every hour of the disastrous effects of the torrential rains that had ended the long dry summer, but Thornhill seemed anxious to return.* He left with Mrs. Thornhill on the afternoon of October the twentieth and took the road to Gerona, from which he must have branched off in the direction of Vidreras and San Felíu de Guixols. Stranded for several hours at Llagostera they set off in darkness for a place called Cassa in an attempt to get back on to the Gerona road. At night conditions were even more chaotic than in daylight. Either there was no road closed notice outside Toroella de Sta Barbara or, as seems more likely to have been the case, it had been blown down and he failed to see it. The bridge there, over a tributary of the Río Ter, collapsed at about 10.30 p.m., which fixes the time of Edward's and Myra Thornhill's deaths. The car was noticed the following morning, upside down and almost completely submerged, about a quarter of a mile downstream of the place where the bridge had been. The bodies were recovered at mid-day and placed in the church of Sta Barbara. Señor García identified them twenty-four hours later and at once informed the British Consulate in Barcelona. When he died,

* Playa de Faro is the name Thornhill invented in his first attempt at a new novel he had been trying to write. It has been substituted for the purposes of publication for the name of the actual resort which appeared in the original manuscript of *The Plaza de Toros*.

Thornhill was aged sixty. His wife was twenty years younger. It was then over four years since the publication of his last novel, *Cassandra Laughing*.

All that was known about his work-in-progress was that it was to have been a story about 'two people who turn up somewhere in disgrace'. According to Señor García, Thornhill said in Barcelona that although the work had made no real progress he had now resolved most of the problems connected with it. Señor García got the impression that Thornhill's anxiety to return to the villa was due to his fear that his notes and preliminary work might be lost for ever if the storms continued as destructively as they had begun. Consequently, it was thought at first that the most to be expected from an examination of any holograph manuscript left behind would be notes for and passages from an uncompleted work of fiction that would be of interest mainly to his biographers. The actual examination, however, revealed quite a different state of affairs, although it was more or less by chance that the manuscript of the narrative that forms Part Two of the present volume under the title *The Plaza de Toros* was discovered.

It had always been a joke of Thornhill's that he visited Spain 'especially not to see the bulls'. For the last four years of their lives, he and Myra were in the habit of spending a month or two each summer at the villa Vora la Mar.* Señor García, being something of an aficionado, had a number of books on the subject of the corrida in the library of this villa which he rented to friends and acquaintances, but seldom stayed at himself; and it was in the study where Thornhill worked, on the shelves devoted to the literature of the bulls (supplemented by similar books in English that Thornhill had bought himself) that the manuscript of *The Plaza de Toros* was found, in a thick-spined, feint-ruled, buckram bound volume. If, as must have been the case, this work was written after Thornhill's visit to the corrida in San Felíu de Guixols on Sunday, September the ninth, it was completed in the few weeks between that date and his departure on October the sixteenth for Barcelona.

Before *The Plaza de Toros* was found, an examination of the foolscap holograph manuscript in the drawers of the desk had already brought to light the apparently unconnected

* Vora la Mar. Again, a name invented by Thornhill for the novel, now substituted throughout this volume for the name of the villa he and Myra Thornhill actually stayed in.

stories and two attempts at the novel about two people turning up in disgrace that form Part One of the present volume under the titles: *The Leopard Mountain, The First Betrayal, The Arrival in Playa de Faro*, and *The Arrival in Mahwar*. Among these papers there were, as well, autobiographical notes about the writer's early life. It was already recognized by those who knew him that *The First Betrayal* in spite of its third person narrative technique was autobiographical. Although the notes provided no positive evidence, it seemed fairly certain for instance that the girl Lesley in *The First Betrayal* who is sexually awakened by the young man whose name is withheld but who was, in reality, Thornhill himself at the age of twenty-three, was a girl he actually met in India in 1925. He probably called her Lesley because he had already chosen that name for her when making a second attempt at an opening of the novel – both versions of which it is safe to assume may be placed chronologically earlier than the composition of the allegorical *The Leopard Mountain* and the autobiographical *The First Betrayal*.

The supposition that Thornhill had begun to work on something intensely personal was therefore not difficult to make and so the discovery of *The Plaza de Toros* came as an excitement but hardly as a surprise. That Thornhill in placing the buckram bound volume among the books in the shelves had put the manuscript away as something that could never be published during his own or Myra's lifetime is borne out by the fact that in Barcelona he referred only to having resolved most of the problems connected with his novel, although in fact this full-length manuscript had by then been completed.

The novel he planned was certainly never written, but the preliminary stories, completed or scarcely begun, and *The Plaza de Toros*, a personal investigation into his obsession with the incapacity of men and women to love unselfishly with its curious and colourful imagery, that of the corrida – 'the last Pagan spectacle in the civilized world' – may be reckoned to stand in its stead. Although the separate papers and *The Plaza de Toros* were not conceived artistically as an organic whole there has never been any real doubt in the publishers' minds that they should be published together. They are, it is suggested, complementary and interdependent. It is, however, necessary to supplement them with a brief account of Thornhill's background. To do that the author of this preface depends not only upon the notes that Thornhill left behind (which, when used directly, are indicated in the following passages by quotation marks) but also upon knowledge gained of Thornhill through a long personal and business association.

Edward Thornhill was the only child of Frank Thornhill, a missionary, who was the eldest son of one Edward John Thornhill who came to London from Northumberland in 1870 and set up in business as an educational and medical publisher with the aid of money borrowed from his father-in-law, Professor Ewart Craig, a rich man as well as a distinguished scientist and lecturer in physics. By the turn of the century Thornhill & Company was firmly established.

Edward John Thornhill was a radical and an atheist. His early medical and scientific training, interrupted through lack of family funds, his work as a medical student among the poor of the north of England, had convinced him that the future happiness and well-being of mankind depended upon the dissemination of factual and scientific knowledge. An anti-colonialist, he cynically courted the missionary societies, printing their texts and eventually succeeding in supplying them with works like Busteed's Simple Arithmetical Method and Singleton's Primary English Course, adapted for use in Mission schools from Africa to China.

After the birth of Frank, his eldest child, in 1872, Thornhill and his wife had five other children, all girls, three of whom survived. In 1885 their last child, a second boy, James, was born. The Thornhill inheritance now looked secure, which it had not done before because Frank was a sickly boy whereas James looked like being robust. Because of his sickliness Frank, Edward's father, was educated at home by private tutors, no doubt carefully selected by Thornhill senior for the radicalism of their views as well as for their academic qualifications. When he was eighteen he entered the family business. The year was 1890. Ten years later he was married to one Hannah Blake, and the two of them were on their way to China as members of one of the missionary societies the elder Thornhill had so carefully cultivated for reasons of his own.

'Does it need an explanation? It's the kind of thing that happens. He had rejected his sickliness, his past, my grandfather's right, bright, factual world. In 1902, in a remote part of the province of Szechwan in China, Frank and his Hannah

10

had a gift from God of a boy child (myself) whom they christened Edward, as if by doing so they were giving my grandfather another chance at heaven.'

Two years later they were stoned out of the Mission House and walked fifty miles to safety where they both died of fever. The two-year-old Edward was cared for by Catholic nuns and later sent home to England in the charge of a senior member of the Mission and delivered to his grandfather, at the house in Richmond.*

Edward John Thornhill was then fifty-seven years old. His wife Gertrude was dead and his three surviving daughters married, 'two well, one badly, but all scattered'. The youngest child, the robust James, was now nineteen. Little Edward called him 'young Uncle James'. There was a housekeeper, Nanny Martin, who was Edward Thornhill's mistress: 'Not quite a New Woman because she was ostensibly in service, but New Woman enough to stand up for her rights in all matters that related to personal freedom. Sometimes she walked out of the house, taking Cook with her, but she always came back and then we had plum pudding again. It was, of course, a disgraceful ménage, but in all other ways delightful. I was happy there. I was happy at school, a poor left-wing but a good full-back. I fought boys who said my grandfather lived with a whore, but that was no skin off Nanny Martin's nose, only off mine. My grandfather told me what had happened about father. He said he wouldn't make the same mistake again. He told me I could believe in God if I wanted to. That's why he sent me to conventional schools. I was turned out of one because other parents objected to Nanny Martin. But we had enough money to overcome that kind of minor obstacle. I wasn't sure whether I believed in God, but I believed in the garden of the house in Richmond and I believed in Grandfather and in Cook's plum duff.† At first I liked and believed in young Uncle James, but when I was older I realized he didn't like me and never had, so I stopped liking him but still believed in him because he looked as if he wanted things. He was afraid I might get some of the Thornhill money. He was seventeen years my senior – a man of nineteen jealous of a boy of two. But then Uncle James was

* 'The garden sloped down to the river. Marvellous for a child.' (See: *The Plaza de Toros.*)

† The image of the garden where he 'first saw the little black hunchback' is a recurring theme in his last work.

the kind of man who couldn't bear the thought of anything belonging to anyone else.* He must have been as pleased as punch when his weakling elder brother walked out of the House of Thornhill and into the House of God. But who knows what agonies of envy Uncle James experienced as a child? Of course he had despised my father for being a weakling, and had hated him more than he despised him, and had feared him more than he hated him, and thought that the appearance from China, aged two, of the despised, feared and hated brother's son was the last straw. People are very complicated and mysterious. Poor father! I'm sure he never said boo to a goose, let alone to his tough little brother James. But there you are. There's a devil lodging in our shoulder-blades. He hunches us up with inexplicable miseries. When Uncle James was nineteen he wanted to go right into the business, as if it might run away from him given the chance. He wanted to get dug in before I was within sight of joining it too. He hated going to University. He spent all his vacations in the City, at the Thornhill office. He hated University so much he flunked out and was never so pleased in his life. He was reading economics. He shouldn't have read economics. He loved money too much. That Law of Diminishing Returns must have killed him every time he read about it. When he was twenty-one or -two he got his heart's desire. Grandfather took him in, and not at the bottom either. A year later he married the first girl who ever looked at him twice, just so that he could start in building up a thick fist of male children. You can judge what despair he was in when Aunt Gwendoline wouldn't produce. They didn't have a child until after the Great War (which he found a way of not being in) in 1920, when he was thirty-five and she was thirty-two. She didn't survive the confinement. By then I was in the business too, just. At the bottom. Uncle James said if I had to be a printer I'd better get my hands dirty. I wasn't any use academically. I read too many novels and too much poetry.

Grandfather must have thought he'd sired a bunch of duds. The child Uncle James and Aunt Gwendoline had in 1920 was poor John who became as good a business man as his grandfather. Uncle James was too grasping to be a good businessman. He nearly ran Thornhills into the ground buying up other firms. If I'd stayed in it we'd have run it into the ground

* See: *The Leopard Mountain.*

together, Uncle James buying the firms up and me letting them go to ruin. He died in 1946, just in time to hand over to his son, my cousin John who got a D.S.O. at El Alamein.* Grandfather, of course, died in 1925, the year after Nanny Martin had a heart attack in the punt and came ashore dead. When Grandfather died I was abroad, preaching the faith according to Busteed and Singleton in Africa, India and Malaya, to the schools, the missions and the colleges.† He sent me out because he knew I was no good at home and he thought it better to get me out of Uncle James's hair a bit. But Uncle James's hair was very long. It stretched far East of Suez. He wanted me out of it and out of the business, not just out of the country. I don't think I much resented his attitude. I'd got used to it. The business wasn't my cup of tea, anyway. They were the wrong sort of books for me.

Edward Thornhill was twenty-three when he went on this tour of Thornhill & Company's overseas distributors. It was in Madras that he had news of his grandfather's death and in Kuala Lumpur that he had a letter from his Uncle telling him the elder Thornhill had left him Five hundred pounds and that he was to come back to London at once or resign from the firm.

'I went home, seeing as much more of the world en route as I could. I wanted that Five hundred pounds. I went home only to collect it. I thought if I didn't go home I'd never get it. The day I collected I resigned. Uncle James smiled. Well, that Five hundred pounds lasted me more than three years, which wasn't bad going, was it? But then by this time I knew what I wanted to do.'

He lived in Paris for a while and then in 1927 he came back to England. He had written some poems and several satirical sketches of colonial life and one or two of these had been accepted by left-wing reviews. But he was already at work on his first novel, *The Dark Mission*, and it was in his then capacity as an outside reader for the house that was to become Thornhill's British publisher throughout his life that the present writer read the complete manuscript and recommended it

* 'Poor John.' John Thornhill who became chairman of Thornhill's in 1946, was killed in a car crash in 1950. Just prior to his accident he had merged Thornhill's with the printing and publishing empire of Thomas Broderick Taylor, Ltd.

† See: *The First Betrayal.*

for publication. A few days later he and one of the firm's directors met the young Thornhill over lunch.

They saw a young man well over six foot, broad-boned but curiously gawky and dressed in ill-fitting clothes. Although his manner was friendly and he talked about any subject that came to hand there was an inner restraint that seemed to be due to some underlying disquiet more than to shyness. He did not seem to want to talk about his work in any detail and parried questions about it so skilfully that it was only when the meeting was over that his hosts realized they had spent most of the time talking about themselves, and had done so in response to what had been equally skilful probing by their young discovery.

In *The Dark Mission*, Thornhill (drawing on the firsthand knowledge he had gained of the country as a representative of his family's firm) told the story of a middle-aged English missionary in Africa called Biddle who began to be plagued by dreams of God and the angels dressed in white robes but with skins as black as those of the men, women and children who came to his mission school for instruction in the gospels. Presently, Biddle found himself unable to teach them divinity because he 'felt naked in front of them in his white skin'. It also seemed to him that they were the figures of his dream, that he was therefore teaching the gospels to those who had given them to him. He took to drink but the dreams continued, and in the way that his pupils began to grin at him during the arithmetic and English lessons he gave in a drunken stupor, so did God and the angels grin at him in his dream. His Negro servant offered him a black woman. At first he furiously rejected her but later he thought of it not as temptation by the devil but as 'an offering by a black Saint Peter of the keys to the kingdom of an African Heaven'. Having slept with the woman he abandoned the Mission house, and made off with the Mission funds to live 'the true religious life of ease and luxury in Mozambique'.

There Biddle's dream underwent a subtle metamorphosis. The black faces of God and the angels reverted to white faces, but their white robes changed to black. He took a mistress, half Negro, half Portuguese, and then tried to sell her as 'a true child of God' to the young white man who narrates the story both as he divines it and hears it from Biddle himself. When the stolen money ran out his coloured mistress made charges against him to the authorities. At first the authorities took no

14

step but sent an inquiry to the headquarters of the Mission. Having obtained confirmation that Biddle was a thief they arrested him. He was dragged out of the bungalow shrieking 'Judas!' at both his mistress and the young man, but when the young man visited him the following day Biddle had become calm and sane.

He said, 'I dreamt last night and they were gone, all of them. There was nothing, nothing. Just the forest. Just the animals. Thank God! Now I can have a bit of peace.'

The Dark Mission was published in the autumn of 1928 when Thornhill was twenty-six. It was attacked by *The Sunday Times* ('Blasphemous, vulgar, disreputable'), *The Daily Express* ('Filthy and obscene') and *The Times* ('Curiously perverse'). Without these attacks the book would probably have got by with a few respectful notices and proportionately low sales. But the violence of the attacks promoted equally violent counter-attacks in Thornhill's favour, and within a few weeks of publication the novel had gone into its fourth impression, an American publisher had outbid his rivals, and Edward Thornhill found himself with what he called money of his own and somebody else's reputation.

In 1931 he went back to Africa after completing his second novel, *Incident in K.L.*, and was abroad for the next five years. In 1936, when he was thirty-four, he came back to Europe having travelled most of the world on what he called 'lovely, stinking freighters'. He brought with him the manuscripts of twelve short stories which were published that year under the title *Spades and Shovel*. He went to Rome, and then late in 1937, to Berlin. For the time being his interest in Africa and the East was exhausted. 'If you scratched my Gentile skin what kind of a Jew would you find?' he wrote in one of his letters from Germany. It was in Berlin that he began to work on the first draft of his anti-Fascist novel, *The House of Cards*; and it was in Berlin that he met the woman who was to be his first wife.

The allusions to this episode which occur in *The Plaza de Toros* (both directly, and indirectly in the character of the Eurasian girl, Leela), are, perhaps, incomprehensible without some advance knowledge of the affair, although the story is obscure because he spoke very little about it to his friends. The girl Mitzi, to whom he refers in *The Plaza de Toros*, was half-

Jewish. Her parents – a Jewish professor of Geology and his Gentile Austrian wife – were both dead. They had lived in Munich. The father had been arrested, having spoken out against the National Socialist Party to a group of students he thought he could trust. The mother stayed on in Munich but sent Mitzi to Berlin to live with her sister, a non-Jew like herself. In Berlin, Mitzi and her aunt had news first of all of the mother's arrest and later of the two deaths. By now the Berlin aunt was too frightened for her own skin to be of any comfort or protection to her niece. The girl herself suffered not only grief for her parents' deaths but also fear that her aunt would procure her arrest in order to absolve herself from any suspicion that could fall on her for having non-Aryan in her care.

Edward and Mitzi were married in the summer of 1938. They honeymooned in Paris. When they came to England they lived in a flat in Holland Park. About four months later Mitzi committed suicide.

'She was ashamed to have escaped,' he wrote in one of the notes found among his papers, 'and towards the end she created a fantasy that her parents were still alive in spite of the fact that she had received the ashes and an official note of regret. She said she felt that they needed her still. Of course, what she meant was that she needed them. If we had loved it might have been different, but what there was between us was my pity for her and her gratitude to me. At the time it seemed like love, but when we crossed the Channel and the last link was broken we both knew the truth, and then, after a while, I think she hated me. She was pregnant when she died.'

After the affair of Mitzi he went back to Africa and began work on the first of the trio of novels about colonial life, *The District Officer*. Meanwhile, *The House of Cards* had been published successfully on both sides of the Atlantic. *The District Officer* came out in 1941. It made little impact at first, but remained in print throughout the war and was reprinted again shortly after the appearance in 1945 of the second book in the trilogy, *The Commissioners*. The publication of *The Administrators* in 1950 completed the sequence. There was then only one more full length novel to come, *Cassandra Laughing* which appeared in 1958, in which same year he was granted the honorary degree of Doctor of Letters by the University of Durham.

During the war he worked variously for the Foreign Office, the Ministry of Information and the War Office, and travelled again all over Africa, India and Malaya. In 1940 he visited the United States for the first time and returned there in 1947, 1950, 1954 and 1961 on lecture tours. He was never reconciled to his Uncle James, who sneered at his nephew's literary success, and who died in 1946, but he occasionally visited his young cousin John in Richmond when he was in London. And it was there 'in the garden that sloped down to the river' that had been 'marvellous for a child' that he met Myra Benson. The year was 1950. She was at that time personal assistant to the editress of a fashionable woman's magazine, and was engaged to be married to John.

At the end of his 1961 tour of American universities, when he was fifty-nine, a friend who met him in Paris where he and Myra were staying before leaving for Spain described him as 'a bit stooped, as if tired of standing six feet and more high'. He said that the young people on the campuses had called him 'sir' and treated him kindly, 'like a man not yet quite old and not yet nearly grand, but give me another year or two and they won't know the difference'.

According to this friend of his Thornhill at this time gave the impression of a man undergoing a process of what is called agonizing reappraisal, reappraisal of himself, his talent, his beliefs, and of the work he had done and wanted to do. There have been suggestions that in leaving Llagostera in darkness he deliberately sought the occasion of his own and his wife's deaths – and perhaps a reading of the papers and an interpretation of the conclusions he reached in *The Plaza de Toros* may give support to such a theory. It is no secret that he had become a heavy drinker and his reappraisal may well have been made more agonizing by the depressive effects of alcohol. This view, though, is not the one held by those who knew and worked with him closely.

In his last lecture tour of America he said on one occasion: 'There are young men and women here who look at me where I stand from where they sit, and on their faces I see that young man's and that young woman's challenge to me to prove to them why they should take me and my work seriously. And afterwards they will ask questions calculated to expose me as a man of an obsessed generation. And this is good for me. It reminds me that anyway writing a novel is a private game, that all art is play, that we play the game in the only way we can, obsessions and all, and it reminds me that the last thing I want is to be taken seriously in my life and work. If you're taken seriously you're treated with awe, or with disdain, and both those are corrupting experiences for a human being. Naturally it gives me pleasure if someone says to me, Mr. Thornhill, I liked that last book of yours about the woman who stood by her husband through six of his adulteries and never once thought he'd not come back to her. They would mean, of course, *Cassandra Laughing*. If they say that about it they can take it as seriously or unseriously as they please. But I don't want to be treated seriously because I wrote it. I don't want to be asked serious questions about why I wrote it or what I think its significance is. I don't know why I wrote *Cassandra Laughing*, except that I was what I suppose you'd call obsessed with the vision of this mythical figure, this dark prophetess of doom, suddenly lit from inside by the knowledge that Apollo had forgiven her and that what she prophesied would thereafter be believed, and this making her so happy that she laughed and said everything would work out fine in the end. *Cassandra Laughing* was a novel about human optimism, fear, courage, loyalty and madness. I don't know whether that is significant. If you think it is don't tell me. I don't want to be elevated to a position of social and cultural distinction on the shoulders of my work. The work is all that matters. It stands or falls by itself. But it stands or falls as a game. As a writer I do not feel that I have any special duty to society or feel, as a writer, that I should have any expectations or desire or hope of improving it or making it wiser or more tolerant, either by example, entreaty, satire, castigation, cheers or catcalls. I do not see myself, as a novelist, as a man whose opinions on the burning questions of the day are of any outstanding importance. As a man in society I vote, pay taxes, have opinions and argue with my neighbour when sober enough to understand what I am asked to support or drunk enough to find colourful words to refute. But as a man who writes what is called fiction I play no tune and dance to none, for in that capacity I am concerned not with panaceas but with questions unsusceptible even of formulation.'

To those who knew him well, the image of him driving through rain and rockfall in an attempt to get back to the work that mattered much to him, even though he could call it publicly 'all play', is far more convincing than that of a man driving recklessly to end his own and his wife's lives. As a man, Edward Thornhill had no time for death by decree, and is unlikely to have signed his own warrant.

The Leopard Mountain

The Leopard Mountain was a wild uninhabited place where no white man ever went because there was nothing there except scrub and desolation, and no black man because of the legend of the leopard who thought of the place as her own and saw off all comers. The story of the female leopard who lived on the mountain and lorded it over the surrounding wilderness was old, unlikely to be true, but harmed no one unless he happened to be a man like Saunders, who couldn't bear the thought of anything belonging to anyone else.

Saunders was a scrap merchant who had quickly made a small fortune in the nineteen twenties. Now he owned most of the good farmland in the valley and held in mortgage a high proportion of the rest. There was precious little left that he could get his hands on that he hadn't already managed to. And it was about this time, after a native boy swore he had heard the leopard calling in the night, that Saunders decided a leopard, real or imaginary, had no business owning anything, even a wilderness. He made up his mind to go after it, kill it and hang its skin on the walls of his living-room as proof of the futility of possessiveness in all dumb creatures.

He needed a gun-bearer and tracker, and a cook, but there wasn't a boy within miles who would go with him. He thought they were frightened of the leopard. In fact it was Saunders they were frightened of. He lived alone in a bungalow on the outskirts of the town and nobody ever called there except on business. He had one servant, an old Kaffir who was stone deaf and, being uncommunicative, as good as dumb. Saunders knew that there were still some things that would never be his because they belonged to other people in a way that couldn't be got round, so he had taken a bit to drink in the last few years. The town boys didn't mind him drinking: drink, after all, was the white man's courage: but the rumour (put round by Englishmen who disliked him for his success but even more for his common accent, which made his success indecent) was that he was the worst shot you'd ever clapped eyes on, and the combination of whisky and bad aim was more than any of the native boys were prepared to face. It was clear to them that if the leopard didn't get them Saunders would.

When he got over the annoyance of finding no volunteers he announced his intention of going alone, and congratulated himself on saving the cost of the wages. He bought what supplies he needed on tick as usual from Ali Mohammed, borrowed a couple of spare wheels from his friend Thompson, loaded his truck and set off early the following morning.

Thompson was his friend because Thompson had nothing left that Saunders seemed to want and had an accent even commoner. His meagre little farm had long ago been taken over and absorbed into Saunders's holdings. Thompson always had been, and still was, up to his ears in debt. Since his wife left him he had had three mistresses, lost two and buried the other. When Saunders foreclosed on his property he had gratefully accepted the offer of a job as foreman of the junk and scrap-metal yard that had formed the basis of Saunders wealth.

There were no serviceable spare wheels in stock in the junkyard, but to give Saunders the two he wanted as an insurance against blow-outs on safari, all Thompson had to do was take the remaining two from the hubs of his last possession: an old farm truck that was jacked up in the yard on bricks, waiting for the new engine it would never get because the money put by out of what he could save was regularly appropriated by the court to pay off arrears of alimony to his ex-wife, a blonde woman now in middle-age who lived far away, in Cape Town, on what Thompson privately suspected were immoral earnings.

Thompson was a simple, homely-looking person with rangy limbs and large clumsy hands. An orphan, he had been brought up by hardworking, indifferent relations, to respect his superiors, to be honest, kind to men and animals, and never to cry but to face up to life like a man. So he did not cry when his wife left him or when his favourite mistress died, or when Mr. Saunders, who was shorter by a foot and neat in all his calculated movements, foreclosed on his farm. Thompson, who loved the farm, had had very few experiences of life that weren't unpleasant and he might have been forgiven for losing his temper when life dealt him this final blow. As it was he turned out to be the only man Saunders had foreclosed on who didn't threaten to shoot him, or black his eye, or have his liver for breakfast. On the contrary; to Saunders's surprise he held out his hand and offered to shake, like a good loser who had just had the daylights beaten out of him and blamed himself for his lack of staying power more than he blamed his antagonist for hitting low.

After they had shaken hands Saunders offered him the job at the junkyard. Everyone knew that Saunders had never been able to keep a white foreman for long because of the insulting wage. When Thompson accepted the job Saunders despised him. Nevertheless, there was from then on an association between them that to the outside world looked almost intimate. Saunders had never had a grateful victim before. They had all been either sullen, or pigheaded, and violent. The experience, being new to him, puzzled him a bit. He had an uncomfortable feeling that Thompson, in shaking hands, had put one over on him. He filed the thought away for later reference.

On the day that Saunders came into the yard and said he wanted two spare wheels for his truck Thompson had been working there for more than five years.

All that time the truck in the yard had been the symbol of his survival. Thompson was a man who liked to see green things growing around him and there was nothing in the junkyard remotely like that. Even the weeds that sprang up around the mounds of rusty scrap were brown and withered. But in the cool of the evening he sometimes sat in the cabin of the derelict truck drinking beer and reading the paper, the seat there being more comfortable than the hard chairs provided by the management in the lean-to shack that was euphemistically described as the foreman's bungalow; and when the light went and he had to put the newspaper down he sometimes dreamed that he was driving the truck back home in the dark, up the road to his farm, the new one he would have one day, a green and fertile holding that would be a good place to grow old and die in. He sometimes imagined, especially on days when Saunders had been less grim than usual, that it was in Saunders's mind to give him his farm back as a reward for his hard work and loyalty, or put him in to manage it in place of the red-necked German who looked after all Saunders's agricultural interests and in his cups swore vengeance for something Saunders had once done to him down in Durban.

On the day Thompson drove away from his old home on the farm to his new home in the junkyard, the engine of the truck died with a phut and a clank. He had a tow the rest of the way down the red-earth road, and in the flush of optimistic expectations for the future he called in the expert advice of Mr. Ali Mohammed's brother, Jan Mohammed, proprietor of the Universal European Garage that was on the other side of the road from the Universal European Stores. After inspecting the engine Jan Mohammed prescribed the brand new one that he knew Thompson couldn't afford. They argued the toss for a bit until Jan Mohammed agreed to see what could be done that would be less expensive. He proposed to tow the truck away, but Thompson had already seen the chairs in the shack and insisted on the work being done on the spot. In the end they reached a compromise, and only the engine was removed.

After a few days Jan Mohammed reported that the engine would cost more to repair than to replace, and sent in his estimate. Thompson considered the estimate and said he would let Jan Mohammed know. A year went by. Sometimes he called in at the garage to pass the time of day, to discuss the new engine and to make sure the old one was still there. At the end of two years the old engine had disappeared. It had gone bit by bit. There were pieces of it Jan Mohammed's mechanics found useful for patching jobs. The scrap value of the engine wasn't much, less in fact than the bill Jan Mohammed had sent in for towing and inspection and expert opinion, which Thompson still owed for. By the time there was nothing left of the engine that its previous owner could identify beyond all reasonable doubt, a telepathic understanding had been reached that the bill had been settled valve by valve and tappet by tappet.

By then the truck was supported on bricks to take the strain off the springs. One night a thief broke into the yard and removed the front near and offside wheels. He must have been disturbed otherwise what would have stopped him taking the rear wheels as well? What was to stop him coming back for them some other night?

So Thompson took to bedding down in the back of the truck with a pistol under his pillow. The hood leaked in the wet. In the dry the van was as airless as an oven ready for the Sunday joint. When he was flush at the beginning of each month he thought of paying his boy extra to sleep in the van so that he could get a better night's rest himself, but he didn't really trust anyone but himself to guard it. The kind of boys Saunders allowed him to hire to help around the yard and the bungalow were the kind who would sleep through the sound of the last Trump.

'You should get rid of that old hulk,' friends told him. 'You could get a couple of quid for it. If Saunders ever finds out what it means to you he'll have it for nothing.'

Thompson laughed and said that Mr. Saunders was a badly misjudged man. All the same, whenever Saunders was around the yard he found himself referring to the object of his deepest affections and of his most private dreams with an offhandedness that amounted to mockery.

'They tell me you sleep in it,' Saunders said to him once.

'Oh, they're loose-fingered lot around here, Mr. Saunders,' Thompson said. 'There's a lot of stuff in this yard they'd like to get their hands on. But they know I sleep in the back of that old hulk with a gun. That keeps them away.'

Saunders said nothing but looked at him with his pale expressionless eyes. Thompson had heard everything that was said about his friend and benefactor, but he put his trust in what he called their special relationship. Saunders, who knew all there was to be known about anything that went on in the town and the valley, and a lot of what went on beyond, must know, Thompson told himself, about the business of the engine and the theft of the two front wheels and how it was only after the front wheels were stolen that he had taken to sleeping in the truck. The look Saunders gave him that didn't seem to have any expression was, he expected, really a look of sympathy, the same sort of sympathy Saunders had shown when shaking hands back there on the old farm.

When Thompson heard about Saunders's plan to go on safari to shoot the leopard he was at first puzzled and then upset. He knew that he was round the bend himself about the truck, and that in this country being round the bend wasn't a disgrace, but Mr. Saunders was the last man he had ever expected to find gone out (as they said in Derbyshire where Thompson had spent his childhood). It was sad and incredible that Saunders of all people should want to go and shoot an animal that didn't exist.

Presently he heard that no boy would accompany his friend, and that made him sadder than ever. He told his own recently hired boy to report to Mr. Saunders at once, but the boy rolled his eyes in that infuriating way, packed his blanket and went home to his kraal without waiting for the wages Thompson owed him. He thought several times of going to see Saunders and offering him his company, but decided that it wasn't fitting to push himself forward. That was the kind of thing his wife had always been on at him to do. But the more he thought about accompanying Saunders the clearer became the picture of the two of them together. Today, the next day or the day after, Saunders would arrive at the yard and say, 'Look, I'm off into the bush. What about coming too?'

While he was waiting for Saunders he went through his tin trunk to see whether he had any suitable clothes for the expedition. There was an old khaki shirt that wasn't too bad, and a pair of khaki trousers patched by the girl he'd lived with and liked the best of the lot until she had died and had to be buried. There was also a pair of not too bad boots. He went to the emporium of Ali Mohammed and bought some laces and a first-aid kit with the money his boy had saved him by running away. He looked on himself as a man charged with the health and well-being of poor Mr. Saunders who was momentarily not in full possession of his senses.

Saunders came at five o'clock in the evening before he was due to depart.

'I expect you've heard I'm off on safari, Thompson,' he said, his eyes taking in every corner of the yard and coming to rest on the old van jacked up on bricks with two wheels missing and the engine gone.

'There's been talk around, Mr. Saunders,' Thompson replied.

'That's pretty rough country up there,' Saunders said.

'That's a fact.'

'You can get a puncture as quick as wink,' Saunders said. 'Now my van's almost brand new but it's the same make as that old skeleton. I thought I'd better take those two spare wheels. I'll be back for them in half an hour.'

When Saunders had gone Thompson went to the truck, opened the tool box and took out the brace. The nuts were rusty and took a lot of strength to budge. But within the half hour he had the wheels off and ready.

'They're here, Mr. Saunders,' he said when Saunders was back and climbing out to see what was what.

'Just pop them in the back,' Saunders said. 'Then I'm off to get a good night's sleep and an early start.'

'Good luck with the leopard,' Thompson said, when he had stowed the wheels. He put out his hand.

'Making sure no one creeps in tonight and pinches any of this stuff,' Saunders said, not noticing the hand but looking hard at him with the same grey expression as usual. 'It mightn't be a bad idea to take stock, there's nothing due in for a day or two and you'll have time on your hands.'

'Okay, Mr. Saunders. I'll have a check. And nobody'll have a chance at any of this stuff. I'll be dossed down in the old van.' He grinned. 'It's not going anywhere.'

Saunders drove away and Thompson went into the bungalow. He made himself a cup of tea and sat down to drink it. It was true, after all, what people said about Saunders. There wasn't anything a man could have he didn't want. Nothing was too poor, too insignificant, too paltry.

'Oh, God, Mr. Saunders,' he said aloud. 'I'm sorry. I truly am.'

For the moment he wasn't sure whether he was sorry for Saunders or sorry for himself. He had been taken in from the start. Taken in by Saunders, by his wife Gloria, his mistress Lily and that other one, Miss Rivers, who had been half Negro and called herself Swannee. The only person in the whole world he'd never been taken in by was Mary Dee, but she was dead and buried under the hill. He had even been taken in by Jan Mohammed who had known right from the start that he would get that old engine and use it to repair other people's. Worst of all though, he had been taken in by himself. He had allowed an image of himself to take possession of him. He had been true to the image but the image itself had been false.

He wasn't a simple, kindly man at all. He wanted a share of the world's riches as badly as any man you could point at with his tongue hanging out panting like a dog. He wanted a brand new engine, and four new wheels, and a road to drive the truck on that led from a gate with a name on it, 'Thompson'; and when you thought of that place, simple was the last word you could use to describe it. It rolled from one horizon to another and was as thick with toiling labourers as a hive with bees.

He took a long straight look at himself in the spotted mirror and knew that to get what he wanted he had to cheat and lie and swindle, and that the face he was looking at, being no more than a plain man's face, need not change one line, one wrinkle, to look like the face of a man who would do these things.

He went to the office desk and rummaged among the mess of bills and receipts and letters for any piece of paper that had Saunders's signature on it. Then he sat down at the typewriter and typed a note to Ali Mohammed (copy to Jan). For a while afterwards he practised Saunders's signature and presently signed the note. The note informed the Mohammed brothers that Saunders had decided to take Mr. Thompson on safari and they should therefore provide him with supplies, rifle, ammunition, sleeping-bag and everything he asked for, all of which were to be charged to his, Mr. Saunders's account. Jan Mohammed was instructed to provide him with a vehicle on hire, rental no object as long as it was guaranteed. The vehicle was needed because there would be one day's delay in Mr. Thompson's departure, owing to certain business commitments at the yard.

The following day, after eight, when Saunders had been gone for a couple of hours, Thompson visited Ali Mohammed's emporium. At first the storekeeper seemed sceptical but changed his tune when Thompson for the first time in his long life in the country shouted at him as any other self-respecting white man would have done. The performance was repeated at the University European Garage. Then, equipped and newly mobile, Thompson returned to the junkyard, put up the Closed for Stocktaking notice and had the first square meal he could remember since the early days at the farm. He drowsed through the afternoon, and at night slept the sleep of the just and the strong in the back of his new truck.

At dawn he woke, shaved, dressed himself in his stiff new safari clothes, and at seven was off, up the road, pointing the bonnet in the direction of the Leopard Mountain. As he entered the bush he sang Riding Down to Dixie, and Cut a Little bit off the Top for Me.

He was no longer a fool, no longer to be taken in, no longer round the bend about a beat-up old truck. For the first time in his life he was sane and level-headed and no man's servant. He knew exactly what he had to do. He had to get the leopard before Saunders got it. He had to get it and kill it and skin it and push the skin up against Saunders's nose and shout at him, 'It's mine. It's mine.'

Late in the afternoon he saw the sunflash of Saunders's vehicle. It was parked near thorn scrub. Finding similar shade he parked his own truck. Then, armed with loaded rifle and the fine pair of binoculars Saunders had bought for him, he went to a point of vantage.

It was Saunders's truck sure enough, but there was no sign of Saunders. The ground was rough but the truck could have been driven further, so Thompson knew Saunders hadn't left the truck to go on on foot, but was somewhere in the area.

He went back to his own truck and opened the case of Scotch whisky. For years he had drunk nothing stronger than beer. He wondered whether he should water the whisky down but decided not to. In a place like this water was more precious than gold. He spoke the phrase aloud: 'More precious than gold'; and was pleased with the sound of it and with the sense he had of himself as a man who understood the bush code of survival.

So he drank the whisky straight. He coughed and spluttered over the first swallow. The second went down easier. He lit one of Ali Mohammed's best cheroots, and strolled back to the place where he could watch Saunders's truck without being seen. Saunders still wasn't there. In half an hour it would be dark. He grinned at the thought of Saunders lost somewhere in the scrubby thickets and rocky outcrops. He waited until Saunders's truck began to merge into the uncertain light of its surroundings and then went back to his own. He knew he mustn't light a fire or Saunders would know there was someone behind the hillock.

Climbing in he pulled the tarpaulin cover down to the tail-board, lit the hurricane lantern, keeping the wick low. He opened a tin of cold turkey, one of potato salad, one of tinned apricots, one of Nestlé's milk. As he ate he felt blessed again by youth and irresponsibility. He poured more whisky, lit another cheroot and stretched out on top of his bed-roll and thought of Mary Dee who had had no one in the world to care for her except himself. Presently he turned the lantern out, raised the tarpaulin and looked at the bright stars. When he had finished his cheroot he stubbed it out carefully. He checked his rifle, placed it within reach, slid into his bed-roll and went to sleep.

When he woke the truck was full of milky white light. He sat up and looked at his watch. It was just past midnight. He couldn't make out where he was. When he remembered he began to be afraid. He listened. He could hear shuffling. After a moment he couldn't hear anything. His head was aching from the whisky and his bowels were moving, unused to the richness of the food he had eaten. He wanted to urinate and defaecate. He lay back, hoping the feeling would go away. When he was settled and becoming hopeful he thought what a fool he had been to leave the rear tarpaulin rolled up. Anyone or anything could get in with no more trouble than it took to climb or leap over the tailboard. He had to lower and secure the tarpaulin if he was to get any sleep, but, if he moved, the feeling in his bowels would come back again. He reached for the rifle and held it over his body. He would stay awake like that, on the alert. Anything trying to get in would get a bullet between its eyes. He felt brave again. He thought what a coward he had been for a while there. As if to test his courage the tumbling began again in his bowels.

Cautiously he got out of the sleeping-bag, groped in his haversack for some tissue and then got out, one leg first, and then the other. As he jumped, the butt of the rifle clanged against the tailboard. Standing by the truck he considered each shape, each shadow. He walked round the truck and then, satisfied that there was nothing there, went further into the thicket to find a place. When he had finished he felt better; but he also felt empty, shrunk, diminished. He returned to the truck, opened the cabin door and sat in the passenger seat. At first he felt safe and secure. Then he felt trapped. He moved over to the driver's seat. He went to sleep with his head on his arms over the steering wheel.

He woke. The sun was high. He got out of the cabin and went at once to see what had happened to Saunders. He had made up his mind to shout him up, to have breakfast with him. When he saw that the truck was still there and that Saunders wasn't he felt frightened. Everything he should have seen clearly yesterday he could see clearly now. Saunders had reached this spot twenty-four hours before he had. He had parked for the night and at the time Thompson had set out yesterday, one day behind him, he had gone off somewhere on foot and had not returned. Panic stricken, Thompson searched the sky for vultures. Had there been any yesterday? He could not remember. There were none today, but that proved nothing. They could all be on the ground in a tangled heaving heap, or they could all have gone, leaving nothing behind except Saunders picked clean to the bone.

He ran down the slope towards the truck. As he ran he called to Saunders. When he reached the spot he thought that the truck had that bleak appearance of a possession its owner would never return to. Inside, Saunders's bed-roll was neatly packed away near the two spare wheels he had borrowed. White ashes and charred wood showed where he had made a fire on the first evening. The sandy earth bore clear traces of his footprints. Thompson tried to make out from them what direction Saunders had set off in, and having failed stood still and asked himself what would have made Saunders set off at all? Why had he gone looking for the leopard here? It was too low down in the foothills to look for a leopard. And there wasn't any leopard in the first place. Saunders was crazy; and yesterday he himself had been crazy, off his head, maddened by hate and envy and greed; over a couple of spare bloody tyres.

He sat down on a stone and tried to work it out. Since there was no leopard to see, what had Saunders seen or thought he had seen that sent him off in search of it? What was there in this terrible wilderness to see except scrub and earth and hill and stone and sky? And how silent it was. There was nothing to hear either, except your own breathing. It was only at night that hallucinations came and you woke up thinking there was something shuffling round your truck.

Thompson stood up. He had got it. Of course. Saunders had woke that first night and heard that curious noise that wasn't really a noise if you kept your head and thought sensibly about it. And in the morning, because he was mad and thought the noise had been made by the leopard, he had gone out to hunt and kill it. And had fallen, and broken his neck. Or leg.

Thompson ran back to his own truck. He filled his brand new water bottle from one of the two-gallon cans. He threw some tins of bully into a haversack. Finding Saunders or Saunders's body might be a whole day's job. He checked his rifle and ammunition. As he was about to leave he stopped in his tracks and prayed for the first time since the death of his favourite mistress. Dear God, please let me find Mr. Saunders and forgive me my sins of pride and envy and covetousness and bring us both home safe, amen.

By mid-day Thompson was lost. He knew he was lost because he had just reached a point he remembered passing an hour before. He told himself not to panic. The mountain was deceptive. It looked the same from every angle. So far he had been casting about among the foothills. Now he climbed higher. Presently he was rewarded with the distant sight of the two trucks shimmering in the heat. They were in quite a different place from the one in which he had expected to see them. He fixed their position in relation to the sun and set off towards it, soon losing sight of the trucks themselves as the ground dipped and undulated. But keeping them firmly in his mind's eye.

At one o'clock he stopped and had some corned beef and a little water to keep his strength up. He was very thirsty but he wanted to save the water for Saunders. If Saunders was still alive with a broken leg he wouldn't be alive much longer unless he got help quickly. He packed up his haversack and set off again. His feet hurt and his head ached. He saw how similar the land he was walking over was to the farm in the days when it had been his. Now it was quite different; fertile, bearing good crops. He was glad that Saunders had got it and not another fool farmer like himself. Saunders hadn't taken good land from him at all. He had only taken it as it was, barren, hopeless, heartbreaking, and made it rich and yielding.

'I love you, Mr. Saunders,' he said. 'You are a man. And you are my friend. Hold on, Mr. Saunders. Just hold on. Help's coming.'

It was a rifle shot that led Thompson to Saunders. When he heard it he stood still and then shouted. There was another shot and this time he thought he had fixed its source. He began to run, shouting. Saunders was firing off to attract attention. He had found Saunders and Saunders was still alive. Coming to the top of a hillock he saw him. But he wasn't stretched out in the sun with his leg twisted under him; he was staggering across a piece of open ground towards a thicket of trees, pausing, bringing the rifle up as if it were a dead weight. Thompson called to him but Saunders didn't seem to hear. Saunders seemed to be shouting something himself, shouting to whatever it was he was firing at that had taken cover in the thicket. Saunders went down on one knee and reloaded, then fired again.

As Thompson ran down the hillock, momentarily losing sight of Saunders, he told himself that if you fired a rifle into a

31

thicket you did so because there was something in there to fire at. He heard another shot. Then he knew that Saunders had been right after all and everyone else wrong, except for the boys who claimed to have heard it. The leopard was real. And when you thought about a man like Saunders you realized that whatever the circumstances were he would always come out on the right side. He would always be in a position to say, I told you so, or if not actually to say it, then to look it, and to turn away unmoved by his victory.

All Thompson's fury came back, but it was directed this time at the leopard as much as at Saunders. He was angry with the leopard for being real, and angry that it should be Saunders who had found it and who would shoot it. He was sorry for Saunders, really. A man like that was never happy. Perhaps the truth about Saunders was that he was lonely and miserable and had to prove his superiority all the time to make up for it. He needed just once to be taught a lesson. If he could be beaten at his own game he'd go to pieces. It wasn't nice to see a man go to pieces, but Saunders had to be beaten. Thompson would have to beat him to the leopard. When he had killed the leopard though, he would give it to Saunders so that Saunders could go on showing his face, cheating people and ruining them and living his own miserable, sad, unhappy, dried-out little life. Only Thompson would know the truth. Between them there would be a bond. There had been a bond between them before but that one had been on Saunders's terms. This one would be on Thompson's. Saunders would never be sure where he stood with him. He would get those spare wheels back from Saunders, but it wouldn't just end there. He would keep all the kit and supplies and Saunders would never dare expose him for forging his signature in case Thompson told people the truth about who had really shot the leopard. In time he would be able to afford a new engine from Jan Mohammed. Saunders would have to pay him a higher wage, call him manager instead of foreman, perhaps even take him into partnership. And in the end he would get his land back, not the barren land he had given up, but the fine land Saunders had turned the old land into. 'You see, Mr. Saunders,' he said. 'I'm not as simple as I look.'

Coming to the top of the last hillock that stood between him and the thicket and the open space over which Saunders had been advancing, he went to ground. Saunders had disappeared.

Presently he saw him, so close to the trunk of one of the trees he looked like part of it. If you hadn't been looking for him you wouldn't have seen him. Stay there, my friend, Thompson thought, and leave the leopard to me. You're finished, played out and in mortal danger standing by that tree so close to the leopard.

He studied every inch of the thicket. For a time, then, he thought Saunders might have been suffering from a delusion, and he trembled to think what would happen to him if there was no leopard, nothing to shoot at and kill and hold over Saunders so that he could blackmail his way out of that letter he had forged to Jan and Ali Mohammed. In the back of his mind, too, was a little voice that whispered to him that even if he shot the leopard Saunders would still somehow be able to prove that Thompson hadn't shot it at all, but that he had. Thompson held his breath, praying for the leopard to show. There had to be a leopard. There just had to be. He brought the rifle forward, adjusted the sights, drew a bead. As he did so there was a movement in the bushes. It was happening some fifty yards from where Saunders was still standing looking like part of a tree. Thompson watched every stirring of every leaf. He could tell now just where the leopard was placed, where its head would be. There was another movement and in the second that he thought he saw the leopard's mask in the sights of the rifle he fired. For a moment the bushes were still, and then shook violently as if something heavy had fallen.

Thompson stood up. 'I've beaten you,' he cried. 'Mr. Saunders. I've beaten you.'

But Saunders didn't move from the trunk of the tree. He couldn't because the trunk of the tree was just the trunk and he had never been standing by it at all. Thompson ran down to the thicket. Saunders's arm was out in the open. Thompson stood near it. Then he knelt and parted the branches that hid the rest of Saunders's body from him. He pulled Saunders into the clear. There didn't seem to be much blood, but then people had always said there was nothing but ice in his veins. Saunders's eyes were open, staring at him with that familiar grey look.

'I've beaten you, Mr. Saunders,' Thompson repeated. He wanted him to know. 'I signed your name to a chit.' He enjoyed making the confession because he had always been taught to tell the truth. He offered the water bottle but

Saunders didn't take any notice. So Thompson pulled out the cork and let the water he had saved for Mr. Saunders pour out on to Saunders's unblinking face. 'There's plenty more back in the truck,' he said; and then remembered. 'You signed for the truck too.'

He looked about him. He and Saunders were quite alone. He spoke again to Saunders.

'In fact you signed for everything,' he whispered. '*Even for the bullets.*'

Then he began to laugh. He thought it was queer laughing when your best, your one and only friend was lying like that, as dead as a doornail, but having begun he didn't know how to stop, and when he thought about it he didn't know whether he was laughing for Saunders or for himself, or for pretty little Mary Dee.

The Stones were absurd: as far as he could make out (armed as he was, superbly, confidently, with more than two months' experience of these two cultures) neither Buddhist nor Hindu. Obviously pre-Aryan; palaeolithic. He had expected some jolly Kama Sutra obscenities. The caves were a sell too. In the light of the guide's smelly taper all you could see were some uninteresting red-brown stains that occasionally cohered into the likenesses of horned animals chasing or being chased by something indeterminate that had merged with the rockface.

When he got back into daylight he thought the random group of smooth monoliths looked even less worth spending time on. Phallic of course; the old john thomases of the jungle. They said the stone wasn't indigenous to this part of India so that it was a mystery how they had got there. You had to admit you'd do yourself an injury just dragging them up the track from Darshansingh; and whoever manhandled the Stones as far as the clearing and set them up in the positions you now found them in would have been too exhausted to appreciate them. Later, of course, there would have been some pretty gruelling orgies. There was clearly a fertility cult connexion between the cave paintings and the monoliths, unless both had been manufactured simply to get people up here to stare at them, have picnics in the shade like that mixed party over there and hand out rupees to the fellow who had been clever enough to think the whole thing up: a fellow like the one at his side now, holding his hand out.

'Thank you,' he said, making payment. 'It was all very interesting. When I get to Madras I shall write to the Principal of the Laxminarayan College in Durrockpore and tell him he was quite right. To pass near Mahwar without stopping off to see the Stones of Darshansingh is nothing short of criminal.'

The man pocketed the money and turned away with no sign of having heard the voice, let alone understood the language or the sarcasm. But it was a bad year for white people, so there was no point in getting upset.

He walked back to the place where you had to leave the ponies. There was more money to pay to the man whose job it was to mind them. He minded them by tethering them to a rail and sleeping in the shade of a tree; although, presumably, with one eye open, because he got up in time to sort out the reins.

There was no denying it: equitation just wasn't his cup of tea. The ponies he got never seemed to have any necks or, if they had them, they kept them low and left him without any feeling of having something to fall forward on. But at least, through perseverance, he had acquired the knack of getting up into the saddle without looking as if he were climbing a five-barred gate. From this superior height he grinned at the – what would you call him? Syce? – and started off without having, as it were, actually given the word, but fortunately at a slow enough pace (the pony's own) for his departure to look intentional.

The soft floppy hat that he chose to wear (who had never worn a hat since taking off his school cap for the last time some five years ago) because he thought it more suitable to his age and temperament than a solar topee (the specimen of which tried on in Bombay giving him, he had noticed, the air of a man who had just become badly lost on the upper reaches of the River Amazon) had come rather too far forward over his eyes for comfort and clarity of vision, but both his hands were engaged, for the moment, in trying to stop the pony from jerking its head up and down. While it jerked its head it frothed rather unpleasantly at the mouth.

'Rajah Sahib,' he said (the man who hired out ponies in Darshansingh, probably a cousin of the syce and the guide who took your money at the Stones, said that this was the pony's name), 'if you don't give over I shall beat your arse,' which he wouldn't have done for the world, having no crop, or even a conviction that the outcome of such an action would have been peaceful.

So the pony continued to jerk its head; but at least it walked sedately, and presently he was able to remove one hand from the reins and put his hat into a better position.

Riding towards him were a white man and woman. By a lucky chance the track was wide enough at this point for them to pass one another with several feet to spare. If they had met lower down where there was scarcely room for two and the ground was steep, he – as the gentlemanly youth of the trio – would have had to manoeuvre his pony off the track, cause it to halt and, while they filed past (she with a nod and a smile, her husband with a nod and a grunt of approval at the lad's manners) maintain his seat, keep the pony still, and generally behave with quiet but watchful assurance; manage to convey, in fact, his absolute readiness to provide succour and support (by catching her pony's bridle and saying: Steady boy?) should the lady's mount suddenly turn awkward; because she, naturally, would be several paces in front of her husband and utterly dependent on the tall young stranger for aid.

When the meeting was about to take place (in the broad part of the track, thank goodness) Rajah Sahib began to walk sideways and so he scarcely had time to sketch even a salutation. It was returned not by the woman but by the man. The confrontation over, and gone not too badly, he realized he had seen them both before in Darshansingh, although neither was stopping at the hotel. He had seen them in the bazaar, and again outside the town, in the field with the temple in it; the man with sketch-book and easel and black umbrella to keep the sun off, and she with a parasol sitting nearby on a little canvas stool, doing nothing. Since they weren't staying at the hotel they must either be living in the area or spending a night or two at the Dak bungalow on the road between Darshansingh and Mahwar.

The Dak bungalow was even older than the hotel. Years ago, before the British abandoned the civil and military cantonment of Mahwar, which they had found an endless source of trouble one way or the other (Durrockpore, fifty miles to the north, providing better facilities) the Mahwari Hills had afforded rest and relaxation for several hundreds of people, from April to September; and in those days the hotel, as well as the Dak bungalow, was always full, and Darshansingh gay – sometimes scandalous, what with the Stones and the caves and the picnic parties. So it had been according to Mr. Croft (M.A., Cantab) who had steered the Laxminarayan Christian College in Durrockpore through a number of vicissitudes for twenty years, had always sworn by Busteed's Simple Arithmetical Method and Singleton's Primary English Course to give a boy, even an Indian, a good grounding, and who was altogether very friendly if, in the event, demonstrably misleading when it came to describing the kind of place a young man could profitably stop off at.

The truth was that the hotel was empty. Given the choice of living in the depressing main building (a wooden construction that looked as if it had been shipped from Switzerland or the

Tirol and reassembled not wholly accurately, there being a balcony at first floor level that none of the rooms on that floor gave access to) or in a room in the annexe, reserved in the old days for bachelors, he had chosen the latter. There were three apartments in the hut, which was all the annexe amounted to, each incorporating a bedsitting-room and a bathhouse. The annexe was isolated, hidden from the main buildings by trees, because bachelors more than any other species required privacy. From the annexe he had to walk up an overgrown path to reach the hotel dining-room, and eat there alone, unless a party of Indians had come up for the day from Mahwar and brought no picnic lunch. There was such a party on the day of his arrival. They were friendly, asked him a lot of questions and had even heard of Busteed, although not of Singleton. But their place was taken the following day by a party of three men and two women who looked politically-minded and talked in voices loud enough to be overheard about the bloody British. He didn't mind, but thought it unfair of them to keep looking at him as if he were personally to blame.

When he heard that you could only go up to the Stones astride a pony he put his visit off until he had got some practice in and felt himself proficient enough to get there and back without actually falling off. He visited the bazaar, led by a syce who hit the pony's nose and dragged at its bridle, and next day attempted a solitary walk-trot-walk as far as the Dak bungalow and back. The Dak bungalow looked as empty as the hotel, but the ride was quite a success, although the walk was more enjoyable than the trot.

When he got back to the hotel and paid off the pony's owner he ordered a mount for the following morning early so that he could get the Stones over and be back in time for tiffin. In the evening he got mildly drunk, had his fortune told and was persuaded by one of the ubiquitous boxwallahs to buy brass and sandalwood souvenirs. He also bought some feint-ruled violet notepaper, there being no other kind, and sat up in his room until after midnight writing down his impressions of Darshansingh, and of the hotel as it presently was, and as it must have been at other midnights long ago, with the wood and timbers contracting as they were doing now after the heat of the day, but with other sounds as well: of lusty escapades (remembering his own) with sporty girls in darkened bachelor bedrooms.

When he got back from his abortive visit to the Stones he

decided to leave Darshansingh in the morning. The distributors of Busteed and Singleton in Madras would be wondering what had happened to him. He told Yusuf Ali to be back with Rajah Sahib immediately after lunch so that he could go down to the bazaar and book a place on the Indian bus that left at ten every day. He ought to be able to get a train the same afternoon from Mahwar to Kotimala Junction, even if it meant spending several uncomfortable hours at Kotimala until he could travel on south. When he reached the place in the bazaar where the bus stopped and turned round he found the little office closed. He thought he would do better to inquire at the hotel at dinner time. Perhaps even now, in this bad year for white people, you could book a seat simply by sitting in the dining-room and announcing in a loud voice that this was your wish.

As it was only three o'clock and Rajah Sahib was tired and docile, he decided to go down again in the direction of the Dak bungalow.

Although the road from Darshansingh to Mahwar was on a generally downward slope and tortuous in many places, that stretch of it that led out of the bazaar was comparatively straight and flat, and the last half-mile to the Dak bungalow, with its avenue of trees, and wide strips of sandy earth on both sides of the metalled surface, was a perfect place to give a pony its head. He decided to have another go at trotting as soon as he came to it, and gave Rajah Sahib ample warning of his intention.

He had now become quite attached to the bony animal and this afternoon hardly noticed the height from the ground. Although the muscles in his legs were still inclined to show a spasmodic life of their own for several minutes after dismounting, today they didn't ache too badly and the feeling that his riding muscles were hardening rather pleased him. He pulled the brim of his hat down over his nose to show he hadn't a care. The hat was made of green tweedy cloth, his shirt was of blue cotton and his trousers of tropical khaki twill. He knew he must look pretty comic, but this was the only way to look when you were stuck up on top of a ribby horse like this one.

As he neared the bend that led round to the long straight section of road he thought it would be a good idea to enter the straight already on the go, because then, who knew, Rajah Sahib might develop a turn of real speed and the rider a real sense of balance, and it would be a pity to leave Darshansingh without having put man and mount to a proper test. So he tapped Rajah Sahib's flanks with the heel of each shoe, and then tapped again, the first tap obviously not having been felt. The second tap caused Rajah Sahib to come to a standstill. He kicked with both heels and shook the reins and said, 'Move, you bloody dope.' The pony began to skitter. Another kick set it in motion, not quite at a trot, nor yet at a walk. Its legs were probably moving in the wrong order. But presently Rajah Sahib seemed to get the idea, and at the same time, quite fortuitously, the rider got the knack of rising and falling in rhythm with the saddle. What a marvellous feeling it was. 'Oh, boy!' he shouted. 'That's it! That's it!' and they rounded the bend going steady if not exactly strong. Ahead, galloping towards them was another pony ridden by a girl.

It may have been the attraction of one animal for another, or the jealous instinct of that animal to match a performance that threatened to put its own in the shade; or it may have been his own delirious sense of achievement, his whoops and his heel thuds, that turned Rajah Sahib from an obstinate nag into a reincarnation of some distant forebear long since dead on a field of glory in Arabia. Whatever it was, Rajah Sahib put himself at the stretch and headed straight for his rival with teeth that were probably bared judging from the flecks of spittle.

This swerve, this apparently intentional cutting in on the other rider's territory was, he knew, quite unforgivable. He tugged hard on the left rein, with no effect, and then tugged hard on both, an action that brought Rajah Sahib's head up but didn't stop him galloping and closing rapidly. They were close enough now (and he sufficiently alarmed to look hard and straight at his victim) for him to see that the girl was reining in and shouting something. But seeing itself charged her pony took fright and got up on its hind legs. At this show of retaliation Rajah Sahib veered away at such a sharp angle that he lost a stirrup and a rein, and it was probably this – the feeling of there being only half a rider – that made Rajah Sahib cavort, buck and set off at a brisk gallop leaving him on the ground momentarily stunned.

When he came to his senses the girl was still mounted, patting her pony's neck. She looked very young, not more than eighteen or nineteen. Her cheeks were flushed, her hair very fair and her eyes very blue. Her expression was one of contempt.

Whatever she had thought him when he first appeared – a young man maddened by the heady air of the hills, a tribesman sweeping down on her from the steppes of Central Asia – she obviously knew now that he was simply an idiot, dangerous on horseback but of no account off.

He got into a sitting position and smiled at her.

'I'm sorry about that,' he said. 'The damn' thing developed a mind of its own. Are you all right?'

Actually she didn't look half bad. She might even turn out to be pretty dressed like a girl instead of in a white shirt and fawn jodhpurs. She looked quite capable of coming and beating him over the head with her crop, but on the other hand she also looked capable of putting her own head in the air and galloping off. So far she had done neither.

'From the way you were acting,' she said, 'I wouldn't have thought you cared who was all right and who wasn't.'

She had a hard little voice. Using it seemed to remind her that she was over her fright and really in a very bad temper.

'If you can't do a simple thing like ride an old hack like that without nearly killing people,' she pointed out, 'you ought to take it into a field and fall off there. Or try walking.'

Before he could think of anything suitable to say she had guided her pony round with a lot of graceful expertise and set off at a trot and then a canter in the direction of the bazaar.

The Dak bungalow lay back from the road in the shade of some big old trees whose names he hadn't yet learned. It was no longer deserted. On the open ground immediately in front of the bungalow Rajah Sahib was cropping the grass and being laughed at by three or four Indians in white uniforms and broad sashes; obviously members of the bungalow staff. When they saw him limping towards them they gave him a cheer. One of them caught hold of Rajah Sahib's bridle and led him over.

'That's very civil of you,' he said. 'Here is a chip.' He handed out a soiled rupee note. The man said, 'Salaam, Huzoor,' and then added something voluble, very expressive, word for word unintelligible but clearly having to do with the sudden alarming sight of a runaway horse and the gallant action of the chokra (the grinning ten-year-old boy who now came forward) who had somehow managed to stop and pacify the fiery animal.

'Then you should give the chip to the chokra,' he said, making a guess and pointing from the man who held the rupee to the boy who really deserved it if he had understood the story correctly and the story was to be believed. In the end he parted with another rupee, knowing that only his Uncle would have felt mortified at such careless and random expenditure of the firm's money. The next problem was how to get back on. The foot that had to go into the stirrup first was on the leg that was hurt. It was difficult to raise the leg and bend it at the knee. For a while all the help he got was good-natured advice that he suspected would be vulgar in translation, but then they gathered round him and hoisted him up with more strength than was quite necessary. The chokra stood by Rajah Sahib's head as if waiting the sign to let slip.

'I say. Just a moment there.'

He looked round. The man who had called – much too loudly to sound polite – was coming down the steps from the verandah of the Dak bungalow. The servants stopped grinning.

'Did that pony come in by itself?'

He was still some distance away. He would have to come nearer before he got a reply.

'The reason I ask,' he said, 'is that I saw this pony about five minutes ago on the grass here and wondered who it belonged to.'

'It belongs to a man called Yusuf Ali.'

'But you're riding it.'

'That's right.'

The man was tall and bony. Below thinning sandy-grey hair his prominent forehead and bushy eyebrows were counter-balanced by a clipped pepper-and-salt moustache and a jutting chin.

'I take it you mean you've hired it from a man called Yusuf Ali.'

'Why do you ask?'

'I ask because a pony doesn't usually bolt without a reason. Where did you come off?'

'About half a mile up the road.'

'How long ago?'

'Ten minutes.'

'Then you must have seen my daughter.'

42

'Oh. Is that who it was?'

'Am I to assume from your tone that whatever made this one bolt didn't make hers bolt too? You may appreciate that as her father I'm naturally anxious to know.'

'Oh, yes, you can certainly assume that.'

'Are you by any chance an officer?'

'No.'

'I see. Perhaps you would tell me your name?'

'My name,' he said, lifting his hat and kicking Rajah Sahib into action, 'is Busteed-Singleton.'

In the bazaar he thought he saw the girl's pony being held by a little boy, but there was no sign of the girl herself. She was probably shopping and beating somebody's prices down. How unsufferable the English were abroad. His grandfather was quite right. Colonials were hell. The girl's father was almost certainly Army, and what had riled him more than anything else was not being called sir, and being talked to straight by a man much younger than himself. It was a pity he would probably never know he'd been palmed off with a false name.

When he got back to the hotel Yusuf Ali's boy was waiting. Getting off was easier than getting on. He handed over the reins and some more money, gave Rajah Sahib a valedictory pat on the nose and limped down to the annexe. After his bath he went back to the hotel and sat on the verandah and ordered beer. He asked about a seat on tomorrow's bus. The bearer said he would see. The verandah overlooked the grounds at the front of the hotel. The smells of evening were peculiar but not unpleasant, and it was now cool enough to wear a jacket. The Indians who had been picnicking at the Stones that morning arrived before dark and made a lot of noise without directing any of it at him.

Over dinner (brown Windsor soup, meat and two veg., tinned peaches) he asked about the bus again. The waiter said he would see. A quarter of an hour later the waiter returned holding an envelope. He said it had been delivered by hand and was it for the Sahib? If it wasn't for the Sahib the boy was waiting and would take it back. It was addressed to – Busteed-Singleton, Esq.

There were two temptations: to hand it back and tell the waiter he ought to know his name by now; or to open it. The latter temptation proved stronger. So he nodded and the waiter went away. The waiter probably couldn't read the name anyway.

The letter went:

'Dear Busteed-Singleton,

My daughter has now told me of this afternoon's events. I propose to call on you at the hotel, where I fancy you must be staying, tomorrow morning at ten o'clock.

Yours truly,
Something Clubby-Smith.'

Clubby-Smith? Climpy-Smith? No matter. At ten in the morning the most Clubby-Smith would see of him would be his rear view climbing into the bus.

But when the waiter who had promised to see came back and said that he would go down to the bus station in the morning and reserve a seat for the Sahib he said, 'No I've decided to stay for another day.'

There were some experiences that not only shouldn't be run away from but which were potentially too interesting to miss. He was filled with curiosity. Who could tell but that Clubby-Smith, notwithstanding that this was the year 1925, would come armed with a horsewhip?

The name on the card that a bearer brought to the annexe at five past ten the next morning was Major W. A. Clipsby-Smith, M.C.

What a tongue-twister. Clibsby-Sbith, Clwpbsy-Smith. If the W stood for William it made it worse; and Bill worse still. On his way to the main building (limping more than he needed to) he decided to say no more in greeting than 'Good morning.'

Clipsby-Smith was standing on the verandah without a horsewhip, but with a stout stick, admiring the view of the Mahwari Hills. He was wearing a check shirt and flannel trousers and was bare-headed. On leave he was undoubtedly a great walker. He stood as walkers do, left hand on hip, left leg crossed over right, leaning his weight on the stick which he had in his right hand. Hearing dot-and-carry footsteps he uncurled himself and turned round, presenting the formidable brow and chin. Close to, and in the morning light, his eyes, deepset though they were, looked as blue as his daughter's.

'Good morning,' he said. 'You got my note?'

'Yes, I got it last night.'

'Good. Then you weren't puzzled by my card just now.'

'No. I was expecting you.'

'These chaps here didn't seem to know who I wanted, but they said there was only one chap staying here so I knew it must be you. Look, Singleton. I wonder whether you would be good enough to tell me what happened yesterday from your point of view?'

'I thought your daughter had told you.'

'She did. But I want to hear your side before I say anything.'

'I don't know about my side. It was all quite simple. The pony I was riding or trying to ride made straight for hers then veered away and left me on the ground.'

'Yes, I see. Look here, I won't pretend your attitude yesterday didn't annoy me, but after I'd spoken to my daughter I realized you might have had cause to be abrupt with me, especially after you knew she and I were related. You're new to the country, aren't you?'

'Comparatively.'

'Not much of a horseman either. I could see that for myself yesterday. And I thought you were just being insolent but as soon as my daughter told me your pony came straight at her I felt she should have seen for herself what the trouble was. What she did was unforgivable. Leaving you in the road like that. Directly I got her to admit that the first thing you did was apologize and ask if she was all right I sat down and wrote that note. And I've told Lesley that if I can persuade you to call on my wife and myself this afternoon and have some tea she's to apologize to you personally.'

'I don't think that would be very fair.'

'Why not?'

'Well I did nearly run her down, and she did wait to see how I was.'

'The pony nearly rode her down. I don't say you were entirely innocent in the matter. Could make out a case advising more caution and less high spirits until you know horses better. But these hill ponies have iron mouths and wills like mules, and you weren't to know that, whereas Lesley was. She took unnecessary fright and unnecessary umbrage. If she'd been a man instead of a girl, well, all right, she'd have cursed you up hill and down, but at least she'd have got off to see you weren't badly damaged and then gone after your mount.'

'Yes, but she is a girl.'

'When you're in the saddle that's not a distinction you can

45

always afford to make. Perhaps I'm being hard on her, but she's at a headstrong age and I've told her more than once I won't tolerate bad manners in these sort of circumstances. How was she to know you weren't concussed?'

'Well I sat up.'

'Your sticking up for her does you credit, Singleton, and if it would embarrass you to have her apologize we'll say no more about it. I think you can take it she is sorry. It's not the kind of thing she's likely to do again in a hurry. But if you're not otherwise engaged Mrs. Clipsby-Smith and I would welcome you to tea at the Dak bungalow.' He smiled. 'Although I don't recommend your riding down with that leg of yours. You'd better come in a gharry. How is it by the way?'

'Oh, much better. The bruising has come out.'

'Ah well, you're on the mend. If you're here for a few days more we might get up a picnic. There's not much doing here for young people. We're going on to Mussoorie presently. But we've got a motor with us so we could run down through Mahwar to the Kotimala Lakes.'

'I'm afraid I'm off tomorrow.'

Clipsby-Smith looked quite disappointed.

'That's a pity,' he said. 'Never mind. Shall we expect you this afternoon?'

'Thank you very much.'

'Say four o'clock.'

Clipsby-Smith offered his hand. When they had shaken he said, 'By the way, how old are you, Singleton?'

'Not quite twenty-three.'

'That's about what I thought. The fact is, although we rather crossed sabres yesterday, I like a chap who won't be bullied, and I was bullying you a bit wasn't I? Failing of mine. But no more of that. I know you appreciate the anxiety I felt. Until four o'clock then.'

All of which showed that you should never judge by appearances. Old Clipsby-Smith wasn't a bad chap after all, although you had to recognize that behind the apology were some pretty complicated motives. In the first place Clipsby-Smith was a snob. Faced by a young man with the right sort of accent and a double-barrelled name (imaginary though it was) and a built-in resistance to being bullied, Clipsby-Smith had probably gone searching through the Army List or whatever it was called to see whether he had tried to browbeat the son of a general or a relation of the Viceroy. What a laugh it would be if there actually were a Busteed-Singleton, some pot on the General Staff with a row of ribbons and connexions in the House of Lords. In the second place, apart from being a snob, Clipsby-Smith no doubt believed (especially in this difficult year) in white solidarity. The Clipsby-Smiths, young 'Busteed-Singleton' and the elderly man who sat in the fields and painted while the woman looked on, were the only Europeans in the district. In the third place, Clipsby-Smith was a father with a marriageable daughter. It didn't matter if you'd nearly killed her so long as you'd also apologized and asked if she was all right as soon as you'd got your breath back. Her bad manners were then the only flies in the imperial ointment.

Poor Lesley! She hadn't acted as a white man should. He almost felt sorry for her. Feeling like that towards her he remembered his first impression: that she didn't look half bad and might even be pretty dressed like a girl. He wondered whether she had cried herself to sleep last night at the injustice of it all, and with what shame and misery she anticipated the hour of four o'clock. The kindest thing to do would be to beg off, to send a note down after lunch saying his leg was worse or that he had been called away. But the Clipsby-Smiths would know there wasn't another bus until ten in the morning, and a plea of increased lameness would inevitably result in Lesley being brought to the hotel by her father with some kind of offering for the invalid that she would be forced to hand over with every sign of being humbled and sorry for what she had done or rather failed to do, even if she weren't made to apologize in so many words. The kindest thing to do after all, then, would be to go to tea and be nice to her, even show her that if he had to be left to his fate by a girl he'd rather have been left to it by her than anyone else he could think of, now that they knew each other better.

And so at half-past three he sent a bearer down to the bazaar to fetch a horse tonga, and at a quarter to four he set out in one of these jingling and smelly contraptions to take tea with the Clipsby-Smiths under the treacherous but now indispensable banner of his assumed name. Perhaps lacking the nerve, he realized, he had let go by the opportunity to come clean about 'Busteed-Singleton'. But he would be leaving Darshan-singh tomorrow, so what did it really matter? Actually it was a bit of a lark. During the journey he decided to say 'Ned' if they asked him what they should call him, and worked out a family history that rested upon a quite fictitious but interesting alliance between the daughter of Professor Busteed and the son of Professor Singleton whose famous text books he now had the honour of helping to promote abroad on behalf of the eminent Victorian printer and publisher who had first given them to the ignorant world.

He did not leave Darshansingh the next day nor the day after. Within half an hour of meeting her again he felt himself violently attracted to her.

It was really extraordinary. He hated her hard little hands and her horrible chewn nails; he hated her high complexion, her embryo-memsahib voice, everything she said, everything she looked as if she stood for, the way she walked, the way she sat. He hated her grudging, sulky reception of his well-meant conversation, her refusal to look him in the eye, her rudeness to her mother, her defiance of her father that she just managed to make look like dumb obedience. The fact was there was nothing about the damned girl anyone in his senses could possibly like. There was just this one thing which, when he was within a few feet of her, even a shirt and jodhpurs and the smell of horse didn't stop him from sensing: her overwhelming aura of *girl*, of being his physical opposite. Astonishing. She wasn't even well-built. Her breasts looked as if they would be disappointing. He couldn't see her legs. The puppy fat hadn't quite gone from her face. Perhaps the sensations he experienced could have been traced to her slim waist and the way the jodhpurs suggested an accommodating broadness of hip and generous display of buttock. Or was it her hair? It looked as if she washed it every night and brushed and brushed. Or perhaps it was her mouth. Obviously she cleaned her teeth regularly. They were very white. Mane and teeth. She looked after herself as she would a horse.

She was late for tea which was served on the verandah at the back of the bungalow. She arrived at four-fifteen and went away almost at once to wash her hands and came back after ten minutes still dressed for riding. She was told off for being late, told off for not having washed and told off for not changing. He would have been sorry for her if she had looked sorry for herself, if she had seemed upset by this criticism of her behaviour in front of a stranger; but she didn't. Asked by her father why she was late she said she had forgotten the time. When her mother – an unlikely little sparrow of a woman to be married to a man like Clipsby-Smith and to have a daughter like Lesley – told her to wash her hands and face she got up with a secret little smile, and he felt it was only his presence there that stopped Clipsby-Smith from telling her to sit down again and get up without that smirk on her face. When she came back her father said, 'You might have changed.'

She said, 'I thought you all thought I'd wasted enough time,' and then sat down, her arms on the arms of the wicker chair and her jodhpured legs stuck out so that the bearer, replenishing the tray, had to lean over them. During the rest of tea she said nothing except Yes, No, Not that I know, I don't remember, I suppose it's all right (India), actually I prefer Murree (to Mussoorie), No, I hate it (dancing).

Her mother was a bead twister. She had a stringy neck, no bosom and a habit of never keeping her head still. You might have thought her observant, but when you had a good look at her eyes it was apparent they were seeing nothing that didn't relate to her husband's desires or Lesley's shortcomings. For the rest of the time they were staring into those vague mists that swirl about the private twilight world of unaccountable failure and distant deprivation.

The story of the alliance between the children of Professor Busteed and Professor Singleton had been received with such interest by Clipsby-Smith (who remembered those two text books from his prep school days) that he was almost persuaded himself of its veracity. The story took on a life of its own. Professor Busteed, the friend and rival of Professor Singleton, had only consented to the match between his daughter and the Singleton boy on the understanding that the young couple should join their names as well as their flesh. But alas for the vanity of human wishes. Soon after their marriage the son and daughter abandoned their own academic careers and went out to China as missionaries, where they died in desperate circumstances. Both the professors immediately died of broken hearts. The only child of their son's and daughter's union, now an orphan, was sent home and adopted by the eminent publisher who had cause to regard a child bearing both those worthy names with more than ordinary affection. He had always been well looked after and was lucky to be sent out so young to tour the distributors.

He told this pack of lies with just the right mixture of humour and seriousness. Clipsby-Smith smiled and nodded and looked at the well-breeched orphan with sympathy and – what was it? Calculation? Mrs. Clipsby-Smith also smiled and nodded, having heard nothing, but taken her cue from her husband. If Clipsby-Smith had thrown crumbs on to the table she would have pecked at them dutifully until they were gone.

Only Lesley remained unmoved. Once he caught her looking at him with a very odd expression. He wondered whether she had seen through him. She was the kind of girl who would ride up to the hotel, stride into the reception office and look at the Visitor's Book where his real name was written: illegibly, but not to be taken for the name he had given them. Perhaps she had already done so and was waiting her chance to face him with it.

At half-past five he got up to go, but by then he had committed himself to stay for at least another day and go with them on the morrow to picnic at the Kotimala Lakes.

Why? Why? Why? he asked himself all the way home in the tonga.

He knew why.

The car was an old-fashioned touring model with a canvas hood and no windows. He sat in the front with Clipsby-Smith. At first sight of Lesley that morning he had hoped like anything to sit with her. She was wearing a loose blouse and skirt of the same creamy white silky material. The collar and the neck of the blouse were vaguely nautical. She had silk stockings on and white shoes with two little straps across the insteps. At first he thought the smell of lavender water came from Lesley but it came from her mother, who had to be careful about headaches. The two of them sat in the back with a hamper and an icebox on the floor. For the purposes of the picnic even Lesley was considered a member of the distaff side.

On the winding road to Mahwar they saw langur monkeys in the trees, and parrots, and the shimmer of the rice fields below on the plain. Avoiding Mahwar itself they came out on the road to Kotimala at a junction where there was a roadside temple. They passed a line of ox-carts and heard the tinkling bells on the beasts' necks. At eleven they stopped where there was some shade. The men drank cold beer and the women iced lemonade. They could see the lakes gleaming in the distance.

They reached the lakes at midday. It was very hot. A smell of stagnation came from off the water. They parked under some trees near a ruined temple where there were monkeys that sat and watched them and leapt from the broken pillars to the ground and back again making no sound.

Everything looked old; older than the Stones of Darshansingh. The whole place was under sentence of silence. Only the monkeys moved. It was like a dream. When the Clipsby-Smiths talked their voices sounded like rubber, muffled and bouncing away without any echo. His own voice was the same. They ate cold chicken and salad and fruit and drank a bottle of claret. And none of it was real. Somewhere hereabouts a terrible peace, an awful wholeness had been achieved, a union between man and nature that left them excluded, dangerously exposed. After they had eaten they settled down to sleep.

When he woke the two elder Clipsby-Smiths were snoring. He could see Lesley down there by the lake, under a tree. He got up and went to join her. She did not acknowledge his arrival. He sat down next to her. They watched the lake together. Her cheeks were paler than he had seen them. He wondered what she had been thinking. When she was ten they had sent her home to school. She had only come back last year. Perhaps she was thinking of England, trying to make sense of the years of separation.

'Why are you so unhappy, Lesley?'

'What makes you think I'm unhappy?' she asked. Her voice, as hard as ever, broke the spell. She was her own savage little self again. He hated her and wanted her more badly than ever. He longed for her more than he had ever longed for anything or anybody. The very air around her made him want to enter it. It was air different from any other because it surrounded her. He looked at her closely. What a marvellous girl she was! A horror. A squat tight little bitch with nothing to be said in her favour except that she made him rigid with desire just being near her.

Suddenly she stopped looking at the lake and looked at him instead. And at that moment he was sure that she knew the effect she had on him, sure that she enjoyed treating men like dirt but even more enjoyed watching them eat it. And she knew why they ate it. How she must laugh up her sleeve at her father who had spent years trying to turn her into the boy he had never had.

The question was how much dirt did she make men eat

before she called quits? How many insults to their pride did they have to swallow before she chalked up another score against her parents and allowed herself to be kissed and fondled? Did she enjoy it when she finally let it happen? Had she ever let a man go further?

'I asked you a question,' she said.

'I'm sorry. I thought it was really an answer to mine.'

She looked at the lake again.

'Besides,' he went on, 'something else put it out of my head.'

'Oh?'

'Would you like to know what it was?'

'I don't think I'd be interested.'

'How can you tell before you know?'

She said nothing. He couldn't actually blame her. It was a very childish conversation.

He said, 'I was thinking you're really very pretty dressed like a girl.'

Still she said nothing. But she picked up a handful of stones and began to throw them into the water. He wondered whether he was supposed to catch hold of her arm so that she could say, 'Do you mind letting me go?' The temptation to do so was great. He resisted it and got to his feet instead and left her to it. When he got back to the car he looked round. She had stopped throwing stones and was just sitting there, staring at the lake. It was damnable. Whenever he wasn't actually near her he was sorry for her. He wondered whether he was in love.

At four o'clock they started for home. Clipsby-Smith made him sit in the back with Lesley, but he talked over his shoulder all the way back to Darshansingh as if he knew there wasn't much change the young guest would be likely to get out of his daughter. Mrs. Clipsby-Smith twisted her beads and looked intently at the passing scene as if she had lost something on the way out that morning and was hoping but not expecting to find it again before the journey ended.

He had quite forgotten the existence of the two other English people: the man with the sketch-book and easel and the woman who accompanied him: but as they drew up at the Dak bungalow these two people were just coming into sight, riding at a walk down the road from Darshansingh where the man must have been painting the Stones.

Clipsby-Smith said, 'I say, some more people have arrived.' He

52

probably thought they were staying at the bungalow. He and Mrs. Clipsby-Smith got out and stood, ordering the servants and watching the approach of the strangers. When the two riders were closer Mrs. Clipsby-Smith put her little claw-like hand on her husband's arm and said something. In a low voice, he said, 'What? It can't be,' and then, 'Good Lord. You're right.'

Mrs. Clipsby-Smith turned away and went on up to the Dak bungalow taking Lesley with her. Her husband busied himself unnecessarily, supervising the unloading of the basket and the box. As the horses went by he straightened up. His face was pink from the exertion of bending and helping to pull out the box. He raised his hat. The man raised his in return. His painting equipment was stowed and lashed in front of him on the saddle. He was about Clipsby-Smith's age, with a long thin melancholy face. Neither smiled. It was all over in a few seconds. The woman rode on past without looking. Her face was shaded by a wide-brimmed solar topee.

When they had gone Clipsby-Smith looked at his watch. 'Come and have a peg,' he said. 'Then I'll drive you back to your billet.'

Before dinner he wrote a note to the Clipsby-Smiths thanking them for taking him on the picnic to Kotimala. He told them that he would be in Darshansingh just one more day and wondered, now that his leg was better, whether Lesley would like to ride up with him the next day to see the Stones and come back to the hotel for tea; and if, in the evening, they would all have dinner with him. Falling into their idiom he said, 'The food here's not much, I'm afraid.'

When he signed the note he felt rather ashamed writing Busteed-Singleton. He sent a bearer out with it and took an opportunity to go to the Visitors' Book and add, '& Co', and 'E.B-S. Rep.' to the name he'd correctly written there. It was too late now to tell them the truth. And anyway, what did it matter one way or the other?

Within an hour, just as he was finishing a solitary meal (solitary, that was, except for the four white-uniformed bearers who stood by one of the dining-room pillars watching every mouthful and taking it in turns to clear each plate the moment he'd done with it) the boy came back with Clipsby-Smith's reply.

The letter was very friendly and began, 'Dear Ned.' Clipsby-Smith was afraid, however, that the journey in the car had rather unsettled his wife who had never been a strong traveller and she doubted she would be well enough to dine out on the morrow. It was very decent of him (Ned) to think of returning hospitality, but quite unnecessary because the pleasure had been all theirs. In any case if he was leaving the day after he would want an early night to be fresh for the trip. However, Clipsby-Smith said, he didn't want to spoil the day for the young people. Lesley would be glad to accompany him to the Stones and it was nice of him to ask her back for tea. She would ride over to the hotel at about two-thirty and perhaps he would be kind enough to deliver her back safe and sound about six pip emma and have a farewell drink with them all? He was, sincerely, William Clipsby-Smith.

Clearly, Mrs. Clipsby-Smith's indisposition was due to the presence in Darshansingh of the two people she had cut dead. She would probably stay in the Dak bungalow until the time came to travel on to Mussoorie, and so make sure of avoiding them. He wondered what the man and woman had done. He wondered what threats Clipsby-Smith had had to employ to get Lesley to agree to accept his invitation. He also wondered whether her fair little head would rest sweetly on the pillow that night, full of plans for ways and means of working him up to fever pitch while treating him like something brought in by the dog.

It occurred to him that none of the Clipsby-Smiths knew that he slept in the annexe, unless the bearer Clipsby-Smith gave his card to the morning he called had said so. If he hadn't said so then Clipsby-Smith may have thought his appearance from the shrubbery indicated no more than admirable morning exercise.

He looked at the bachelor quarters with fresh interest. They could have tea on the verandah and be quite alone. He wondered whether there was a private way in to the grounds from the track that led up to the Stones and whether there was a place where you could leave the horses unnoticed. He wondered how much it would cost to bribe the bearer to keep clear until nearly six o'clock.

The answer was ten rupees.

For that amount tea would be waiting at ten to four and would be taken away at six o'clock. Between those two times the bearer would not be anywhere near the annexe but chatting to his friends in the back of the main building. The man was elderly and spoke almost fluent English and grinned. The good old days were back.

But was the bearer to be trusted? In broad daylight the whole business looked unlikely. And what was the whole business anyway? A ghastly ride up to the ghastly Stones with a girl who wouldn't speak a civil word, an even ghastlier tea followed by an attempt to see how far he could go with her. The consequences of going even a fraction of an inch further than she would permit were too distressing to contemplate. There would be a horde of Clipsby-Smiths about his ears. You could get drummed out as quick as wink. The wrath could follow him to Madras. If he ever got to Madras. The whole sordid story would come out. The false name, the ten rupees to the native servant. He wouldn't have a leg to stand on. And when you thought about it, thought about her, what she was, the game probably wasn't worth the candle.

But it was a question of what was felt, not thought. He felt it again, at half-past two precisely when, mounted on Rajah Sahib, he met her near the bazaar. He had trouble turning Rajah Sahib round to ride by her side. She waited patiently: too patiently: not exactly looking him up and down but taking him all in at a glance and finding nothing to be said in his favour. The impression she gave was of knowing exactly what he was doing wrong with the pony but of it not being compulsory to tell.

When he was facing in the right direction at last, he said, 'We could always cut out the riding lark and go for a walk instead.'

She didn't reply. So they rode together, passing the almost hidden track that led off into the grounds of the hotel which he had reconnoitred for and discovered that morning.

'I say,' he said, again conscious of using their idiom, 'who were those two people who went by the Dak bungalow last night?'

'I don't know.'

'Your father seemed to know them.'

'Did he?'

'But he didn't seem to want to say.'

Silence.

'I suppose,' he said, 'they've commmitted some awful breach of the rules and regs. I mean people have sent them to Coventry and they've come all this way to Darshansingh to hide their faces. I wonder where they're staying? Probably some bungalow in the jungle between here and Mahwar, full of ghosts.'

The image pleased him. He expanded it. He tried to get a rise out of her by using what he imagined would be the Clipsby-Smith brand of rather old-fashioned slang. The woman had well, you know, gone the pace a bit. Not that she looked that kind, at least not from what you could see of her under that topee which was probably the only hat she had now because she'd thrown her other over the windmill for some chap in the regiment. Or perhaps they were brother and sister, not husband and wife, and she'd made an ass of herself over some fellow who was already married. Perhaps the brother was a school-teacher, dedicated to Busteed and Singleton, and then his sister fell in love with the head boy.

He looked at her.

She said, 'You don't have to talk to me.'

'Oh? Why not?'

'I only came because my father told me I had to.'

'Well, thanks.'

'So you can let me go home now if you want, or we can go on with it. But you don't have to talk. In fact I'd rather you didn't. All you've said so far has been pretty disgusting.'

'Well, I'm a disgusting sort of fellow. I mean I can't even ride a horse.'

When they reached the narrow part of the track he let her go on ahead. They reached the Stones without saying another word. If she had any sense she'd find the Stones disgusting too.

This afternoon there were two parties of Indians having pic-nics. Beside those graceful women with long braided hair and coloured silks Lesley looked awful: like some farm girl who'd just been mucking out the pig-stye. She refused to go into the caves. She looked at the Stones as if they were so many minia-ture Nelson's columns without the lions and without the Ad-miral. It was possible, he supposed, but not likely, that she had no idea what they represented.

He said, 'Well if you won't go into the caves, let's sit down.'

He sat down under a tree. She sat down too, several feet away. He offered her a cigarette which she refused by shaking her head. While he lit one for himself she examined a scratch on her left boot. Her hair fell over her cheeks. He wanted to get his hands into it.

'Why won't you go into the cave?'

She said nothing.

'It's all right, you know. There's a guide. You wouldn't have to be in there alone with me.'

She continued to examine the scratch, bending her head low to get a closer look at it. 'Not,' he said, beginning to lose his temper, 'that I imagine there'd be any pleasure in taking you into the bloody caves, guide or no guide. If you've finished staring your boot out I'll take you home.'

He stood up, and threw the almost whole cigarette away.

'Come on, then,' he said, more kindly, remembering the annexe, and tea for two. He waited, then bent and caught her arm. She pushed away. He tried again. Still she pushed. He knelt by her. Her face was turned from him. One hand covered it, hiding it.

'Lesley?'

She said something. It might have been, probably was, 'Go away.' But he could have sworn she said please: Please go away. He remembered how she had said, You don't have to talk to me. In retrospect it sounded sad instead of rude. And he also remembered how, after he had left her yesterday, she had stopped throwing stones and just stared at the lake.

'Look,' he said. 'You may have come only because your father told you to. But nobody told me to ask you. I asked you because I wanted to see you.'

'Don't,' she said. 'Please don't tell lies.'

'I'm not telling lies. I know you don't like me, but I like you. As a matter of fact I like you very much.'

He put his arm round her, which after all was one of the things he had come for. She pulled away. For an instant he could see her face. Her eyes were brimming.

'How could you like me?' she said. 'How could anyone?'

She was on her feet and away, running for the place where they left the ponies. He went after her, not calling because the Indians were watching and smiling, waiting for further proof of a lovers' tiff. She didn't wait for the syce but uncurled the reins from the post herself and was off. If she galloped down the track she'd break her neck. He had to pay the man. By the time he was mounted she was out of sight.

All the way down, going as quickly as he dared, there was no sign of her. The noise of Rajah Sahib's hooves made it impossible to hear the sounds of her own pony. The track curved through the forest, barred by strips of shadow and sunshine.

On the flat, just short (as if she knew it existed) of the private way into the grounds of the hotel, she was waiting for him. She had a high colour, higher even than usual, but her eyes were dry and her mouth was set like that of a boy waiting to be punished.

'If I go home alone they'll think you've fallen off again,' she said.

'Then let's have tea. I've ordered it for four o'clock but we can get it sooner.'

She began to ride forward. He stopped her by calling, 'It's quicker this way.' He pointed out the narrow track. 'Come on. I'll lead the way.'

The track led round to the back of the annexe. Dismounting, he tethered Rajah Sahib to the post that was still there: a relic of old bachelor delights. She followed suit.

'This way,' he said, and led her round to the front of the hut. The bearer was laying the table on the verandah. He salaamed. Tea, he said, was just coming. He went away smiling. It was only half-past three.

'You'll find the bathroom through there,' he told Lesley. She went into his room. He stood by the open door. He heard the bathroom door shut. There was that old boathouse smell coming off the timbers of the annexe. He stepped into the room. Before he left he had closed the cretonne curtains. The room was full of amber light. He went further in, attracted by sounds from the bathroom. Lesley was crying. She probably had her handkerchief stuffed in her mouth. That's what it sounded like. He came back on to the verandah and sat on the rail, lit a cigarette and waited. In five minutes the bearer came back with the tray. He kept his eyes on the tray and said 'Thank you,' and let the man go away.

After a minute or two he went back into the room. He could hear her splashing her face; pouring water away and then pouring fresh from the jug; getting rid of the tearstains and delaying the moment when she had to come out and face him. Going out again he poured a cup of tea and put some chocolate biscuits on a plate. He took them in and put them on the table by the armchair. He tapped on the bathroom door.

'Lesley,' he said, 'there's a cup of tea for you on the table here. Drink it up when you come out, then if you like I'll take you home.'

A shadow had fallen on the afternoon. He didn't know what to do for the best. He felt himself floating in the vacuum of his inexperience, realized how young he was still, remembered she was four years younger. A lifetime. Poor Lesley. How could a child like that be such an enigma? He went out on to the verandah, disturbed by the thought of what he might feel directly he saw her again. He drank a cup of tea.

When she came out he looked at her without taking her in, and looked at the tea-table again, and said, 'Would you like another cup?'

'No, thank you.'

For the first time her eyes were on him straight, uncritically. They said nothing for a while. From several feet away he felt nothing. A constriction, an emptiness; that was all. It must be the distance, he thought. You couldn't suddenly feel nothing.

'Shall I take you home, then?'

'There's no need for you to come.'

'Don't be silly. Of course I'll come.'

He went first, down to the place where they had left the ponies. He untethered hers first. As she came close to him he waited for the flood of sensation, of his own body needing hers. It didn't come. She was only a child. Why was she a child? She couldn't be.

'Lesley,' he said. He took her in his arms. She was warm. Her flesh was her flesh. There were bones beneath it that he could feel with his fingers. Her hair smelled of soap: clean, soft, fragrant. The hair of innocence. And her eyes: blue, puzzled, wondering, innocent too. He kissed her. Nothing. Nothing. It had gone. When he drew away her lashes were upon her cheeks and her cheeks were burning. He watched her for a while in dismay, and all that time her lashes were upon her cheeks as if she dare not look up. He had been quite wrong. She knew nothing. She was waiting to know.

He moved, and she turned, mounted her pony without looking at him but with an air all the same of seeing him, accepting him, giving herself to him. He remembered the arm he had put across her shoulders and the words he had spoken: I like you very much. He wished that he could forget them. He did not *like* her. He had only wanted her. Now he didn't. He led the way back to the track and waited for her there and rode by her side down to the bazaar where he stopped and got down and made her get down too.

'Come on. I'm going to buy you something.'

'But I don't want anything,' she said.

'Yes, but I want to give you something. A goodbye present.'

They went into a shop where you could buy handkerchiefs,

scarves and sarees. There was a scarf decorated with horse's heads.

'It's too expensive,' she said. 'Everything's too expensive. We oughtn't to stay.' She was in a panic.

'This,' he said, and chose a length of fine silk that could have been passed through a wedding ring. The owner of the shop began to get out his treasures.

'Please let's go,' she said.

'These,' he said, a bit panic-stricken himself; and picked up a box of handkerchiefs embroidered with an ornate letter L. 'L,' he said. 'Obviously they're meant for you.'

He paid the man what he asked. Lesley was out in the road by the time the deal was settled. He gave her the box. 'Here,' he said. 'You hold them. You don't need as many hands as I do.'

When they got back to the Dak bungalow it wasn't quite half-past four.

'I won't come in,' he said. 'Your parents will be having a nap I shouldn't wonder.'

'They're expecting you.'

'Not until six. Tell you what. I'll come back about then and have a drink. I've got my packing to do and to see about a seat on the bus.'

'I think my father wants to drive you to Mahwar.'

'Oh no. The bus will do me fine. See you about six.'

When he got back to the hotel he knew he couldn't go at six, or at any other time. The whole treacherous little episode was over.

But not quite over. At seven o'clock as he sat on the verandah he heard the sound of a telephone ringing inside the hotel. It was quite a shock. He hadn't known there was a telephone, although he remembered, now, telegraph poles all the way to Mahwar. He knew, without really any doubt at all, that the call being put through was coming from the Dak bungalow, He guessed the manager would answer it, that he would deny the existence of a guest of the name asked for. At the eleventh hour. Almost he was glad. He made his way inside. The ringing had stopped. The manager was saying, 'No, no, sir. There is no one of that name.' Then he gave the real name, and paused, and said, 'Just a moment,' looked up and saw the wanted man through the open doorway of his office and smiled and made him welcome inside.

'Hello?'

'Hello,' Clipsby-Smith said. 'Those chaps up there seem to be in an awful muddle, I suppose you put the name of your firm down in the book as well, and that's all that's sunk in. I just rang to see if you were all right.'

'I was about to ring you. I'm awfully sorry —'

'That's all right, old chap. All that packing. It's best to do it yourself unless you've got your own man with you. But we're sorry to have missed you. Look, what about that bus?'

'It's all arranged. I'm off at ten.'

'Meant to say when I saw you I'd be glad to give you a lift into Mahwar. Never mind. The other thing is I wanted to thank you for all you've done for Lesley.'

'Well, it was —'

'She seems to have enjoyed this afternoon. Sorry it was cut short. These wretched headaches she gets. All the same, decent of you to look after her. And that was a jolly nice present you gave her.'

'I hope she's better now.'

'Oh, she's perked up. Disappointed you couldn't get down for drinks though. We all are. Well, look, I mustn't keep you. Have a good trip.'

'Thank you, sir. And you.'

The sir had slipped out. After five years.

And even then it wasn't over. At eight o'clock a package was delivered. It contained a bottle of Scotch for the journey with Clipsby-Smith's card (the regimental address in Marapore), some fruit and a note from Mrs. Clipsby-Smith (the holiday address in Mussoorie). He replied on Hotel notepaper saying he would try to write to them in Mussoorie and indicated (by omission) that his own forwarding addresses were uncertain.

At five to ten next morning he took his seat on the crowded one decker Indian bus. At ten past the bus moved out, blowing its klaxon horn all down the narrow street of the bazaar.

There was only the Dak bungalow to get past. As the bus drew near to the place it began to slow down. It hadn't occurred to him that the bungalow might be an official stop, but it was. Two of the bungalow staff were waiting for it, to go down into Mahwar for supplies. And the Clipsby-Smiths were there, waiting to wave him off. He was hemmed in by passengers, but there wasn't any glass in the windows. They called goodbye and he called goodbye back.

She was wearing a coloured cotton dress. Her father had one arm across her shoulders and one across his wife's.

She had one of the handkerchiefs in her hand, ready to wave. He could see the blue initial. When the bus moved he shouted goodbye again, and thanks, and waved, and Clipsby-Smith took his arm from Lesley's shoulder and waved too. Just before they were out of sight Lesley raised her own hand, tentatively, and then let it fall to her side.

You should not have waved. Lesley. You should not have stood there waving in the morning sunshine. You should have stayed in your room in the dark with all the shutters down.

The Arrival in Playa de Faro

Centuries ago the bay of Playa de Faro was scooped out of the shoreline by the hoof of a giant horse that came across the Mediterranean from Poseidon's stables with the water scarcely reaching its trembling white flanks. At Playa de Faro it stood on the water's edge, whinnying softly down at Spain, stamping one leg because the grazing looked lean and hungry. At last, rearing and twisting, it plunged back into the sea, its golden mane sparkling with jewels of light and water. When the turbulence set up by its arrival and departure had died away two black-eyed children ran down through the pines to stare open-mouthed at the distant apparition and at the impression of the brazen hoof and the now calm water standing in it like an inland lake embraced by the curving promontories of broken red rock. As they watched from the brow of the higher promontory the earth shifted under their feet and a piece of rock slithered from the precarious position it had been left in by the last stamp of the white horse and splashed down into the bay to lie there undisturbed; so that it could still be seen today, half in the sand and half in the tideless sea, gathering molluscs on its under side.

Facing the beach were three hotels: Hotel Playa de Faro, Hotel Brava and Hotel-Pension Royal: built as one in a block upon whose flat but slightly irregular roof there were poles and lines to hang and dry the linen. Wooden balconies, painted for the current season red and yellow, jutted from the upper-storey windows in the white and blue stucco façades. Below them was the long roof of the porticoed terrace beneath which meals were served on little tables covered by gay cloths that whipped up whenever the breeze caught them. In front of the hotels, separated from them by a narrow lane (a lane made even narrower by rows of potted plants, vagrant chairs and tables, billboards advertising the corrida at San Felfu and the flamenco at the nightclub Faro), concrete floors had been laid on the sand and roofed over on wooden log supports with a material that looked like asbestos but could only be seen from below because the tops were camouflaged by pine branches that were green in April but quickly turned brown.

Under these raffish Mediterranean roofs the tourists drank

and sometimes ate when the height of the season filled the dining terraces beyond their capacity. From under them watch could be kept on what went on beneath the coloured umbrellas a stone's throw away, and between the dry-beached boats that were clustered at the north-easterly end of the three-hundred yard wide bay, the end where there were old fishermen's houses that faced the setting sun that once dried the nets and warmed the nimble stitching fingers of their laughing women, but which had now been turned into bars and shops: shops that sold souvenirs of España Brava, bars that had their own pine-log and bamboo terraces on to the beach, almost to the water's edge, and played fiery Andalucian music into the sunshine from their dark interiors.

The sand on the playa was gritty, but there were patches that had been ground to velvet where the boats were dragged. As well as their names the boats carried registration numbers on their prows. The registration numbers were prefixed by the letters BA which stood for Barca. There were two boats larger than the rest. They went out at night two or three times a week with scratch crews of men and youths. Crowds collected on the dark playa to watch them light the pressure lamps that were fixed to the iron contraptions in the bows, three or four to each boat. The lamps illuminated the sea to show where the shoals were. The boats came back before dawn. You could hear the sailors sing. They unloaded the fish in boxes and sent them to the markets in Palafrugell and Palamós. In the early hours of the morning the long nets were spread across the sand to dry, and later gathered up to make room for the tourists, the locusts of the sun and the grape who came in summer swarms to fill their northern veins with the lifeblood of the south.

The quietest hours were between three and four in the morning and three and four in the afternoon. At four in the afternoon the kitchen boys came from the hotels, taking time off. Most of them were from distant parts of Spain. They were very poor and worked hard and looked happy. In the winter they went home and laboured with picks and shovels for a subsistence wage. They ate well in summer anyway. At four in the afternoon they came down to the playa to swim and play football and size up the muchachas. They wore smart slips but their bodies were pale. What tan they picked up between four and five they sweated out the same night in the kitchens. Coming out of the water, though, they were sandungos, muy machos. Their game was Reál Madrid. It took them closer and closer to the likeliest among the daughters of the turistas who lay prone, eyes closed, showing their round bottoms, knowing themselves chosen.

In time the boldest of the boys deliberately took a tumble, spraying those delectable bottoms with sand. Pardon was asked and perhaps granted. It needed only to be granted for the boy to remain and only for the boy to remain for the game to end and the players to sit, close to the girls, naming objects in Spanish in exchange for the same objects named in English, French, Dutch or German. At five, one by one, the boys said goodbye and returned to their hotels to stoke up the fires in the cooking ranges, leaving the girls burning with a sense of impermanence.

Behind the hotels there were narrow lanes that were full of hard sunlight and sharp black shadows and sudden openings between white stucco walls on to the steps that led to the newly built villas of speculators in Barcelona and Gerona; and doorways no longer screened by the old fashioned heavy bead curtains but by long spaghetti strips of green and yellow plastic. Crackling through those curtains you entered dim and musty rooms whose tiled floors were roughened by sand brought in on the soles of bare feet and on the soles of canvas espadrilles, and there made purchases; huile-filtre, sunglasses, pairs of castanets, schnörkel tubes, beach wear and picture postcards of the glossy panorama of Playa de Faro, and of Spanish girls with cheeks of carmine and mantillas stuck over with scraps of real lace. You could buy bottles of Andossino and Rocabardi, Castellblanch Espumoso, Cointreau and Courvoisier, suede jackets, onions, bread, fruit, sweets and postage stamps showing a saint or a Madonna, or General Franco looking into the middle distance of history and thinking his thoughts.

Here in this complex of doorways, sunshine and shadow, where the gamine faces beneath straw hats from the civilized capitals of Europe met but did not merge with the strong Catalonian faces, where the mule cart took garbage past the parked dusty automobiles of the tourists, there was to be found the entrance to the nightclub Faro, and beyond the nightclub one road leading to the Correos, the Apartamentos and the Camping, and another away from Playa de Faro, past a row of white villas with green shutters, up the hill, away into the red rock and green pines of the southwest arm of the rugged horseshoe, and eventually past the gateway that was the official entrance to the terraced grounds of the Villa Vora la Mar.

Here there was scent and silence. Through the pines came the blue of the sea far below, mottled by currents, and the red brown of the rocks, perhaps a cry, and a murmuring from the shore.

Ice-buckets of Spanish champagne at six shillings a bottle were being brought down to the beach when Bruce and Thelma Craddock came to the playa. They arrived by boat, sailing in from the north round a promontory of the terracotta coloured rock that surrounded the bay. It was a clear, hot day. Out to sea there was a breeze and a swell, but the surrounding hills kept the wind out and the heat in.

The boat that brought them was one of three motor launches that ferried passengers from one to the other of the half-dozen or so popular resorts on this part of the Spanish coast. Anyone who watched the arrival from its beginning would have known that the boat entered the bay from the north, but it was the kind of boat you usually noticed only when it was almost upon you, coming in rather too quickly, scattering the swimmers and the paddle-rafts, making for a point on the beach where shingle had piled up into a ledge to form a natural landing place.

Later, when rumours began to tangle in the oil and garlic scented air, there were some who said that the boat had come in from the south, even that it had been a private boat, and then a whole field of conjecture lay open. 'South conjured the Algerian coastline, brought Spain into closer proximity with the Kasbah, and the hot oven-breath of Africa; and inquisitive people would watch for the Craddocks to come down from the villa that stood isolated, white and Moorish, perched in the shade on the side of the southwestern promontory in a green nest of pines, trees with which the hills were thickly strewn. You smelt the pines immediately you drew beyond range of the hotel kitchens. It was a dry, warm, lemon and sweet-pea smell that made the limbs heavy and the blood restless.

The boat ground to a stop with its bows dug into the shingle, its stern swinging and bucking to the miniature combers which on days such as this played hit-and-run with the shore; and Bruce and Thelma disembarked, followed by their luggage and the eyes of the basking tourists.

Thelma was dressed in white slacks and a white husky

sweater with blue buttons. The men on the beach waited for her to turn sideways to them. Before she followed Bruce down the little gangplank that had been lowered from the sharp end she stood at the head of it, letting the breeze that had sneaked in with the boat lift her hair, pivoting round to take in through large sunglasses in thick tortoiseshell frames a panoramic view of the resort that some years earlier had been a fishing village of twenty-five souls. A gold charm bracelet jingled on her wrist when she put her hand up to stop a lock of hair from whipping her cheek. Her brown arms were bare to the elbow, the sleeves of the sweater rolled up into soft white corrugations.

'Wasn't I right, Bruce?' those within earshot heard her say. 'Wasn't it right to come in by sea?'

The breeze all but blew her voice away. More people heard Bruce's reply than heard her question.

'Old thing,' he said, 'when were you ever wrong?'

The top of his head reached just short of the ship's prow. He carried his sweatshirt in one hand, was mahogany naked from the waist up. Washed out blue jeans cleaved his buttocks. His feet were bare and apparently undaunted by the shingle. They must have come that morning from another playa. When Thelma was on the gangplank he put out his hands, took her weight and gathered her into his arms. Three flatchested English girls eyed the play of his muscles. He carried Thelma to the soft sand, put her down gently like something delicate arrived safely at the end of a perilous journey, hugged her with one arm. Then they faced the sea, side by side, while the luggage came down, some of it so encrusted with travel labels it looked as if it belonged to a party of vagabond harlequins.

Her hair was a curious colour. In certain lights, when it was a bit untidy, sticky with salt from the sea winds, it had that glowing gold-in-the-iron sculptural quality you associate with the word bronze. But it was thick, water absorbing hair, and whenever she flung it over her face and bent her head to be dried by the sun or the fire or Bruce's towel, you could see how pale and yellow it was at the roots in the nape of her neck.

Again, in certain lights, it gave off a here-and-gone impression of redness, as if the bronze had been warmed by a memory of fire. Evening was best for this effect, or early in the morning before the sun was up and the ghost-whiteness on which her head lay began to harden to the real whiteness of a linen pillow, while the hair itself, taking shape and acquiring substance, softened from moment to moment until, leaning close to it you would have seen each separate strand and the redness catching it.

'What colour would you call your hair, Thelma?' another woman might ask, although Thelma being the woman she was had little need of conversation with her own sex.

'Tortoiseshell,' she would answer. 'Like a cat. It depends on the time of day and the mood I'm in. Doesn't it Bruce? Bruce, isn't that so?'

It seemed that she couldn't be near her husband (if he was her husband) and not speak to him, leave him out of a conversation for long. But when they were alone they sat for hours, silent, hand in hand. Strangers were not to know this. In places where the Craddocks stayed the gossip was that she kept her eye on him. Women didn't blame her for that. They didn't thank her either. Bruce's hair was the kind that women had difficulty in keeping their hands off when they passed the back of his chair. He used no brilliantine but this didn't stop it from being glossily black and curly. He kept it cut short, unfashionably so about the neck.

'You've had it cropped again,' Thelma sometimes wailed. 'It does date us so.'

And then she would put her forefinger low down on his bare neck and run it upward, pushing against the stubby grain in a way that never ceased to thrill either of them, although now there was something almost valedictory in the way she did it. Words like date, time, soon and later were not, to use their own just outdated slang, okay words; but they would slip out and, having slipped out, had to be left to wriggle away like tiny creatures making for cover when a stone is lifted. Strangers were not to know this either.

The top of her head came to his shoulder. She had the figure of a girl in her early twenties and he that of a man under thirty. In fact she was thirty-nine and he forty. 'At forty, old thing, we'll be in our prime,' he used to say. They now seemed to be, but did not refer to it. His musculature was well defined but unobtrusive unless he bent, or stretched, or lifted anything heavier than a bottle. He wore his upper body bare without self-consciousness and did so not to peacock it about but because he liked the freedom of movement and the healthy satiny-glow of clean tanned skin. His features inspired confidence in men because they indicated frankness, and sexual admiration in women because they were regular, handsome, and suggestive of that irresistible combination: a warm heart and intemperate blood.

Rosa, chambermaid at the Hotel Playa de Faro, paused in her sweeping of one of the four hundred peseta a day bedrooms with balconies, and watched Bruce trudge up the sloping beach. Downstairs in the patio a cluster of white jacketed waiters looked at Thelma with their sombre manqué-bullfighter's eyes.

Thelma now unbuttoned her sweater and took it off. She had on a floppy sky blue cotton shirt with short sleeves that looked as if it had once belonged to Bruce. It had, but not for more than a minute or two.

'Oh, Bruce. Sky blue?'

And he had given it to her without a word, with a half-smile, and gone out and bought sky-blue jeans instead. Of these she approved. Usually he did not much care what kind of clothes he wore. Just occasionally something would take his fancy and then he set about getting it with a singleness of purpose which once she found endearing, but now no longer did.

'It's me,' she sometimes cried. 'Me. It's because you've only got me. It's not enough for a man.'

'That's it,' Bruce said, pointing at the white villa on the hill. 'Let's see about transport and get up there.'

She said, 'Is it really it? But then it must be. It's how I imagined it. How I hoped it would be.'

For a second or two, as they looked at the villa, arm in arm, the smiles they wore constantly in public faded.

'I won't,' Thelma said. Her voice was hoarse, cracked by her public years and her private anguish. 'I won't stay in this terrible place.'

A packing crate, sent ahead of them with four others, had arrived undamaged but alone. She sat on it, one survivor of a journey making contact with another, bent her head, hiding her plain face under the wide brim of her old-fashioned sun-helmet.

The boy was coming in from the compound with the first load of suitcases from the Ford. Craddock told him to get out. The boy, afraid of the gaunt white man, let the suitcases fall on to the floor of the verandah and went. In the silence that followed there could be heard in the Panther House the sound of small, damp, clawing animals fighting their way panic-stricken out of the dark corners where they had lived long in peace.

When the sound had stopped, and the animals had died, dry and blind in the sunlight, Craddock said, 'We'll both stay. For the rest of our lives, probably.'

For a while she was silent, considering what he had said. Then she began to laugh, making for hysteria like someone swarming up a flexible ladder in a high wind. He took her by the shoulders but she only laughed louder. He jerked her rag-doll body. The sun-helmet fell off. Her hair clung to her scalp. It was brown, lustreless, lighter at the ends where bleach that marked the ebb of a once fulltide of vanity had not yet grown out.

'Ned!' she called. 'Oh, Ned, come and take me away!'

Craddock struck her on the cheek. The rag doll was turned to one of wood. Its mouth was open. For a moment or two they stared at each other.

'It's because of Ned you're here,' he said.

Presently she shut her eyes and put her hands up, feeling for the helmet, the lost carapace of a hermit crab; and knowing it gone, pressed her hands to her head.

'I know what you're thinking,' she said. 'You're always thinking it. How Ned could bring himself to touch me. But Ned didn't see me as you see me. He didn't see me as I am. He told me I was pretty. He filled me with warmth and love, night after night. And I was pretty then.'

Even before Thelma Craddock sat in the entrance hall on a packing crate calling out to poor, dead Ned, the Panther House existed as the repository of a human as well as animal sense of deprivation.

The house was approached by the road that led from Mahwar through the Mahwari Hills to Darshansingh where there were the Stones which the Craddocks were to visit later, he with his sketch-book, easel, canvas stool and the black umbrella that kept off the glare, she with her thoughts that were more dangerous than the heatstroke against which she wore the old-fashioned helmet, shielding her neck from the sun and her plain face from the world.

The Mahwari Hills were forested. The Darshansingh road mounted by way of one of the many spurs that convoluted the course of the Mahwar river down in the plain which stretched southwards. The river watered rice-fields which in the transplanting season reflected rows of women moving and bending, feeding the mouths of hungry creatures beneath the surface. When the road turned the spur, the view of the plains was lost. There were glimpses of terrace-cultivation on the foothills, but the balance of power between man and nature was unmistakably shifting. Among the trees the wings of parrots and the black, grey ruffed faces of langurs announced the frontier between two kingdoms, and here was to be found the turning into which the Craddocks drove in the Ford, a turning into a garden that had no wall other than the one provided by an embankment of earth and of roughly hewn stones held firm by creeper and the partially exposed roots of trees.

The path to the house levelled off and then led through a shadowy, sun-lanced garden of fleshy plants that gave off odours a traveller once described as those that Adam must have smelled in Eden. Some of the plants were taller than a man and they grew in the indigo shade of trees from which ropes of green liana hung motionless, like relics of some primitive attempt at campanology.

An Englishman who lived in Mahwar for many years called it when he wrote to friends, 'this lonely place', even, 'this murderous spot'. But after he died his diaries showed another side of the coin.

'Today I watched the mist and noticed how it is striated by the sun. It is made of some pale blue substance, opaque, elastic; and when the sun gets hotter it gives along the striations, elongates, tautens. Entering the mist it feels like a frost on your eyelids, and eyeballs. But the inner surface of the lid is still warm and when you blink the frost is melted. Tears are simulated. But there is no sensation of sadness. The mist on the Mahwari Hills as the sun gets up is a lovely sight.'

But it was mid-afternoon when the Craddocks arrived. Shafts of sunlight penetrated the wilderness. Neither of them spoke. The track curved and brought them abruptly to the clearing in which the Panther House stood.

It was an old construction, a bungalow of stuccoed brick with rounded pillars supporting the roof of a verandah that shaded all four sides. Above the roof there were to be seen the small fanlight windows that lit the rooms during the heat of the day when the louvres of the wooden shutters of the doors and windows that gave on to the verandah were closed.

The white stucco was faded and cracked. The round pillars were in the grip of vines and creepers, Tendrils of these hung from the verandah roof and betrayed the slightest wind. The movements of the tendrils suggested the sound of distant bells, and there seemed, therefore, to be some connexion between the tendrils on the verandah and the lianas in the overgrown garden.

The door was open. A boy was waiting, and came out to help them with the luggage.

'He told me I was pretty,' Thelma said, but he was no longer there to tell her anything. Ned Pearson had shot himself because of the disgrace.

Loss of favour, downfall from a position of honour, ignominy, shame: that is how disgrace is defined by dictionaries. But words have meanings as an onion has skins. Ned peeled himself away analysing the nature of his disgrace. You can picture him at it, a blond good-looking man in his middle twenties, taking his coverings off all through one of those hot nights that come before the rains, until they lay like snake sloughings on the floor of the monkish, military room that was his office.

He had put on his old uniform and set that room up, they said, as if for a court-martial, which proved to them that he was off his rocker. But he had had a classical education as well as an experience of arms, and he knew the names of all the gods who were destroying him. Perhaps he anticipated as he took and told off his skins, loss of favour, dishonour, downfall, ignominy, that in the end there would be left a kernel of hope or even of absolution, but there was only the last skin of his disgrace and inside it the seed of another. So he tidied the pencils and pads on the table which had three wooden chairs behind it and lacked nothing appropriate to the occasion except his accusers and a green-baize cloth; removed his buttons and insignia of rank, went out, stood himself against a wall and shot himself through the head.

He left a widow. She was young, pretty, harmless; a girl who came of good parents who had wanted boys but made do with her, and regarded her with affection as well as exasperation. They had christened her Lesley.

She climbed trees as a child, shot pigeons with an air-gun, rode ponies as if pursued by cossacks or the shrieking hordes of Ghengiz Khan, and wept alone where none could see, but for what she did not know. Tears, she found, quickly healed a passing grief but left exposed the scars of deeper and more mysterious wounds she knew she had but did not remember getting.

But Lesley exists only on the periphery of this tale, although without her there might have been no tale to tell, which is why she enters now: a girl with fair hair and cheeks flushed by the wind, a small fragment of tense flesh and tingling blood who emerges from the hot, dust-storm landscape of her youth, with a firm hand got of horses, to take her place, as demurely as her little breasts have taken theirs beneath her cotton dresses, in the bright clear handsome sunshine of being Ned Pearson's wife; and then with a shriek of incredulous rage at his infidelity, his adultery with a woman as old, as plain as Thelma Craddock, of whose like by this world she had never been warned, she is gone, back into the creating chaos, white-faced from the sight of Ned's body, holding herself up, but feeling herself betrayed by the tears her bird-like mother lets fall and by the haggard look her father has, standing by the grave like a man deprived by telegram and battle of an only son.

Taxed with the violence as his fingers still trembled from contact with Thelma's cheek, Bruce Craddock would have been hard put to it to explain why he hit his wife, for he was a

73

man of peace, getting on, come far from impetuosity and the bare restraint of passion such as in this climate marked out younger men.

And later, when they were both calmer, in a limbo of time between the days and nights when the Panther House was full of subtle scents and low noises such as might come from an animal that was dispossessed, restless and inquisitive, and the days and nights when the animal seemed to have gone away and there were no scents or noises other than those of their own occupation; between these two periods of time, if Craddock had been reminded of the day his wife sat on the packing crate and of how he had hit her, which he had never done before, he might have found reasonable explanations but he would not have told the truth which, being a territory, is explored more easily than told.

Four people; one dead; Bruce and Thelma Craddock. Ned and Lesley Pearson. These are not their real names. With the exception of Ned they are still alive and so it is necessary to create a correspondence of reality that won't cause them pain. But in going about their business and in describing their circumstances to each other and to themselves, people are endlessly inventive. It is they who set the precedent, not the storyteller who, as a consequence, is bound only by his version of the truth and by the words he can muster to record it.

'Playa de Faro'
April–September, 1962

Part Two

The Plaza de Toros

'*Playa de Faro*'
*Between September 10th
and October 16th, 1962*

1

To see Ordóñez at the corrida twenty miles away in San Felíu de Guixols it would cost five hundred pesetas for a seat at the barrera, sombra y sol y sombra, or four hundred pesetas at the contrabarrera which was two hundred pesetas more than the weekly wage young Miguel and his twin brother Domingo earned between them for fetching and carrying at the Villa Vora la Mar.

At five in the afternoon, on Sunday; six bulls, six Bravos Toros and Ordóñez: maxima figura, maximo triunfador en todos los Ruedos del Mundo. The posters had been up since Monday, showing Ordóñez gold-jacketed and expressionless above a convolution of pink cape and black bull, gracefully transfiguring a moment on the journey to the grave occasion. It was forbidden to throw cushions at the toreros, on pain of arrest by the Guardia Civil; and who would wilfully get on the wrong side of the brown-skinned lads with the flat eyes and the shiny black hats? But it wasn't forbidden to throw money or roses, to mix the scent of the roses with the blood of the bulls. At five in the afternoon, on Sundays, all over Spain the spectacle begins. In how many places? At six bulls to the plaza, how many bulls? How many roses?

Myra said, 'We'd like to go. What about you, Ed?'

There had always been an understanding between us that I came to Spain especially not to see the bulls. Below her tall-crowned sunhat and her black sunglasses there was nothing to see except her smile.

'Yes, what about it?' the young man said. He was fair-haired, tanned and vigorous, perhaps ten years younger than Myra, which would mean that when he was born I was already thirty, looking at the world from the decks of tramp steamers and noticing how most parts of that world looked like others.

75

He sat close to her. His teeth flashed like those of a novillero. 'You could tell us what to look for,' he said. During my absence in Ampurias he had seen the books about the corrida in the study.

For three of us it would cost twelve hundred pesetas at the contrabarrera. For tourists the cost of death in Spain was obviously higher than the cost of living. Twelve hundred pesetas was more than three months' wages for Lola, our maid of all work. For the same figure one of us could have stayed for three or four days full pension at the Hotel Playa de Faro, with a private bath and shuttered windows that opened on to the Mediterranean and the Prospero music of the transistors that came in on the ancient wind with the smells of pines, garlic, cooking-oil and abre-solaire.

'It's up to you, Ed,' Myra said. 'We're for it.'

'You're not for it,' I said. 'Neither are we. It's the bulls. They're for it.'

We were sitting on the terrace of the Villa Vora la Mar which Myra and I had rented for a year from Señor García at the end of the last lecture tour. We drank Cinzano Bianco in tall glasses. In the six o'clock light the three of us were caught in a glow like that which might follow a swirl of Ordóñez's cape: my wife Myra, whom a man at the Consulate in Barcelona once mistook for my niece; the young man from the beach whose name I hadn't caught; and myself, an ageing animal at the hour of aperitif, observing these two others from the safety of his querencia, which is the name given to the particular spot in the ring the bull likes to go back to because he feels safest there.

In the end for reasons that will become clear, I went alone; but I was late, and missed the paseo, the march-on of the cuadrillas. I filled the absent picture in for myself from what I knew of the bearing of matadors when they enter the arena abreast to music, their arms wrapped and stiff as if they have already suffered wounds.

It was four years since I had finished a novel. Perhaps I had written myself out. That was not an unfamiliar nightmare, but four years was a long time. I went into the study at seven every morning and came out three hours later. Myra had virtually stopped asking how things were going. If we talked about work at all we did so in terms of another lecture tour in the States. The money they pay is good. That was understood, but the inference was that the new book would be finished by then.

The book I'd been trying to write was about two people who turned up somewhere in disgrace; people called Craddock. In Playa de Faro there is a passenger launch service, the Cruceros Costa Brava, that takes people from one playa to another, and that was what I first pictured the Craddocks turning up on: one of those boats, coming in from the north, from somewhere like Estartit, and living in a villa like the Vora la Mar. A nice looking couple, Thelma about thirty-nine, Bruce forty, just right for each other. They were the sort of attractive people you sometimes see who strike you at once as ideally matched. You wonder what obstacles they've had to overcome, what they've had to throw overboard, whom they've had to hurt, just in order to be together. People like that in places like Playa de Faro always look as if they're living on borrowed time. You wonder what they've run away from, how much time they've got left.

For Bruce and Thelma, Playa de Faro, or somewhere like it, it, was the last stop. There was nothing ahead of them, although to watch them arriving on the beach no one would have known there was anything wrong. But they knew. As they stood on the beach looking at the white villa their smiles died away. Perhaps the money was running out and it hadn't been theirs to spend in the first place. Perhaps Bruce had embezzled the money and stolen Thelma from another man: from his brother as likely as not. It's extraordinary how frequently melodrama crops up in life, even if it no longer does in books.

But when I analysed this version of the Craddocks's story I realized that it wasn't right. It wasn't a story about two people turning up in disgrace at all. In a place like Playa de Faro, Bruce and Thelma weren't capable of supporting the penitential load I tried to put on them. They kept wanting to shrug their shoulders, go out and around and have a good time for as long as they could. It threatened to turn itself into a story about what happened to people like that when the money was gone and they had to think seriously about what else they had, apart from what they felt for each other, to make a go of it together.

If I'd told Myra what had happened she would have said: Well, that's fine, Ed, it means those two characters have got wills of their own, they're running away with you. So I didn't tell Myra. They don't run away with you. You have to lead them carefully step by step to their logical conclusion, and you have to stop leading them if the conclusion you're leading them to doesn't fit in with the original picture of them.

I think the idea of two people turning up in disgrace came to me the first time Myra and I visited Spain on what must have been our fourth or fifth honeymoon, after she'd rejoined me in Rome at the end of an enforced separation that had lasted more than two months. I had been putting the finishing touches in a book called *Cassandra Laughing*. Myra was at an hotel in London. We have never had a permanent home. We are both too restless, although I suppose if Myra had married a steadier man she would have been content to settle down. As it is, we have lived in hotels, furnished apartments, and have rented houses from absent friends.

Leaving Rome together we drove into France and then turned south, for Perpignan and the Spanish frontier. As soon as we'd crossed the Pyrenees I stopped the car and asked her whether she couldn't smell it too: poverty, and the blood of bulls, the scent of roses; the smells of pride and sorrow. I had always kept away from Spain. For me it was the graveyard of the Thirties and the literary preserve anyway of poor old Ernest. We had come to Spain because Señor García had offered us his villa for a month. And that is when it began: with this idea, of two people; turning up.

But the Bruce and Thelma Craddock who turned up in a place like Playa de Faro weren't in disgrace at all. Once I'd accepted that I told myself that the word disgrace was inapposite when used to describe the kind of situation people find themselves in nowadays. After all, disgrace presupposed a state of grace you could fall out of, and which of us had ever been in it in the first place? But we all knew what we meant as human beings by disgrace. Loss of, or downfall from, a position of trust or honour. But who is trusted? Who honoured? I decided that Playa de Faro was probably the wrong place in which to write about this kind of thing. People went there for a good time.

And that definition of disgrace, that, surely, was disgrace defined by the people who weren't in it but who were describing to themselves the state of the people they said were? The word disgrace, in a tolerant age, seemed to smack of intolerance. We could be in bad odour, get kicked out of a job, feel it wise to make ourselves scarce or even necessary to get out of the country, discarded by our wives or our lovers for infidelity, laughed at, accused, given a bad time generally for behaving reprehensibly or for refusing to conform or for being found out in some nefarious practice, or for having the wrong number of heads or the wrong colour skin. But ninety-nine times out of a hundred we would have our excuses ready. It was the hundredth time I was thinking about, the time when there wasn't any excuse.

I meant disgrace that went deep, that they felt deeply, those two people; disgrace they accepted and had no answer for, disgrace they experienced sharply every morning when they woke up. Eventually they would have got over it, and I anticipated that. People have a basic resilience. But when they arrived, when they turned up, they were shattered by it.

That was as far as I got. I thought that Spain was bad for me. The wine was too cheap and the sun was too hot. The words evaporated before I could get them down. But I knew that Spain was good for me, too. Here they understand about the Duende.

It means imp, ghost, goblin. The Spanish poet Lorca wrote about it, the one who died mysteriously. They never found his body. He said the Duende burned the blood like powdered glass. Someone else, Manuel Torres I think, said that everything that had dark sounds had Duende. I think this is true. The Duende is inside, so the sounds that come are bound to be dark. It's easiest in music and singing to say whether a work or a performance has the Duende, but whatever type of work or performance it is it counts for nothing unless the Duende is heard.

I think of my own Duende as a little black hunchback who draws pictures on the walls of his dungeon. When I find the pictures moving he shrieks with laughter. When I find them comic I hear him weeping in the straw. There's a chain on his left leg and there's one part of the dungeon wall he can't get at to draw pictures on. I shout at him to break the chain. He curses me and tells me to break it myself. We both bleed from the strain. The book I would write is the picture he would draw on that part of the wall. You wouldn't recognize them as the same, but he's got to. If he does the chain is broken and he leaps across the page too quickly for you to see anything but his shadow. He draws his pictures and I write my words. Then you feel him.

To the Duende the physical world is bare, ugly, beautiful. He is naked, disarmed, crippled; aching with the pain of his imprisonment and his deformity. What is inanimate in the world – trees, hills, mountains – they kill him with their tranquillity. At night the Universe looks intolerable to him, unbearably indifferent. There's nothing, nothing he can do to molest or change or halt it. What he paints or draws or sculpts or writes is done with this knowledge, but to make his life bearable.

But it is only paint, only words, only thought, only imagining. It is an artifice, a malformation, a malpractice, a mask, a joke, a game. If he's lucky some of his games are good enough to be handed on as proof of what can be done when you play the game hard enough, well enough.

I had always said that I came to Spain especially not to see the bulls, but on that first occasion when I crossed the frontier, I think I guessed that the time would come when going to the corrida would be obligatory, symbolic of my submission to an old habit of curiosity. Secretly from Myra, I began to read books about the corrida so that I should know what to look for. Reading books about it became as compulsive an occupation as not going to it. Perhaps the thing that fascinated me most was this business of the bull's querencia, which is the name they give to the particular spot in the ring that the bull favours.

The matador must detect the querencia, not only so that he can try to keep the bull away from it but also so that he doesn't inadvertently stand in the way of the bull getting back to it. If he stands in the way neither the cape nor the muleta will distract the animal. The torero will be up in the air or stuck on the horns. And even when the matador knows the primary querencia he must watch for signs of the bull choosing a secondary. They say a cowardly bull has no querencia at all, which makes it difficult to fight him, because he is unpredictable. The brave bulls always adopts a querencia. He establishes a claim to a personal territory; and once he is in it he only leaves it to charge a man or a cape or a horse. He is then difficult to cite, to make responsive to the lure. And so it is a contest of wills, and of cunning.

You can stop him going to the querencia, provoke him to leave it, distract him from finding a secondary querencia, but the mystery of the animal's choice remains unsolved. A shadow on the sand, a damp patch, a blood stain: any of these may mark the spot. But why? A bull that chooses the centre of the ring is thought the bravest of all. Perhaps he is also stupid. There is no mystery in geometry.

If a matador who has detected the bull's querencia is out to make a show for the patrons who don't know a cornada from a cogida, he stations himself between the querencia and the bull: not quite in a direct line but close enough to make it look risky when the bull charges. The bull is indifferent to the matador when he charges in these circumstances, he is intent simply on regaining the querencia and he makes for it like a steam-engine. The matador fakes it up with some fancy cape work as the bull goes by and the crowd who thought the bull was accepting the lure goes mad with enthusiasm.

I have been faking it up with the cape for a long time. In Playa de Faro, from the shelves outside Señor Rojas's bar, and from one or two of the shops in Barcelona, you can buy Penguin editions of some of the novels. The photograph on the inside was taken some years before the war. It shows a man already in his middle thirties but looking as optimistic and confident as a young novillero at the beginning of the season in which he is to take the alternativa: take the estoque, the sword, from the hands of a full matador and make the kill in the matador's place, and so become a full matador himself, a new Manolete or Belmonte, or an Ordóñez: to be judged for ever afterwards not only on the sublime poetry of a series of tenderly confusing verónicas, nor merely on the skill and grace and fine male arrogance of a set of well and dangerously placed banderillas, but pre-eminently on the sad passion, the punishing absolution of his performance in the faena, which is the name given to all the work done with muleta and sword in the last third of the combat.

Ten minutes after the start of the faena the aviso sounds: the first trumpet warning to the matador that death cannot wait for ever. The second warning comes three minutes later, and the third and last two minutes after that; and then if the bull is still alive it is herded from the ring by steers and killed by the butcher. Time tells for the matador, as for the man, as for the lover.

Today the face in the mirror is that of a man who took the alternativa years ago, who has killed well a few times and survived his frequent gorings. It is upon the face rather than the thighs that I bear the visible scars of my cornadas. Even with the face in repose, with the eyes shut, I can feel the depth of the lines from the outer flesh of each nostril to the corresponding corner of the mouth. They are lines of inquiry and rejection, and have deepened in the flesh as the flesh has thickened and coarsened. Hidden in these crevices, perhaps, is the residual optimism of youth. The black curls on the head of the younger man in the outdated photograph (which preserves, I have always felt, the constant image of the sitter's potential promise) have thinned and straightened and made way for wiry grey intruders. Those poet's eyes are now the eyes of a writer of prose, and that youthfully pro-consular nose the nose of a man who remembers every smell there is. It is the face of a man ruined by his own curiosity.

Before I abandoned the attempt to write this book about two people who turned up in disgrace, I tried it another way. I placed the Craddocks in the kind of old-fashioned society that took its pleasures in private and paid for them in public. They turned up now more than thirty years ago in India, in a place called the Mahwari Hills. Thelma was plain instead of attractive, hiding her face under one of those old-fashioned solar topees in the way that Myra hides hers under her Vogue beach hat; only in Myra's case the hat is worn to preserve her complexion.

Craddock was older, about my age. You could see he had been an administrator from the way he walked and stood and relaxed, always on the qui vive, as they were, even when out strolling, as if a messenger were likely to arrive at any moment, especially at sundown, with an urgent minute. Only now, for Craddock, there was no messenger to arrive. They had been sent to a backwater to wait for the scandal to die down. His wife had had an affair with a goodlooking boy on his own staff called Ned Pearson who wasn't quite young enough to be her son, but young and handsome enough to make people wonder what on earth he had seen in her, in Thelma Craddock. Well, such things are unaccountable, but people are always being surprised. In this case they were additionally surprised because he was already married to a pretty girl called Lesley, a girl you would have said was made for him if you'd seen them together.

It was Lesley who found out about Ned and Thelma. She was only a kid. She should have spoken first to her parents and asked their advice because there was Craddock's as well as her husband's career at stake, but there were reasons why she didn't. Instead she kicked up a terrible row and filed a suit for divorce. Poor Ned shot himself. Perhaps he was already over the worst of his infatuation. Perhaps all he saw was the horror of being found out sleeping with the wife of his superior. Perhaps her plainness made it seem worse to him when he stopped, to think about it. He might have wondered about his motives.

Lesley hadn't anticipated a violent end to the affair. She hadn't stopped to think. She had been cheated, done out of something, that was all she knew. Ned was the first person who had really seemed to belong to her. He was proof that she was a woman and not the half-boy, half-girl her parents had unconsciously tried to turn her into because they had wanted sons. So she ruined her life, killed Ned and ruined Thelma's husband.

If Craddock had divorced Thelma he himself would have ridden the scandal. But he didn't divorce her. He took her back. The station couldn't stand for that. They both had to be got rid of. Which is where we came in, in this godforsaken spot in the Mahwari Hills, with Bruce and Thelma Craddock turning up with all this scandal behind them still festering inside them. People had explained his taking her back by saying that obviously he couldn't live without her in spite of what she'd done. But Thelma knew this wasn't the reason. She wasn't sure why Bruce had taken her back, but she knew it wasn't because he loved her. She had only to catch him watching her to know that he was thinking how plain, how old and ugly she had become. She knew he was astonished that anyone, let alone Ned Pearson, should have thought of her as pretty. She felt responsible for Ned's death and disgraced by it. She had never felt disgraced by their loving each other or going to bed together or even by their being found out. But when he killed himself she felt as if he had rejected her from the grave, felt as if she had been turned down by a corpse. She knew that this was a disgrace, and she knew that being taken back by a husband who didn't love her was just as bad. When he took her back he seemed to bring to light something discreditable about their life together.

This Bruce and this Thelma seemed closer to the original image I had had of two people turning up. The house they came to live in was called the Panther House. There are places in the world, so I have noticed, where a terrible peace, an awful wholeness seems to have been achieved, a union between man and nature that excludes intruders. The Panther House was like that. It seemed to resist the Craddocks's occupation. Although I used to work mostly in the mornings only there were occasions when I came back into the study, after dark, and sat, and listened to the sounds of night, and it occurred to me then that it was not just those two people who had turned up, in that place, wherever it was, and not only they who had cause to be ashamed.

It was the hunchback who, drawing on my own recollections of something that happened to me years ago as a young man in India, first drew pictures of the house and the panther,.and these latter in turn reminded me of a story I heard once about a leopard: panthera pardus fusca. The Natural History people say there's no difference between panther and leopard. Some of the people who shoot them say there is. They call the larger specimen with the longer skull the panther. Panthers (or leopards) are less intolerant of the sun than tigers, less nocturnal; bold, brave, and fond of the flesh of dogs. They enter huts and tents and have been known to seize men from machans. Langurs would be safe if they didn't panic, but they do; they jump or fall to the ground when leopards are nearby, and are taken.

The story about the leopard is supposed to be true. There were reports of it in the Journal of the Bombay Natural History Society. It happened in Assam, in the North Cachar Hills. Some men from a village found the lair. The male parent had left the district, and the mother leopard was out hunting. When she came back she was too late to save her cubs, but she saw the men who had shot them and followed them back to their village. She lay in wait for two days, watching. If she had been out for nothing but revenge she would have tried to enter one of the huts. But she didn't. She was seen in daylight, but not caught. They thought she had gone away. On the third day a woman working in the fields left her child playing close by.

The leopard came then, took the child and ran off with it into the jungle. The men searched but found no trace of the animal or the boy. Three years later the villagers killed a female leopard. It was the same one. In the new lair they found two cubs and the child. He walked upright but ran on all fours. He had a powerful sense of smell and was partially blinded by cataract.

I can't remember what happened to him. I think he died. Tuberculosis probably. But I wasn't really interested in the boy. I was interested in the leopard. So was the hunchback. He called it panther and painted it black, because that is the colour of mourning (although not in China). The blackness in a panther is due to melanism, the deposit of a dark pigment in the hairs that are normally yellow or white. This obscures the rosettes, or spots, although in certain lights on some black animals the spots can still just be seen. It is thought that melanism is associated with localities where there is a heavy rainfall. The percentage of black specimens increases southwards, down through the Malay peninsula, until they become dominant.

And having given it the colour of mourning the hunchback blinded it, pearled both its eyes over with shining cataracts. The passion of the leopard in the true story ended when it found and took the child, but the passion of the panther drawn by the hunchback never came to an end. It was the ghost of a blind black panther padding up and down, robbed of its cubs, unable to find a substitute. It always seemed to be in the same vicinity, hiding in the undergrowth of a wild garden, and at night coming into the open, circling the house, an old building of white stucco that shone in the moonlight. And it was here Bruce and Thelma came. And sometimes the hunchback drew pictures of them groping for each other in bright sunshine, blind as bats, their eyes covered with cataracts too; pearly blue ovals in white faces.

Sometimes it is the animals I'm sorriest for: those birds, if you can still call them birds, gross creatures of the air, flying over that island we turned sour with one of our experiments. But who would champion a grotesque bird, a blind panther, a brave bull?

There was a bull called Civilón.
This was in 1936, just before the outbreak of the Spanish

Civil War. Civilón had been raised on a ranch that bred fighting bulls down in Salamanca, on the Ganadería of Don Juan Cobaleda, whose colours are green and scarlet.

The cows as well as the bull-calves are tested for courage. I suppose Civilón had been tested in that way, that is to say charged by men on horseback with blunt poles that resembled picas. He was described as noble which seems to prove he had passed the test. The calves are tumbled over by the men with the poles. When they get up they will either run away or show fight. If they run away they are marked for the butcher. If they show fight they are marked for the corrida.

One of Cobaleda's employees, Isidoro Alvarez, who had fought in the ring as a novillero, took special notice of Civilón. He found he could approach him on horseback and feed him. Later, he used to dismount, go close to him, even rub the bull's neck. Some men have this kind of rapport. Perhaps in Alvarez's case it explained why he had given up fighting in the ring.

When Civilón was full grown Alvarez could still feed him like that. They used to let children come and stand quite close. They took Civilón's picture and wrote him up in the newspapers. He became famous. He was lovable and laughable and disturbing to the human ego. And so it was bound to happen, wasn't it? That someone would get the idea of having Civilón fought by a matador in a regular corrida? Even if it turned out to be a shambles it would be worth it. The plaza would be packed because everybody in Spain would want to know the answer to the questions: When is a fighting bull no longer a fighting bull? So of course it happened; not far from here, in Barcelona. The matador was a man called Luis Gómez, El Estudiante.

After the paseo, after the parade, the ring is empty. They empty the ring in the way they douse the house lights in a theatre. They empty the ring after the paseo and again after each bull is dragged out by the mules to the cracking of whips. Then the new bull makes his salida. I wonder how Civilón came out? If he had nobility he must have been levantado, head high. Alvarez was there, watching from the callejón. Gómez's peons would have gone in first, trailing their capes, catching the bull's attention then making a dash for it while Gómez studied the way the bull charged, which way he hooked with the horn, whether he had a tendency to go for the man instead of the cape. After a while he would have signalled the peons to finish, and gone into the arena to get to know Civilón himself, and start the business of confusing him, winding him, stopping him in his tracks.

This is the stage where to the bull the capes are like a plague of flies, an annoyance, not easily got rid of but not to be taken too seriously. But towards the end of this first third of the combat the bull wonders. Nothing he has done to see the capes off the premises has worked. He begins to feel frustrated, but his head is still levantado and the tossing muscle on his neck makes him feel supremely confident. And curiously this means he is far less dangerous to the man. The head is too high and the bull isn't attacking as he would if he felt any serious need to defend himself. The sport of the corrida is bringing the head down, making the bull dangerous. To do this they bring on the horses and the picadors, for the climax of the first act, La Suerte de Varas, the trial of the lances.

To the bull, after the confusion of the pink capes, the horse is a recognizable enemy. The horse is an outrage. They say that any bull, brave or cowardly, will charge the first horse. But it is what happens when it has got there that counts, because the man on the horse, the picador, has to lean over and spear the bull with the pic, right in the tossing muscle. There are rules and regulations about the length and thickness of the spearing point of the pic and there is a circular flange that stops the point going deeper than the specified number of inches. But it makes a wound the blood flows from. It weakens the muscle. The head comes down a bit, and that brings the horns nearer to a man's belly. When they fought Civilón in Barcelona no one could be sure he would charge the picador's horse. After all, Alvarez had fed him from the saddle. But if he charged the horse and took the pic in his tossing muscle would he charge again? Would he charge the other picador? Or would he retreat into his querencia, to the barrera or to the now closed gates that led back into the toril, wanting only to get out of that place and be off, away to the grasslands of Juan Cobaleda? Even after they had played him effectively with the cape, the spectators in the plaza must have felt that when the horses came on there was a good chance of the whole business ending in farce. Perhaps there were some who hoped it would. If so they were disappointed.

Civilón charged the first horse and took the pic. He charged the second horse and took the pic there too. And the whole crowd rose calling for the indulto, the reprieve, and this was granted. I don't know how many times in the history of the bullring the bull has been given the indulto. Perhaps you could count them on the fingers of one hand.

When a bull has been reprieved, or when the matador has failed to kill it in the time allowed, or the picador has ruined it by pic-ing it in the ribs instead of the muscle they bring on steers to herd it out of the ring. Normally Civilón would have been led out like that, but this was a very special performance.

Alvarez, who had been watching from the callejón, was dared to go into the ring alone. They wanted to use Alvarez as a steer. Because he was Civilón's friend he accepted the dare. He took a handful of hay and walked out into the arena. Civilón came towards him. Alvarez had nothing to defend himself with. When the bull was close he stopped, and then – they – say – he nuzzled the man who was offering the handful of hay and they walked out of the ring together. The bull's flanks would have been streaming with blood. There must have been a lot of applause.

Cobaleda wanted to buy him back for stud. And that would have been a happy ending, wouldn't it? Even though Civilón was wounded by the pics. It was because he was wounded that they kept him for a while in Barcelona, to recover. And it was because they kept him in Barcelona that the ending wasn't happy.

On July the eighteenth, 1936, rebel soldiers entered the city. They were hungry. They went to the corrals. I don't know how many bulls they shot and butchered, but Civilón was one of them.

The bullfight has been called a sport. It has been called a tragedy. It has been called Art. It has been said simply to illustrate life, and perhaps that is nearer the truth, because it is foreseeably to end in death and what lies between the beginning and the end is therefore an exhibition of mystique and vanity.

2

There had been no rain for months. The light was intense. Myra hid behind dark glasses, even after five, when the beach began to take the shade of the hill on which the villa stood, a white focus for the eye among the pines, los pinos, that shed soft-pointed needles and distilled aromatic gums.

The kitchens of the Villa Vora la Mar were light and airy. They opened on to a courtyard. Our two serving boys, Miguel and Domingo, sang there in the mornings, bare-chested and peeling vegetables, and unlike the kitchen boys in the hotels they were as brown as berries.

Lola sang too while she cleaned and ordered the household to Myra's satisfaction. The boys slept in a corner of the store-room among the sacks and the bottles, and prepared coffee and fruit juice that I took into the study every morning at seven after swimming in the warm deserted sea like an old coela-canth with an instinct for self-preservation, an atavistic mem-ory of what the oceans were like before they became infested. Lola lodged further up the road in a little pink house that belonged to Señor and Señora Sarbosa. She came to the villa at eight o'clock to begin her day by making Myra's breakfast, and sometimes Señor Sarbosa, the traffic policeman, called in for coffee in his smart white summer uniform before going on down to the playa where it was his job to see that the tourists didn't park their cars in the narrow lane between the hotels and the terraces, and observed the efficient oneway system he had devised that took them round the little complex of dirt roads with ease and comfort and without encountering ob-stacles.

Fat and smiling, Lola loved as her own those twin sons of the woman I had never seen but thought of as the Dolorous Widow of Figueras. Lola said she prayed for us all every night, but especially for her nephews. In twin brothers, Lola said, the passions of the sea could run strong. Perhaps her prayers were less for Miguel who was the studious, thinner one, and more for Domingo, whose wine-dark eyes were already hot with the knowledge of the power he would wield without burdening himself with an education. In a few years he would be hand-some. At sixteen he was beautiful, a creation of Michelangelo.

He was aware of himself, especially, in relation to Myra. Neither Myra nor I commented on this, although we joked together about his brother's more open and comical devotion to her. Bookish Miguel blushed and fumbled when he served her and she rewarded him with a smile that marked her affection but confirmed, in a kindly way, how hopeless any expectations would be. Her mouth alone often sufficed, being all she had left to communicate with under her Vogue beach hat and the black sunglasses. But when it was Domingo's turn to wait at table and he bent over her, helping her to portions not heaped as Miguel fondly tried to heap them, but exactly, almost insolently calculated to conform to the rules of her diet, there was a wariness in her manner that told me she felt what I divined: an unmistakable heat, remarkable in a boy so young, that she knew she would be wise to do nothing to encourage.

We ate out always on the terrace: at lunch under an umbrella whose fringe Miguel (but never Domingo) seldom ducked under without untidying his dark hair. At night the umbrella was furled and taken away and we dined in artificial light that spilled from the lighted rooms of the villa and glowed from the almond trees: The terrace was a small flagged square, walled by a stone balustrade on which there were pots of cactus and urns of flowering shrubs which Myra watered fastidiously at ten in the morning when I came out of the study to drink more coffee and read the mail and talk to whoever had turned up: the mechanic tinkering with the radio or the refrigerator, the girl with the washbag, the boy with the octopus caught early that morning on the playa.

On its pine covered hill, with its view across the bay of a once little known but now popular resort, its private steps to the beach cut out of the hillside and shored up with bits of wood, the Villa Vora la Mar never felt isolated, even in the year we first spent a month in it and there wasn't another villa nearer than half-a-mile and our supplies came mostly by mule cart instead of on the back of a Lambretta or in the back of a truck. But this is a peculiarity of pine trees – they always seem to be shielding other things from view, even when there is nothing there, no close neighbour.

The pines. Los pinos. The Spaniards pronounce every letter of their angular language. They know that words come hard and don't waste them by throwing parts of them away. The stones are in the soil of their speech, like the other stone that you can smell as soon as you come down through the Pyrenees. You can still smell it far beyond the mountains: seeds and shards of shale and granite that crab the vines and embitter the harvests. From the lion hills to the terracotta, bastions that are sucked and slapped by the blue and emerald waters of the coast of Catalonia the rock is there, just under the earth, like the long memories of the Civil War, thunder waiting for a storm, holding on to the roots of the cactus and the pines, los cactos y los pinos.

It erupted through the thin soil out of which the steps had been cut to make a private way up to the villa: steps which from half-way up gave a view of the curve of the chameleon sand that was tawny from dawn until eleven when the sun began to extract its colour, leaving it as dazzling as frost crystallized and heated by ultra-violet rays, white against the clear blue-green of the sea. At two o'clock the whiteness faded to ochre and at four the ochre warmed to pink. And all day it was marked by footprints and mushroomings of gay umbrellas that shaded bodies as brown and limp as strips of anchovy.

Because the villa was half-way up the hill of the southwest promontory, at five its upper storey still took sunshine on the side that faced the continuing slope to the winding road that brought traffic to the playa. The sound of the traffic was muffled by the pines and the traffic itself was mostly invisible except at night when its course could be mapped by the switchback glide of headlamps. But at five, the hour of the bulls, the hillside tingled with stillness and the chanting of the cicadas, and the sun slanted through the louvres of the shuttered french doors of the bedrooms.

The Reglamento Taurino lay down that the matadors and their cuadrillas must be present in the arena fifteen minutes before the beginning of the corrida. But these were early days. The posters announcing Ordóñez at San Felíu were not yet up on the billboards opposite the Hotel Playa de Faro. If at this time you had watched us coming out of the villa and going down to the beach, returning, it would have seemed that Myra and I were alone, except for the servants. But that would have been to reckon without the Craddocks, or Ned and Lesley Pearson, without any of the people I take with me wherever I go, the shadowy figures of my imagination and of my curious and disastrous history.

And it would have been to reckon without the solider figure

Myra suddenly conjured, as if to convey a warning.

Sometimes, when she sat on the playa staring through those dark glasses beyond the bathers to the horizon, or on the terrace gazing down through the gap in the pines to the mottled currents far below, I fancied she was looking for her image in the sea, identifying herself with its immense wastes and extraordinary untapped fertility.

Her parents separated when she was eight or nine. The father was quite rich, but he left his money to a mistress. Myra spent six months of the year with one parent and six months with the other. I used to have a picture of her in my mind, travelling from mother to father and back again, with her child's nose close to the window of an express train, her love held in abeyance, parcelled up and lying on her lap like a bag of biscuits one of them had given her to ease the tedium and hunger of the journey. When she was old enough she stopped seeing either of them. By old enough, I think I mean the day (and there must have been such a day) when she looked in the mirror and realized that she had something of her own that she owed to neither parent: extraordinary physical beauty.

Myra has never been marked by nature as one of the mammals though. Her body has never been subjected to the process of distension and parturition. She had two miscarriages the year after we were married. Her doctor warned me of the dangers. She was not made to be a mother. I was too old to be disappointed. Only a young husband would have been. Only a young man seeks immortality in the flesh. At fifty we are finished with that particular delusion. But for a time there was for me in making love to her a bleak sensation of arid devotion only to the machinery of copulation. In a primitive tribe she would have died in childbirth, or been cast out.

When I first knew her I noticed something odd about the way she held her head, as if it were one too easily broken off at the neck, and so never to be moved without major considerations for its safety and for the delicate balance of its classical features. Sometimes it looked like a head of pale creamy wax with articulated eyelids that would close if the body were laid flat, but not otherwise, at least not completely, being activated by counterweights only to the degree of inclination, the tilt, the angle of the face as it went through the motions of discriminating observation, or simulated the reception of impressions, the production of emotions, the reflections of passing thoughts. And even when she sat down on the stone bench in the garden at Richmond under the unexpected weight of my proposal, the head itself was erect, disciplined, apparently rejecting whatever curious messages were reaching it telling it to bend, look up, look down, or laugh, or frown. It was a head protected by an invisible carapace of unknown shape, dimensions, texture and strength. I couldn't break through it. I never did break through it.

Before I knew a word of her history I thought I saw in her eyes an understanding, even a horror, of the emptiness of her beauty. She had the kind of looks that made her welcome everywhere and feel welcome nowhere. She filled the void with culture. She had read every book people told her was worth reading and knew the difference between Manet and Monet which in Esher, where she came from, stood her out in a crowd.

She was twenty-eight in those days. For ten years she had known what it was to have men gather round her wherever she went. A human being is not meant to be a decoration. At last a marriage had been arranged with my cousin John, not in desperation but in surrender to a convention. It is often that way with women as beautiful as Myra. Such physical perfection begins by being of a kind its possessor guesses ought not to be squandered and ends invalidated by having been preserved too long. It is the kind of beauty sensible men admire too much to insist on owning when they are young enough to do it justice, and the time comes when it carries around with it its own prickly mask of already being spoken for. The prize, then, often goes to a man like John whose unsophisticated belief that there must still be all-comers to compete against makes him act towards her like the kind of boy she regrets having discouraged when she was young enough to make a match the society she moved in would have approved but would not have dictated. I suppose you could say that John was the brother she had never had, and I was the father-lover she wanted to recapture. But in this century, if we want to feel alive, it is best to forget Freud.

Standing side by side they looked ideally matched: John as handsome as Bruce, and Myra even lovelier than Thelma, the Bruce and Thelma of Playa de Faro, not of the Mahwari Hills; but there was something missing, something I had learned to look for as I knocked about the world: the sense of there being other people they had had to hurt, just to be together. This was in 1950. No one had been hurt. No one really cared. It was the absence of strong feelings that had dictated the engagement. Two questions had been answered: Whom would Myra Benson marry, whom would John Thornhill ask to marry him? and already the answers had ceased to be of interest.

Surrounded as they were by friends on the terrace of the house at Richmond they had already passed over the threshold of their dull but worthy futures: money and executive power for John, perhaps a child or two for Myra, a casual infidelity here and there, a split-level home in the New Forest. I could not help it that I fell in love with her and ached to bring life back into those empty eyes, take that vessel that was Myra Benson and help to fill it with something like a passion for the world it moved in. Did I succeed? At most I think I filled her with a sense of a special vocation, a vocation for being the wife of Edward Thornhill.

The garden of the house in Richmond sloped down to the river. Marvellous for a child. In summer in the dark corners of the boathouse you could smell the mist and damp of winter. In winter if you pressed your cheek against the wood, as children do, you could feel the summer heat trapped in the grain. When I was born, in China, I came with the right number of limbs, but something monstrous attended the lying-in, cursed me with the inability to see only what is there physically to be seen and left me with one of its own dark offspring to follow me and keep me up to the mark.

It was in the garden of the house in Richmond I first saw him, the little black hunchback, capering between the nettles and the dockleaves: the nettles to sting, the leaf to heal – proof of the articulate balance maintained by nature. I saw that good and evil grew side by side and the hunchback hugged his knees in delight and cartwheeled to the water's edge because I had understood. He made faces to amuse my grandfather, covered his mouth to laugh and mock at Grandfather's mistress, Nanny Martin, and stood on his head for young Uncle James so that all the money fell out of his pockets, a faery cascade of pieces of silver that did not need to be counted. He must have been there under the elms picking them up from around the stone bench Myra sat down on when I asked her to marry me.

I think she stopped loving me a long time ago, but how can I blame her for that? Often morose, often drunk, absorbed in my work, restless: even my body hair which has gone grey probably disgusts her. It was different twelve years ago when I turned up, sunburnt from Africa and answering to a name that was on Myra's list of required reading; younger looking than she had been led to expect from what John had told her about where I fitted like a graft of mistletoe on to the family oak, and not making any bones about what I felt for her the moment we stood close, touched hands and exchanged those silent assessments that pass between strangers as doves sent out for evidence of dry ground.

We met once, twice, three times. She and John were the same age, but their conversations were already as stilted as the talk that goes on in visiting hours in institutions for the aged, the sick, the blind and the imprisoned. I asked her why she was marrying him. She said, because she was fond of him. And he is fond of you, I said. I know, because he tells me so, but I am in love with you. There's a difference. Marry me and come to America.

There is always a price attached.

She sat down, then, on the stone bench. She was a child again, in the train between one affection and another.

On the terrace of the Villa Vora la Mar there is a stone bench of the same kind, a slab supported by carved heraldic beasts, under the almond trees, los almendros. Sitting on this she has never been a child. I don't mention childhood to convey an idea of innocence. After all, the rot sets in early. I mention it to reach the furthest point back in time of recognition of our individuality, the time when neither innocence nor experience is relevant to the picture we have of ourselves as uniquely fashioned, and on the bench in the garden of the house in Richmond I touched her on that spot.

Later when John turned away, having at last understood what I was telling him, that Myra no longer wanted to keep her promise to him, but was now betrothed to me, the hunchback stood silent, with a look that seemed to say that in taking Myra away from my young cousin I had got even with the wrong man: cousin John instead of Uncle James, between whom and myself no love was ever lost, although it was a surprise to me to think that there was anything to get even about, because what had Uncle James ever done to me but hasten my departure from a world that meant nothing to me to one that meant everything?

But: It's the wrong man! the hunchback said, and then began to laugh. He went on to his crooked knees, too weak from laughter to stand. It was like a paroxysm. Once he had started he didn't seem to know how to stop.

That empty vessel that was Myra Benson! Well, it was Mitzi all over again, I suppose, with variations, although it wasn't Myra who died, who wasted away once torn out of her native soil; but John; and who can tell whether drunken driving is an accident or not? John was the third betrayal, the second was Mitzi, the first long ago. There may have been, almost certainly were, others. But those are the three that stand out; not like gallows in a landscape but like three isolated little boxwood crosses such as people push into the ground on November the eleventh; small, like that, because everything in human life is really on a miniature scale.

It has been said that an artist needs his still centre, but I've never found mine, except in each book as I write it. My restlessness has been a disease. Perhaps deeply ingrained are recollections of those fifty miles my missionary parents walked after they had been stoned out of their house of cards, only to die, and of the thousands of miles I was taken before reaching what passed for an anchorage on the banks of that slow drifting English river. My first arrival. There has never been a second, but then, as the Chinese know, it is better to travel than to reach the end of a journey.

I turned up in the place and among the people my father had rejected as godless, a small dependent, a little blackhaired wide-eyed orphan who had already felt on his cheeks the whip of winds his ancestors would have thought outlandish and in whose blasts that tough but tender sheep, young Uncle James, hoped never to be shorn. Uncle James always stood foursquare and warm, safe in the querencia of his acquisitive ambitions, building with bricks and straw and good cement instead of cards. There are two kinds of people in the world: those who are embattled in strong citadels which are strong however unjustly or foolishly they are administered, and those who go out like gaunt Don Quixotes on ribby horses to tilt at bulls or the monotonous grinding sails of windmills.

Of the latter, I suppose, were my missionary father and mother; of the former, Uncle James and cousin John, one passionately foolish, passionately unjust, the other just and brave and not to be drawn out of his stronghold by any kind of enticement until he got drunk and climbed into a Jaguar and had an accident at one hundred miles an hour, in order presumably to forget the circumstances of his loss of Myra. Of the former, too, were my grandfather and his mistress, Nanny Martin, that sober keeper of the keys who was always dressed in browns and greys. Years passed, fashions changed, but Nanny Martin stayed staunch to her militant female style: long dresses that revealed the many black buttons on her shining boots and did up at her throat in starched fantasies of lace and mother of pearl. Above the fantasies, her ordinary face gave off odours and other intimations of homely bars of oatmeal soap and honest water got from brass taps that had gurgled with cleanly discipline into white porcelain bowls. To look at her, who would have thought of her as living in sin to establish a principle of freedom? Or as dying of apoplexy under a pink parasol that fell into the slow green water and floated backwards from the punt, riding the river like a crazy owl-and-pussy-cat coracle with a walking stick for a mast, bobbing and bucking, tipping and filling and sinking with an elegant swirl like her own fond, foolish, lively Edwardians, disappearing into the murky depths of their life and times?

Such was the view from the river bank. James poled in swiftly while her ancient lover held her in his arms and yelled across the water to ring for Doctor Beard. In the heat and tranquillity of a summer afternoon in 1924, with the trees glooming over the river, Nanny Martin got her come-uppance, and the era of Uncle James's long-desired iron-clad respectability began at last. Running across the lawn to reach the house and the telephone I knew that my days in Richmond were numbered, and I was glad. The house was stuffy with principles, beliefs and knowledge and I moved in it like a ghost, full of splendid ignorance, disbelief and heretical questions.

Uncle James said to me once, in private, 'You're not wanted. I'll see you're not. I'll get you out. You're sweating for nothing. How does that feel? You should have stayed in China. They bury their eggs there.' When he was married he looked like a totem pole; a piece of wood with a cut-in-smile. When he stood in front of a roaring grate I expected him to get on fire. He must have been doped with that stuff they spray scenery with in the theatre to stop it catching light. He told me once that Hitler 'had the right ideas'. Strength through Joy. Uncle James never laughed. He simply smiled. He was strong though. He used to beat John until the poor boy couldn't sit down. He said my father came to no good because he had milksop tutors and was never beaten. He raised a stick to me once. I kicked him on the shin and threatened to tell Grandfather. Grandfather was indifferent to him. Nanny Martin hated him. Once, as a child he put a worm in her soup. It was mulligatawny. Poor Uncle James. He was a mess. What else in the world was there left for him expect to love money and power? He must have had rich funds of affection that were never tapped and so went rotten. To the end of his days he painted his moustache black. He hated to be old. His cheeks were always flushed, but were smooth, as if they were carved. He treated Aunt Gwendoline, his wife, as if she were a serf who was lucky to be bedded by the lord of the manor. He screwed John out of her as you squeeze a dram from a dry barrel. She carried John like a dying ant staggering under a last load, a speck of grass, a fragment of stick, that had to be added to the other comforts of the nest.

I find the past painful to rake up. It offends me to think they are dead and can't hit back. I rake it up all the time in stories, but that is different. In stories you can deal more kindly with your own and other people's afflictions. In Playa de Faro I began to put Uncle James into a story about a leopard. I've just seen what could be wrong with it. Whatever Uncle James got hold of he went a fair way to making worthless, but the land his story-counterpart swindled other men out of prospered once it belonged to him. If I ever do any more work on that story I must pay attention to this point.

That man, Saunders, might have ended up acquiring land for the pleasure of watching it go to ruin. He might have had a dream of the whole valley gone spectacularly to dust. When it was dust the only creature left to dispossess would be the legendary leopard. Morally, this would be the logical end to the story of a life of greed, for Saunders to be lording it over a dust-bowl and begrudging a non-existent animal a share in its aridity.

On the other hand, the Saunders of the story was shrewd and intelligent as well as mad. Uncle James had nothing of his patience and skill. Uncle James was a child helping himself to the jam tarts and getting belly ache. That's why under his rule things went badly for the business. If he'd been half as clever as Saunders he'd have built up a firm big enough to take John's mind off the personal misfortune of losing Myra, instead of which it was a firm John was glad to see safely under a bigger rival's umbrella. Once he had done that he may have thought there wasn't any future for him. And yet he never looked like the type to take things to heart. Perhaps when he was younger his father had warned him against me, and now he remembered the warnings and thought there might have been something in them after all, that he'd been a fool not to take notice of them. The money he left was divided between three Thornhill cousins. I was one of them. Poor Uncle James! I've often meant to visit his grave to see if the headstone has split from 'op to bottom. In front of such a monument I might pour water on the earth that covers Uncle James's staring face, and laugh, and not know what I was laughing at.

3

In Playa de Faro there was a bronzed godling with whom Myra had earnest conversations she thought went undetected: in the mornings out there just beyond the circle of cork-bark floats that marked the position of the lobster pots, where they met, as if by chance, with thirty feet of Mediterranean beneath them, before swimming to a strip of sand and pebble among the rocks, a place that was invisible from the beach and the flat eyes of the lads from the Civil Guard, but not from the window of the study through fieldglasses.

Upon this strip of sand they enjoyed a drier exchange of gestures than the sea permitted; his hand, for instance, once upon her hip, and hers on the same occasion, on his satin shoulder. From these meetings they swam back together but parted before they reached the shore, she continuing and making land, he treading water to observe no doubt, the still youthful rake of her legs from hip to ankle and the formation of her elegant buttocks, the whole preserved perfection of her physical beauty that he probably guessed, all the same, belonged to a woman of forty. He looked intelligent.

What, I wondered, did they talk about among the lobster pots and on the strip of sand between the terracotta coloured rocks? What conception of the boundaries of friendship led to those meetings in the water and those partings before the shore? What notions of the limitations of human correspondence caused Myra to sit with me as usual over our twelve o'clock champagne at our umbrella-shaded table on the sand below the terrace of Señor Rojas's bar, with her back to the water, the tall sunhat and the large sunglasses back in position, and the dripping godling to pass within a few yards of us without a glance, showing us a chesty profile?

Did she know I would be jealous and not want to hurt me, or did she relegate the godling to the position of a dream she lived in the mornings between the lobster pots and the cove and then forgot? But if he were flesh to her, not dream, what self-denial did she have to exercise to keep to her room while I ostensibly kept to mine, between three and five in the afternoon, while down there on the playa the godling lay spread-eagled in the sun, making motionless love to the sand, playing it through the tense fingers of one outstretched hand as though he were Ned Pearson and the sand a lock of Thelma Craddock's hair?

At five, when the shadow line of the hill reached him, he used to rise and go to the water's edge where he put on flippers, mask and schnörkel. He stopped being Pearson then and became Poseidon, re-entering his kingdom. He swam the gauntlet of siren glances from the rocky outcrops and was gone. It was as if, at five, contact with a world not made up of fish and coral became dangerous to him, as if at five he had duties to perform below. But where did he go and when did he return? Where was he staying, where did he sleep? Perhaps he was a man like Pearson after all, and not Poseidon; a mortal man with an evening assignation on some other part of the coast, a nightly mounting to keep his body sweet, his temper even and his passion in restraint to render innocent those morning meetings with Myra.

But at five he went, and a little after five Myra stirred, returning from the privacy of her dreams to shower and change and join me on the terrace for an aperitif at six.

At forty-eight you can marry a woman twenty years younger and be happy. But that had been twelve years earlier. At sixty I was too old for her. I wondered whether she was plotting to be unfaithful, whether she had been unfaithful before. It puzzled me why she kept him so much to herself. Perhaps she had always managed to keep her men secret and brought them into the open only when I wasn't there to see.

Curiosity, the habit of inquiry; obviously they are fatal to peace of mind. I told Myra I ought to drive down to Barcelona to settle some business with Señor García. It was a city she loved, but now it seemed she preferred me to go alone. She asked me when. I told her: Tomorrow. I checked the sailing times of the Cruceros Costa Brava and instead of going to Barcelona drove up to Estartit and came back to Playa de Faro by sea, turning up like the Craddocks, about eleven o'clock, the time I should have been turning up in Barcelona. As the boat came round the promontory the sandy cove was in view. Myra and the godling were just leaving it, setting out on their swim back to the shore. The boat beat them to it. A few people got off, English tourists carrying packed lunches. Others got on. Show the English a boat and you can't keep them off it. It is as though they are always rehearsing for a second Flood.

Myra made land some seventy yards away, where the fishing boats were beached. The godling followed her out, which he had never done before. It was impossible to judge the situation, though, to tell whether he knew I was in Barcelona for the day or had co-incidentally on this particular occasion decided to push his luck. When she sat under her umbrella he stood for a moment, then leant forward to speak to her, his hands on his knees. Presently he sat down. Her umbrella wasn't in its usual place, but only her own beach bag and towel seemed to be under it.

The gangplank in the prow of the boat was raised and we pulled away from the beaching, stern first. About fifty yards out we came round and headed for Tossa. In a few moments the colours alone made one of the umbrellas distinguishable as Myra's. I got off the boat at Tossa, drank wine and ate a lunch of paëlla at the first hotel I came across. From the hotel I rang Señor García in Barcelona. He was in Gerona for the day. I said I would try to get in touch with him again tomorrow.

A boat left Tossa at half-past two. At half-past three we put in again at Playa de Faro. There aren't so many people on the beach between three and four in the afternoon. Among the scattered sunbathers the godling was there, alone, spreadeagled in the sun, letting the sand run through his fingers, waiting for the shadow line to reach him at five. From the sea, as we put out again, heading for Estartit, the villa looked beautiful, remote, contained by the pines and a sense of slumber. I stayed in Estartit until seven and then drove home.

When she asked how I enjoyed Barcelona I told her I hadn't gone, that I'd driven the long way round, taking the coast road to Tossa, and from there rung Señor García only to be told he was in Gerona, so I'd had lunch, sat in the sun and thought and written a few notes.

Myra said it wasn't a wasted day, then, and I said no, I supposed it hadn't been. We usually slept in separate rooms. It was her wish. That night we slept together. That was mine. Even with the light on she kept her eyes closed.

In the last few weeks of her life Mitzi's face was starved by sorrow. My own is pickled in liquor and ruined by curiosity. You can lose a sense of vocation. Isn't it better to have built one good strong bridge or ploughed one straight furrow than to have scribbled away for years trying to create order out of chaos? When Myra sat with her godling on the sand I wondered whether at last she was losing her sense of vocation for being the wife of Edward Thornhill. She had looked after my business affairs with charm and intelligence, had said the right things to the right people, had been a fine cultural ambassadress in places where they set store by such things. But at the age of forty, so I guessed, she felt the stirrings of adventure. Perhaps alone in her room, close to the window through which she could watch the constant image of the inconstant sea, she looked into the mirror and asked herself what her life really added up to? A childhood spent gathering no identifying moss and a youth and young womanhood preparing to be a beautiful but unclaimed lady, and then twelve years married to a man loaded with the astringent lotions that smoothed and eased her passage to the favour Will knew we all come to in the end.

I had a mental picture of her looking into this mirror and at last raising her hands to hide her head. It is a question of showing humble. None of us does. Why should she? She did not care any longer. Neither did I, or so I told myself. But throw up from the sea a young Poseidon and ah! I cared then. I wanted then. I loved then, and tried to remember occasions when I had slighted or humiliated her, intentionally or unintentionally. This is where women kill us, with reminders of their tenderness, their softness, their physical humility, their absolute nakedness and defencelessness in the face of neglect, unkindness and cruelties. And if at this time she had raised her hands to hide her head, admitted her desolation, I could have admitted mine.

But she did not make this gesture. She had the godling and held her head erect for him. And I was jealous, killed by my jealousy and by the knowledge that I had obviously failed her, probably pushed her into this humiliating liaison through unthinking neglect and selfishness. In my mind it was humiliating, humiliating for her, because she was so much older than he, and in my mind it was a liaison before I even had proof. Even when I knew that he was there below on the sand and she was asleep behind the louvres of the french doors of her bedroom, a dark Brünnhilde resting on her bier, I felt them together, holding themselves apart only in patience and sure expectation of the time presently being ripe for them to enact the roles they had carefully rehearsed.

I did not go to Barcelona again the following day, and was forestalled anyway by Señor García himself ringing to ask why I had called. It was Myra who answered and I took over from her. When she was out of earshot I told him I had rung that day from Tossa because I wanted to see the bulls. He was surprised, but said, 'Come this Sunday. I'll take you to the sorteo first,' by which he meant we could watch the toreros drawing lots to decide which bulls in the toril each matador would fight. They try to pair the good bulls with the poor bulls, so that no man has more than his fair share of fierce bull or cowardly bull. I said I couldn't that Sunday, but might some other time, although it didn't really matter. Perhaps he thought I was drunk, even though it was only ten in the morning.

For three days after my supposed trip to Barcelona she continued to meet the godling, but now he was established as a welcome intruder under her umbrella. I watched them through the fieldglasses from the study which I went back to after the coffee-break, not to work but to answer letters and to read. For years I have worked to a stop-watch time-table. At twelve I was due to join her at our table on the sand outside Señor Rojas's bar. At ten to twelve Myra always looked at her watch and spoke, and he got up then, walked to the water's edge, turned, waved, and then plunged in, and she gathered her things together, towel, book, cigarettes, lighter, sun-oil, and put them into her beach bag. When she had finished I put the fieldglasses away, left the villa and headed for Señor Rojas's.

Antonio Rojas's is the smallest bar on the beach at Playa de Faro. He was an officer in the Republican Army at the time of the Civil War. Captured by Franco's troops he spent several years in jail. Later he ran a bar in Barcelona. Now he runs one in Playa de Faro where there is more money to be made and a long rest to be had between the end of September and the beginning of April. There is a notice up inside the bar that cheap wine isn't served, but this is for the benefit of the fishermen and the run-of-the-mill tourist. When Myra and I weren't drinking Spanish champagne or brandy Tonio Rojas served cheap wine to me, in the back. If it were known that Señor Rojas served wine for a few pennies a glass the fishermen would come. The tourists were afraid of the fishermen. At the end of the season the notice comes down and the fishermen come back and get drunk for a few pesetas.

Señor Rojas's bar is dim and narrow. He and his wife Carmen live in the upstairs rooms. The walls of the bar are whitewashed every March. Señor Rojas himself fixed up the shelves that cover them from shoulder height upwards. On the shelves there are bottles of sherry, Spanish champagne, vodka, anis and foreign liqueurs. There are also stacks of white cardboard boxes containing plain and fancy espadrilles. There are two iron tables to sit at in back. Between the counter and the whitewashed wall there is room for you to stand and drink but not much room for people to get past you to the tables if you are standing drinking. On the counter there is a coffee machine of which Señor Rojas is very proud. It makes the best coffee in Playa de Faro. Behind the counter, blocking part of the window, there is a refrigerator in a wooden cabinet. In this he keeps the tiny bottles of Martini and Cinzano, the bottles of coke and cerveza. The doorway from the bar is narrow. Fifty yards away is the sea. Between the doorway and the sea, on the other side of the arcade that people stroll under, there is a pine-log and bamboo terrace. The terrace belongs to Señor Rojas too. He puts it up in the spring and takes it down in the autumn. All the bars have terraces on the sand, and tables with umbrellas between the terraces and the sea.

Between the doorway and the terrace, under an awning, there are stands on which Señor Rojas displays the other things he has for sale apart from liquor and coffee: espadrilles, sun lotions, trinkets of Toledo gold, picture postcards, beach umbrellas and paper-back novels in English, French and German. There is an understanding between us that he would never give me away to people who buy the Penguins that show that old, virtually unrecognizable photograph on the inside cover.

There are five other bars and two shops and one hairdresser. Before Playa de Faro was a resort these houses belonged to fishermen. Only Señor Rojas's bar retains a feeling of the sea. In the other bars there are neon lights and fancy murals. Each caters for a different type of tourist. Señor Rojas has more middle-aged customers than young. His radio and record-player made only Spanish music. Le Twist is two doors down. Señor Rojas does not welcome what he calls scandal. Señor Sarbosa, the traffic policeman, drinks his coffee and brandy at Señor

Rojas's in preference to elsewhere, and it is the only bar the lads from the Civil Guard come into. Señor Rojas is always polite to the Civil Guard. You remember he was in prison. He is squat, inclined to plumpness and very jolly, but more than any of the men who keep bars in Playa de Faro he gives the impression that in the right circumstances he would make an implacable enemy. He is a good Catalan. His wife is plump too, and pretty, and fond of the bulls. It is she who does most of the running to and fro from bar to terrace with the clinking trays. If you catch her in the right mood and with a moment to spare you could persuade her to go upstairs and bring down her grandmother's black lace mantilla, tortoise-shell combs and black, embroidered fan. One day, she promises, she will dress up in these and give me a close-up view of the old España Brava.

When I reached the table on the sand Carmen was there uncorking the champagne. She aimed the cork at the prow of a dinghy that was named Dos Hermanos, two brothers, and laughed and said Olé! when it went pop and only missed the boat by an inch or two. She poured from a height to ensure the fizz, refused an invitation to join us and went shading her eyes from the sun back up the slope of the playa to the bar and left Myra and me together. We raised our glasses to each other, but what can you see of a woman under a beach hat like that and dark glasses like those?

From where I sat I could see the shop that sold swimming wear and chunky jewellery and suede jackets. A woman with a bare white belly and powdered, presumably painful red shoulders, was rummaging in a wooden box that was full of swimsuits going for a song because September was the end of the season.

By her side, patiently waiting her turn, stood a young girl with fair hair who wore a white blouse tucked into a blue and white dirndl skirt. She had straw-topped sandals on her feet; undoubtedly English like the red-shouldered woman, but from Great Missenden, or Stoke Poges, or just outside Portsmouth. Her brother's name was Simon and their father was a Commander, R.N., axed, devoted now to pigs. It was their first decent holiday for years. At least the pigs had paid off. At home Aunt Evie was looking after the dogs who all had wet tongues and happy dispositions. The mother, a hardworking woman whose only colouring was protective, ran an old black Austin that was called Joppy. The boot was a mess of rope, old sacks and eggboxes. There had been until recently a pony (Loxley) out to grass, but he had died a few months ago which had been a relief because he had outlived his usefulness and knew it and looked at them apologetically because he no longer contributed anything to the family welfare. There were silver cups and rosettes on the sideboard (beans on toast for breakfast and shoulder of mutton from New Zealand for lunch) and the framed picture of Loxley's young rider, serious under a black velvet cap with her fair hair sticking out in little pigtails; whereas now it hung round her neck and looked the devil to do anything with except wash and wash and dry and dry while Simon banged on the bathroom door and the sound of his broken voice reminded her that she ought not to be thinking about her hair but about getting to know a young man with decent manners and parents in Guildford.

The older woman went inside the shop having found what looked like a bargain and the girl – let her name be Lesley – took her place, turning the swimsuits over carefully without lifting them out because she had been trained as a child never to point or to ask why in company, but to keep her wrists low and to grip with the legs from the knee upwards. Bent from the waist the backs of her bare legs were revealed higher than the tops of her calves (backs that were blue-veined and looked a bit like unripe gorgonzola, no stilton, gorganzola was *Italian*) but her bottom, purdahed in folds of floral dirndl, remained a formidable mystery.

The search for a swimsuit that was going for a song without being indecent was given up and Lesley came away from the arcade, stepping on to the sand, into the sunshine, where she put on her sunglasses (Boots, three shillings and sixpence) and her straw hat (Playa de Faro, fifty-eight pesetas) and stood, holding her hands up to its brim. Not finding what she looked for she lowered her hands and turned away, poor desolate maiden, and walked down to the sea, past the umbrellas that perhaps didn't look as marvellous in life as they did in the bright posters, past the boats that were comfortably like the ones daddy and Simon messed about in, sat down in the shadow of Dos Hermanos and unaccountably began to take off her clothes, unbuttoning the white blouse, unhooking the waistband of the dirndl skirt and sliding the zip.

She was naked, amazing, the crimson flush of her open air cheeks now gone completely: whitefaced, breathless, she had the look of a small undernourished saint martyred in a cause she knew she had a duty to but felt she had no understanding of, lying back not looking after the first horrified stare at the transformation from pestering trousered boy to horned satyr, pressing her head back into the pillow, but with her legs obediently open, offering him in resignation the entrance, as if to spare herself the shame of having it taken, because her father had always told her to face up to life like a man, and the subsequent birth of Simon had made no difference to the lessons of her early training.

Trembling, the naked boy lay half beside, half on top of her, and forgot the frigid set of her body, so pleasurable was the shock of feeling for the first time the whole length of a girl, bare, against him. He wanted to turn her head, kiss and fondle her, to express the love and gratitude he genuinely felt for her. He wanted to explore the seemingly infinite number of secondary sensual pleasures her body promised, but the frenzy concentrated in the stiff projection between his legs would not wait, and he changed his position, took hold and set about the business of consummation, and became aware, even while he was at it, that the mechanics of copulation had, for the novice anyway, a clinical and straightforward side to them that made him want to laugh. But he did not laugh. The smile, never quite released, stayed prisoner behind grimly tightened lips as he fumbled and missed and became frantic trying to discover the angle nature had intended to enable male to enter female. She moved her hand suddenly, gagged her mouth with it and bit. And then things were all right, and he felt himself frustrated only by the barrier of her seeming impenetrability. He gathered her bony body tightly in his arms, heard himself saying. Oh, Lesley, Lesley; proud to find himself skilfully articulate in the moment that called, for tender persuasion. With slow and loving deliberation he took up the ancient rhythm, hoping for a more complete enclosing, and then stopped, holding himself rigid in a useless attempt to stop the flow of his treacherous ejaculation. For a while afterwards he lay on her, stirred by a desire far subtler than the one so excitingly but too quickly satisfied.

Presently he moved and looked at her. How small her breasts were. He touched them, looking to be loved and forgiven and made to feel welcome. She still had her hand in her mouth and her eyes were closed, her fair, too fair eyebrows drawn together as if within this contraction she could contain at least a shred of herself that had not been surrendered.

'I'm sorry, Lesley,' he said. 'I'm sorry.' She did not move, or change her expression of concentration. He was, truly, sorry; but later, considering this, he thought that his sorrow must have been for what had not been achieved and not for what had been done. He pulled himself away from her, covered himself with the towel he had remembered to put on the bed in case she bled. She had not. All that riding and jumping. The room was very hot, full of filtered light that comes when unlined cretonne curtains are pulled to shut out afternoon sunshine. The wood walls gave off their familiar saw-mill smell.

Unclothed, she stood up, in the decent dark blue swimsuit, and went down to the sea. She stirred the lapping wavelets with her toes, and then strode in, as she had been taught. Never to hesitate. In, Lesley. In and out to the horizon.

There must have been a couple of thousand tourists in Playa de Faro, tucked at night into the rooms of the hotels, the villas, the apartamentos, the tents and trailers of the camping at a site hidden away among the pines and the hills, who in the day emerged into the cheap sunshine and crowded the beach, the souvenir shops, the bars, the narrow lanes and sometimes packed themselves affluently into cars and went up the hill past the grounds of the Vora la Mar in search of inland pastimes and the pleasures of other playas.

Under the restless weight of the visitors the sand of the playa itself seemed to be shifting. Among them you would sometimes see, hiding like a dog-rose in a flower-show, a girl like Lesley together with her parents and, perhaps, a far from simple Simon. These were my lost administrators, the English who, colonially abroad, aroused grandfather's ire; a dead race now; as dead as the last Romans in a no longer savage Britain, lifting their patched togas up to keep them clear of the mud of an amoral civilization; keepers of the old conscience, puzzled now, beginning to be defensively acquisitive. The fires were dead, the shadows lengthened; the leopards prowled, looking to come into their own, poor dispossessed creatures, lucky if they were disfigured by nothing worse than cataracts. Blind leopards. Hump-backed humans.

'How did it go this morning?' Myra asked.

'It didn't,' I said.

She was ready for more champagne. I hadn't noticed. By speaking she drew attention to her thirst. We had been silent for a long time. She had probably watched me watching the girl I called Lesley. I filled her glass, considering what, if anything, to say.

She bore my silences with patience, an outward show of it anyway. Sometimes I thought that if she complained I would like that better. I couldn't help my thoughts wandering, nor help it if they wandered in directions I got no pleasure from. Old kings, particularly melancholy ones, hired fools to keep them from penetrating too far the bleaker regions of the imagination. What about that for a suggestion? Miguel would do. He would look well in cap and bells, capering on the terrace, tumbling down the steps in the hillside, singing a jingle to bring a smile to the lips of the King and the Queen. Then let his twin-brother brood behind the arras! But if it came to a toss-up for Myra's favours between Domingo and the godling from the beach I fancied the prize would be better off in Domingo's hands. At least, afterwards, he would bathe her in the renàscence light of his boyish adoration, for Domingo was a romantic, and the affair would end for him in a dark corner of the store-room in which he would sit contemplating the enormity of his mistress's sudden coldness, a concern growing in his belly to meet a good death on the horns of a bull. Brave Domingo. Better you should find a pretty peasant girl and turn your wine-dark eyes away from the grosser temptations of the tourist summer.

'It will be all right, Ed,' Myra suddenly assured him. 'Don't worry. You've been stuck before.'

But never for so long. I said, 'Yes, I have, haven't I?' because it struck me as being necessary, at that moment, to raise a flag of self-confidence; to show that the fort was still occupied, still defended, that it would not be true if it was in her mind to say: 'Well, I had the best out of Ed. There was nothing more to come from there.'

The godling was emerging from the sea now, some fifty yards away, showing his blue-satin bulge. He looked directly at Myra's back, and then at me, then walked to the little hummock of his towel, cigarettes and lighter, and sat down, lit a cigarette and watched the horizon. It occurred to me to say:

110

Poseidon's here: to see how she would react. But he was no longer Poseidon, not since he had taken to leaving the sea and joining her in all his muscular mortality under the umbrella. He was Hippolytus, the bastard son of Theseus who was sired by Poseidon, and whom Poseidon sent to destroy with a fierce bull from the sea as punishment for sleeping with Phaedra, Theseus's wife. The roaring of the bull frightened the horses Hippolytus was proudly whipping up from his chariot. Some say that Hippolytus was killed, others that the goddess Artemis wrapped the youth in a cloud, disguised him as an old man from Theseus's and Poseidon's wrath and spirited him away to her sacred grove of Nemi, where she left him in charge of the nymph Egeria, with whom he lived under the name of Virbius, which means 'twice a man'. Once of the godling would probably be enough.

In that version of the story it looks as if Hippolytus had it made, unless looking like an old man he felt like one. But the godling was no bastard son of mine. Poseidon wouldn't avenge me if he slept with Myra. There would be no fierce bull from the sea, no cloud, no Artemis, no nymph Egeria. It was between me and the godling.

If we come out of the querencia of our privacy we are wounded and destroyed. I would stay in mine, say nothing, certainly not accept the lure of the godling's increasing obvious passes at Myra. On every playa there was always such a man, not yet a full matador, but a peón, a banderillero. He was citing to place a pair in a hump already bleeding from the pic-thrusts of the two invisible horsemen of pride and sorrow.

The seat of the torero's courage, so it is said, is in his testicles, his cojones (not to be confused with cajones which means crates or cojines which means cushions; ah, well). But the bull doesn't lack that virile equipment. The bull has his cojones as well as his hump. And if he has no art he has endurance. Both are acquired, both are learned from experience. He also has, finally, his sense of outrage. So it would be between myself and the godling. The longer I stayed in my querencia the more dangerous it would be for him. He would have to stamp his foot and growl Huh! Huh! and come closer, into my terrain, away from his. He would end up having to cite from a position of weakness instead of strength. The sweat would come on to his brow at the prospect of a badly placed pair, or a miss, or a cornada. In this second third of the combat, the act of the banderillas, the animal's head, it will be remembered, is already carried lower because of what happened at the end of the first third, the trial of the lances. The horns will pass closer to the torero's belly.

The banderillas are barbed sticks twenty-nine and a half inches long, inclusive of the two and half inch barb. They are decorated with coloured paper and look like festive decorations. The barbs are designed to penetrate and hold just beneath the skin of the tossing muscle that has been wounded by the pics. They are painful and irritating. They clack and swing as the bull moves. Three or four pairs of banderillas are placed. Sometimes the matador places them himself, but in these days of specialization they are usually placed by the men who have failed to come up to scratch as matadors, the men who form part of the matador's cuadrilla and go under the fancy-dress name of banderilleros.

The ordinary method of placing banderillas is 'al cuarteo'. Cuartear means to dodge. To place a pair al cuarteo the banderillero stands at a distance to cite and begins to run in a quarter circle directly the bull charges. The bull changes direction, following the man. The movement is planned so that at the point of meeting the banderillas can be placed on the run and the man can dodge to one side to avoid the horns. This is the act the crowd finds most aesthetically pleasing. The man is armed with nothing but these frail-looking sticks, one in each hand. To place them in the bull's shoulders the arms must be raised high above the head exposing the encrusted satin-suited body, and the sticks then brought down with one swift stabbing motion, in the way a whimsical butcher's assistant might price and label joints of meat. Sometimes only one stick penetrates, sometimes both fall to the ground. The crowd jeers if either of these two things happens.

Another and more dangerous method of placing the sticks is to place them 'poder a poder'. In this case the banderillero weaves towards the bull instead of running off at an angle to it, and places the sticks head on. The supremely dangerous method of placing is 'al quiebro' where the man stands stock-still to cite, feints with one leg and shoulder when the charging bull is close, in order to swerve him away; then draws the leg and shoulder back to their original positions. He places the sticks as the bull goes by. Before the corrida he has prayed of course.

Until ten years ago there was another kind of banderilla: banderilla de fuego: which incorporated an explosive. Banderillas de fuego were used on bulls that refused to charge the picadors. This was not good for the tourist trade, then just reviving. There were always so many English at the corrida, thinking of the horses, and dogs, and all dumb animals. So now they use a black banderilla with a larger barb and the tourists don't know the difference between these and ordinary banderillas. Wearing a black banderilla in its tossing muscle both the bull and its breeder are said to be disgraced. But the bla.k banderillas are substitutes for the pica. I didn't have to fear the placing of one by the godling. I had been pic-ed before he entered.

He had turned over on his stomach and was watching us, as if waiting for Myra to turn round and beckon him over. Perhaps he had said that morning while they rested in the sandy cove: we can't go on like this. I can't go on seeing you on the beach and not come over simply because he is with you. Tell him about me. Today. Promise. Get him to accept me. Don't worry. He won't suspect. Leave it to me. Trust me. I'll find a way. We'll be together. I promise. I love you, love you. I can't bear to see you together, to watch you drinking champagne, to see him leave you for a moment to go inside and pay the bill, to see that and not be able to come over in case he comes out and finds us. Why are you afraid? I'm not afraid. But I'm lost, lost. I can't bear to see you walking back across the playa, with him, disappearing where the steps turn round on the hill and lead into the garden of the villa, taking you away from me. I lie here sweating, wanting to follow, wanting to run after you. And in the afternoon I lie here alone, thinking of you asleep in the villa. You say you are alone in your room. Are you? How can I bear the thought that it isn't true? I lie here on the sand aching with love and pity for you, married to that old man. I take up handfuls of sand, imagining they are handfuls of your hair. And at five when you say you wake I can't bear the thought of the evening without you because you are with him. I swim for a long time. It's almost dark when I get back. I'm spent. Useless. I want only to sleep and bring the morning closer when we can meet and I can touch you for a few moments. I can't go on like this. We must find a way. Take me to him. Acknowledge me. If you don't I'm not sure I can go on keeping my promise never to acknowledge you.

'Ed,' she said, 'we're almost out of cigarettes. Do you think Tonio Rojas has got the Chesterfields in?'

He got them for us specially, in cartons of two hundred.

I said I would see and got up. The godling looked down, staring at the sand a few inches from his nose. From the table under the umbrella to the doorway of Antonio Rojas's bar was only twenty or thirty yards, but the pinelog and bamboo terrace and the slope of the playa made it difficult to see what went on at the table where I had left Myra lighting one of the last of her cigarettes. A woman was singing on the radio. A gipsy singer, from somewhere like Seville. O blanco muro de España. O negro toro de pena. Those were not the words, but the words did not matter in themselves. Those words would do well enough. They are suitable for most occasions.

I asked for the Chesterfields. Rojas went from behind the bar and out by way of the stairs at the back. I stood near the doorway. I could just see the top of the umbrella. The waist-high windbreak of the pine-log terrace concealed the rest. But if the godling had joined her surely I would have seen, though, if Myra had turned round, shaken her head as if to say: Not yet. Leave it to me. Don't be impatient.

Señor Rojas came down with a large paper-wrapped parcel. A thousand Chesterfields. I paid for the cigarettes and the champagne. They were heartbreakingly cheap. When I got back into the sunshine Myra looked as if she hadn't moved. The godling was still there, staring at the sand. He had begun to play it through his fingers.

'Shall we go back?' I asked Myra.

'Yes, I suppose it's time,' she said. She got up and led the way without a backward glance. I felt the prick of the darts of curiosity he lodged in my shoulder blades.

It was Saturday, September the first.

4

Sunday approaching five. In San Felíu the plaza would already be crowded. This was the week before Ordóñez. In Playa de Faro the bullfight posters announced the rejoneador, Don Angel Peralta, who fought in the Portuguese way, on horseback. In Portugal the bulls are only killed symbolically. Then they are led out of the ring and killed in the slaughterhouse. But the horses of the rejoneadors aren't padded with mattresses and blindfolded like the picadors' horses. The art of the rejoneador is the art of the matador, to provoke, to evade. The horses, like the men, are highly trained. With the picadors it is a different matter. The horses are static objects, candidates for the knacker's yard. The bull has to press up against them trying to get the horn in through the padding so that the man above can lean over and thrust in the pic. Someone told me once that the horses are operated on in the throat so that you can't hear them scream.

Sunday: approaching five Myra was asleep. I left my room and went into the study, which was adjacent. I have never described the study. The walls were plain, distempered white like the walls elsewhere, inside and out. There were bookshelves, and among the books Señor García had left for the amusement of people who stayed in his villa were illustrated books about the corrida. When Myra and I came in April I brought only a handful of my own books with me, a handful because I haven't got many. I have to leave them behind in the places where we live from time to time. There were more books in the shelves now than Señor García had left. People are always sending me books and in Barcelona there are books it is impossible not to buy because they are books and Barcelona is a foreign city and in the midst of its foreignness there are these books in my own familiar, even exciting language. I mean exciting after all these years.

Apart from the books and the bookshelves there was nothing else on the walls. Was nothing? Is nothing? Is nothing. It has become a habit to write in the past tense. The floors are tiled. There are some rugs that were probably expensive to buy because they look like peasant handicrafts. And a table-desk, and drawers in it on either side of the knee-hole; a calendar, marshalling numbers into little rows of anxiety; a chair to sit on and write and a chair to sit in and read; an angle-poise lamp that seems to have become weightless and raises itself until it is sending a beam of light directly into my eyes, like in the third degree interrogation; a shuttered door that opens on to the balcony and the Moorish arches; an arched window through which you can see down through a gap in the pines to the sea and the beach.

– And at five, through fieldglasses, watch the departure of the godling, when the shadow line of the hill reached him, just as at eleven (abandoning the disagreeable mail with its parrot questions: Well, Ed, how goes it? Any news for us, Ed? What about it, Ed?) the meetings by the lobster pots could be observed through the lenses that reduced Playa de Faro to selective concentric circles of moving picture: the two heads there, bobbing above the waves. Sunday: approaching five. I took the fieldglasses out of the desk drawer and went to the window, pretending that the glasses were to be used as they had first been used, to isolate and separate, reduce all that formless unsatisfactory human activity to one self-contained significant image that might move me to create images of my own.

The godling wasn't there. He had been swimming near the lobster pots as usual that morning and Myra had been swimming with him, but now the place on the sand that for days had borne the weight of his body was unoccupied. The shadow line of the hill was just reaching it and he should have been stirring, sitting up, beginning to sort out the equipment he needed to make his rubbery entry into his undersea kingdom.

And then I wondered, was she asleep? Was she in her room or in his room, emboldened by my after-lunch headache to believe that it was I who would sleep and she who was free to come in, freshen up and then take the winding road back to the playa, the apartamento, his arms? In the morning they had swum to the cove. Perhaps, lying close, he had said: This afternoon. I'll wait. And she had nodded. He had taken her wrist. She had said: Not now, not now. Later, later. Be patient. I love you, love you. In your room, oh yes, then, but here, be careful.

I went out to the porticoed verandah that shaded all four sides of the villa and walked on bare feet to the louvred door of her room. From below I heard Domingo and Miguel arguing, then settling their argument with a laugh. 'Myra?' I said.

There was no answer. I tried the door-handle. It was locked. I went through the door that led inside to the half-room half-landing flat that was set with a few chairs and tables and separated my bedroom and bathroom from hers. I tried the other door of Myra's bedroom. It opened. The room was empty. Her bed had not been slept in or lain on since Lola made it that morning. The dress she had worn at lunch was thrown on to the coverlet. I went back to my own room and put on espadrilles. Half-way downstairs I paused. After all, where could I go? Domingo came through the hall from the kitchen carrying a shallow basket of clean napery and cutlery to put ready on the side-table for the evening meal. I asked him if he had seen the Señora. He said she had gone out. He stood close to the bottom of the stairs, clad in black trousers and white singlet. For as long as I stayed there, on the stair-case, he would stay in the hall, awaiting dismissal, staring up at me. He would answer questions, obey orders, but seldom speak or act beyond that. What was he thinking? That the Señor had woken up at last, not from afternoon sleep but from weeks of dreaming? How much did Domingo know of what there was to be known about the godling? Would he have told for the price of a downpayment on a Vespa, or a fancy frilled shirt? He was at an age that had no armour to withstand corruption. He should not have been there at the villa, but on the sea casting nets, or on the sierras, herding goats, and eating his heart out for a wild gipsy girl with eyes as dark as his own. He should not have spent the burning summer eyeing riches and fair-skinned women, and envying men in elegant slacks and expensive shirts. Did he know that these things were bad for him that he belonged to the mountains or the sea, that on the plains, on the playas, and in the hot dusty cities there was nothing for him but the bitter wine of disillusion, the stinking meat of a civilization that felt itself alive because it went through the motions of earning and spending pesetas?

I smiled at him and turned to go back upstairs and then stopped and asked him to bring a bottle of champagne up to my room. When I came out of the shower he was there, at the table by the window, carefully taking off the foil. To come upstairs he had put on his white jacket. He had broad, rather clumsy hands. He covered the cork with a linen napkin so that there would be a pop but no missile. He had watched and learned and in a year or two would make out well as a waiter at one of the big hotels in Tossa or Lloret de Mar. He had put a change of clothes out for me as well; his favourites, not mine, a pair of blue terylene trousers and a crimson shantung silk shirt. He smiled. He liked to do things nicely, to earn praise as well as money.

He went, left me alone with the bottle and the glass. The godling had not been on the beach at five because he was in his apartment. And Myra was in it with him. On the day I ostensibly went to Barcelona he and Myra had been cautious. Myra anyway. He had said: Come to my room. And she had said: Suppose he comes back, suppose he's not gone to Barcelona at all but is spying on us. Be patient. Wait. Treat today like any other day.

So she had slept between three and five and he had lain on the beach, and I had seen him thus innocently occupied when the boat from Tossa put in on the way back to Estartit. And afterwards they had continued to meet by the lobster pots, to swim to the cove and back again, but now he followed her ashore and sat under her umbrella until ten minutes to twelve when she looked at her watch and said: It's time. Now you must go. And he said: We can't go on like this. I can't bear it when I see you together. Why won't you let me speak to you when he's with you? What does he think you are? A piece of furniture? Can't you even make friends on a beach he leaves you alone on for hours? Why can't I come up to your table at Rojas's bar and why can't you say, Ed, this is a friend of mine, we met over at the lobster pots? What's wrong with that? Aren't I good enough? Is there something wrong with my manners or my accent or something? Aren't people allowed to make friends on holiday any longer? If you accepted me as a friend we'd have more time together. We could be together a lot. He wouldn't suspect. Just introduce us and leave the rest to me. I know how to make the running in cases like this.

– Do you? Myra asked. Yes, I suppose you do. You must have lots of experience.

– Perhaps you have too, keeping men dangling in suspense, and hiding behind your husband.

A quarrel. Under the umbrella. He had gone down to the sea and perhaps made a pass at some younger woman so that Myra turned away and blindly collected her things together to put them into the beach bag, making ready to join me for the mid-day champagne. A quarrel. But made up this morning in the privacy of the sandy cove.

I'm sorry, he had said. Forgive me. I'll do what you say. I don't pretend to be good. To have been good. I've had lots of affairs. With married women as well as single. That's why I said I knew how to make the running. But this is different. I'll do what you say. I'll play it your way. It's just that I can't bear to see you with him, to think of you with him, going back to the villa with him, being in his arms.

It's I who should be sorry, Myra said. I've thought about nothing else since you left me yesterday. When we were at Rojas's you came and sat near. I thought you'd forgiven me. But I wasn't sure. I lay awake all night thinking. I can't think any more. I only know I love you. I don't want to hurt Ed, but I love you. I can't fight it any more. But don't hurt Ed. If he were working properly it wouldn't matter so much. But he thinks he's finished. He thinks he's written himself out. He needs me. It used to be I in a curious way who needed him. But that's changed. Now I only need not to hurt him. At the moment everything and anything can hurt him.

It's you who are being hurt, he said.

I'm younger than he is, Myra said. I can stand being hurt. Sometimes I sense him wondering how many years he's got left. He loves life. He's afraid of dying, of being old. He's put everything into his work. He's drained himself. He wonders what it's been worth, what it adds up to. He's driven himself into a corner. He's fighting to get out. He drinks all the time. He watches me all the time. Sometimes I feel he knows what I'm thinking, even underneath my sunhat and through those dark glasses. It's driving me into a corner too because what I needed him for I no longer need. He's tood old for me, and I don't love him. He disgusts me. No. That's wrong. That's untrue. Unfair, I disgust myself. I've grown up, I don't want a father-figure, I want love and youth. They passed me by. I'm forty. There. Now you know. Now you're disgusted too. No. Don't touch me, don't pretend it doesn't matter. It's true. At forty I'm awake for the first time. You've woken me. I dream every night you're making love to me. I can't bear it. To lie here and not to touch you, not to feel you on me and in me. You say you can't bear it either. You could have any girl on the beach, but how many men of your age could I expect to look at me twice, in the way they used to when I was still emotionally a child, looking for something solid, something secure, something to give my life to. Do you know what it means to long and long, to feel physically sick longing for one particular person? How can you? How can you know yet? You won't know for another ten years, if then, if ever. A man like you will always be able to pick and choose. I wake up from dreams like that trembling and ill. Do you know what an effort it costs me to see *him* in the morning? To talk, to smile, to go through the motions of being his wife, and looking after a house that doesn't even belong to me and is empty, empty, because you're not in it?

I know what it is like, he said. It is the same for me. My room. The beach. The whole of Playa de Faro. They are all empty. Only here is any good, here and by the lobster pots, and for a few minutes under your umbrella. Yes, I can pick and choose. Mostly it's been easy. I admit it. Even if they've said no, it hasn't been a disaster. But now I've chosen you. I love you. What do a few years difference in age make? As soon as I saw you I thought: I want her. I followed you into the sea. I swam close to you. But then we looked at each other and it was different from those other times when I've gone after women. I thought: She's beyond me, too good for me, she'll never belong to me. But I wanted you. I wanted to love you, to look after you, to protect you. We've known each other more than ten days. We've never even kissed in all that time, expect under water. If I were what you say, why do you think I still bother? I bother because I love you. I shall go on bothering, whatever happens or doesn't happen. But I'm not here for ever. Even for long. I'm not rich. I've got a living to earn. I don't live here in a fine white villa in private grounds. I've got to go back. There aren't many days left. No one comes near my room after María's gone. Ed wouldn't know. He wouldn't be hurt. He wouldn't suspect. I promise you that. Just give us a chance to be together. I can't wait to hold you in my arms.

– This afternoon, she said, while he's asleep. I'll slip away. Be patient. No, no, be patient until then. I promise. I promise.

And had kept her promise, and gone, and was there now in some unknown room shuttered against the afternoon sun, a room that overlooked one of the narrow lanes and was approached by stone steps, entered by a narrow door past tubs of pretty flowers and spiky cactus: one of the apartamentos where nothing was to be seen of any servant after the beds were made and the breakfast cooked and the soiled linen collected and taken away to be brought back in the morning. It is safe, he would say. Look, here is the door. It is secluded. No one else enters. Only María, but she's gone. There's the whole afternoon. Stay. Don't be afraid. Look, it's dark and cool. I pulled the shutters in readiness. No one can see. No one can hear. I love you. There. Feel how I love you.

And lay afterwards in the shadowy room side by side, exploring and kissing, touching the warm secrets of each other's flesh, whispering, until suddenly they laughed and he said: Why are we whispering! No one can hear. Listen! I can speak your name aloud: Myra. Myra. And only you respond. Say mine. Say my name. Talk to me, as if it doesn't matter what we say or who can hear. Yes like that. And like this. With this. This is a way of talking too. Yes. again. Again. Slowly. To make it last, until dark, until tomorrow, until for ever.

And later perhaps he watched her dressing while he still lay naked on the bed smoking and she was grateful that the shutters were down and the light going, in case in this critical moment of post-copulative regard he was no longer blind to the defects that forty years will lay upon a body however well preserved: and so, dressed, went back to him, sat on the bed and smiling, regarded him, leaning across eventually to kiss him from above, and after a while pulled herself away, against her desire, satisfied that his own was still to be counted on tomorrow, grateful for that renewed tribute he paid her with his vigorous flesh, covering him, making him remain at lazy, lascivious ease, like some miraculous treasure, an astonishing, wonderful mechanism that had to be guarded, tended, taken care of, pampered a bit, shown gratitude and passionately surrendered to on another occasion.

'Until tomorrow,' she said, and from the door blew him a kiss, catching the one he blew back in return.

'The lobster pots,' he said, 'at eleven,' and watched her turn the key, open the door and step out into the evening light, comparing her perhaps with other women who had left him alone like this to contemplate with satisfaction yet another strange room that had been made comfortable and familiar with lingering feminine scents and happy masculine recollections; while Myra walked down the steps and into the narrow lane, taking the long way round to avoid going past Señor Rojas's bar where Carmen, clearing traps, might see from her face that the afternoon had not been idly spent; going the long way, up the hill, along the road that brought traffic winding down to the playa, but at this evening hour was empty.

She returned at half-past six, coming into the garden from the direction of the steps that led from the beach. I watched her from the window of my room, standing in shadow so as not to be seen. She sat on the stone bench. Miguel came out to her. He said something and then she looked up as if she had just realized she wasn't alone. He came away, and she continued to sit there. After a while she took off the dark glasses she looked as if she might have her eyes closed. She moved her head once or twice, to cool it, or to shake out of it some feeling of constriction, or ache, or to clear away recent recollections, or some sense of muddle that spoiled the clarity of those recollections. Then she opened her bag and took out her cigarette case and lighter. Smoking, she rose from the bench and went the round of the flower pots on the stone balustrade, inspecting the blooms. Miguel came out with a glass, a pitcher of ice, a bottle of Cinzano Bianco. He mixed her a drink, then left her. She stood near the balustrade, smoking, drinking, gazing down through the gap in the pines to the mottled sea. When she had finished her cigarette she came to the table, stubbed it out in the ashtray. Then she drained her glass and set that down too. I heard her steps on the tiled floor below and then again as she came on to the landing and opened her bedroom door. I stayed by the window finishing the bottle of champagne and watching the lights coming on in Playa de Faro, scattering my thoughts into the garden and into the branches of the pines to feed the monstrous birds.

That night she said: I went for a walk, into the hills, among the pines, to get some air. I must do something about my weight. I've made a resolution, she said, to walk every day. It doesn't agree with me. What doesn't agree? This lazy life, she said. I shall try to have a walk every afternoon. Into the hills to get some air, to smell the pines. And Miguel, she said, I really must talk seriously to Miguel, and get him to understand that I mean it when I ask him not to pile all that food on my plate. Why does he do it? He must know it's a temptation. I wish he would learn. Why can't he serve me in the way Domingo does? Domingo understands. Domingo is a sensible boy. They are both good boys, but Domingo shows more sense.

Are you going to Barcelona, Ed? If you decide to go to Barcelona I shall have a day living on cheese and lettuce. The boys could have the day off. They could go to Figueras. Their mother would like that. They haven't been to Figueras together since we came. So let me know if you plan to go to Barcelona.

– Is it a break you need, Ed? Is that it, do you think? I was thinking this afternoon, up in the hills, that every day is the same for you. You get up at half-past six. You swim. Miguel and Domingo make your coffee and fruit juice. You go into your study. You come out at ten. We have coffee. You go back to your study and answer letters. You're too meticulous. Let people wait a bit for replies. You never owe a letter. People owe you but you never owe them. It's a sign that you're feeling insecure. Then at mid-day you come down to Tonio's. We drink a bottle of champagne. All those calories. We come back for lunch. You sleep. You get up at five and shower and change and we drink here on the terrace until it's time to eat again. After we've eaten perhaps you go alone to Tonio's, or we go together. At eleven or twelve we go to bed. At six-thirty you get up. And so it goes on, Ed, day after day.

– Then we'll go to Barcelona, I said.

– I meant a break from me as well. It needn't be Barcelona. You could go to Gerona. You could go down to Madrid or up to Perpignan. You've got the car. I'd be all right. I'd go on a crash diet and swim and walk. The boys could go to Figueras. Lola could make my breakfast and do the minimum of what's necessary in the house and have some time off. I'd be all right, really. If I got hungry I could eat at one of the hotels. I could phone you every day wherever you are to let you know if anything important has turned up in the post.

– It would be lonely for you.

– Ed, when things aren't going well with a book it's lonely for me anyway. You look at me as if you don't see me. You say nothing to me, as if you're saying it all in your mind to someone in your book. Sometimes I have to pinch myself to make sure I'm here.

We sit together in the pretty white villa in Playa de Faro, Thelma said. We no longer talk. We sit holding hands. Like that we have proof, reassurance that we still have each other. But for how long? Everything else is gone. In a week, a month, you'll say casually, I'm going to Barcelona, tomorrow. Anything I can get you? And we'll both know that from

Barcelona, you'll send me the last of the money, to pay off the servants and the rent and my fare home and a note saying: I have to go away, please try to forgive me, God bless you, I love you.

– Even now you're not listening, Ed. You're thinking of something else.

– I'm listening.

Listening to the curious sounds that come in the night to the Panther House, Thelma said, the sounds of a man or an animal wandering outside in the dark, snuffling, whimpering, looking to be let in. Or perhaps they are sounds made by a woman, a woman like myself who is a ghost, as I am a ghost. If the world is dead and only you are alive, then you are just as much a ghost as you are if you are dead but still walking in a living world. I am walking in a dead world. Riding in a dead world. I sit like a ghost in the dead fields and Bruce sits like another ghost with his easel and his paints, attempting illusions of life. He does not know that what he paints is dead. He sits under his black umbrella shading himself from a heat and a glare that do not exist except in his mind where they exist as he remembers them from the time before the sun died. But all that exists outside of us is Ned's body. It generates heat in me from the grave. I explore it with my fingers, fingers with flesh on them that touch the skeleton and set it shivering. It is the same with the panther. She too is a ghost, a living animal walking in a dead landscape. The world has come to an end. Only Bruce and I and the panther are left, and Ned's body. Tomorrow, Bruce said, we will go up the track and I will paint the Stones. And I shall ride with him, seeing nothing, feeling nothing, remembering the time I said: It's a break you need. Go into the hills. Take your paints and your easel and the black umbrella. I'll be all right. I have things to do. I will ring you every day and tell you if there are any important messages. You've been overworking. Ned Pearson will look after things. He will come to me every day and tell me if he has any troubles. We will decide together whether any of them are troubles only you can deal with. Then I will ring you. And you can tell me how much better you feel. You can tell me what you have painted, how many sketches you have made. Only of course although I shall ask you to tell me I shan't hear the answers. As I stand at the telephone Ned will be behind me, eager, impatient. His hands will be on my breasts. He has beautiful hands. Strong but sensitive. He will bury his head in the hair in my neck. He will fill me with warmth and love, night after night. He will forget Lesley. When he is with me I make him forget Lesley. At first he was shocked at the things I made him do. But only for a moment. Making love to Lesley he felt nothing but a boy. With me he feels like a man. I have woken him up to know the infinite possibilities of his own body and mine. The exploration is endless. Alone I am ageing and ugly. With him I am beautiful. In the dark his fingers follow the lines and smooth the hollows of my face. With his hands he lifts the sorrow from my cheeks and with the rod of love divines my joy. He moves in me like a giant, and then the world is nothing. Now he is gone. He will not come to the door tomorrow, or the next day, or ever again; except as I conjure him in the dead of night, as now, with the panther snuffling in the garden, whimpering to come in, to be allowed in to find and take some living moving shape on which to expend its passion.

– A week, she said, you could go to Barcelona, or Perpignan or drive to Cannes. I think you need to be alone. Take plenty of money. Buy yourself something extravagant. Leave your manuscript behind. Just take a notebook. Get right away from it. Get right away from Playa de Faro. Get right away from me.

– Why do you say that?

– Because I don't think I'm any help to you any more, Ed. You used to show your work to me. You used to ask my opinion. I know you were mostly being kind, but at least it gave me a sense of sharing part of your life, of not being shut out completely, of not being simply a decoration, Ed, someone you had along so that people could say: Have you seen Ed's wife, she's really something, and he's got it, the dog, how does he do it at his age? No, I'm sorry. That's not kind. But it's true. You know it's true, Ed. But that's not how I ever wanted it to be. I wanted to add something, give something, to you, not add something to your distinction. And I wanted you to add something, give something to me.

– Something has happened, I said, to make you talk like this.

– No, she said, nothing has happened, nothing. That's what's killing us. It is to make something happen I'm asking you to go away, to give yourself a break. This villa – sometimes it seems to me that everything round it is dead, that we are dead too. Yes, I shall walk every day. It renews the circulation. Tonight, Ed, I'm thinking clearly. If going away will bring us alive again, you must go away, alone, or with someone.

– With you, I said.

She shook her head.

– Not with me. Alone, or with somebody, or alone to find somebody. But don't tell me. I don't want to know. But I want us to be alive.

I didn't go to Barcelona, or Madrid, or Perpignan, or Cannes, or buy myself anything extravagant. I went instead just for the day to the excavated city of Ampurias, to the Stones of Emporian; Emporium; Greek stones, Roman stones, the stones of conquest and history and of dead religions. I went again the next day, and the next, and the next, because there among the ruins, among the Stones, I saw the correspondence between Bruce and Thelma Craddock's situation and mine and Myra's. And the time drew nearer for me to go to the corrida, the corrida at San Felíu.

5

The animals moved in great herds on spindly legs, sweeping through the defile across the motionless rock-face into the grasslands. She caught her breath, waiting for the clang of their hooves and the metallic odour of sparks, the twang of bow-strings and the sizzle of swift spears, the cries of men, the bellowing of the beasts, the darkening of the sun as the dust rose in the immense savannah.

Fifty thousand years ago men penetrated deep into caves and drew pictures on the walls of their mortal enemy, pictures of the aurocks, the bulls. This was their wish-fulfilment, their compensation fantasy, their sympathetic magic. By drawing pictures on the walls of secret caves, pictures of bulls wounded in combat and killed with darts and arrows, they believed this gave them the power to wound and kill them in reality.

The guide lowered the smelly taper and the herds were gone. Strings of smoke curled from the point of the flame. She followed him out of the cave, ducking her head, holding the old-fashioned topee carefully with two hands by the brim and came again into the unreal world of daylight. The guide stood waiting for money. She had none.

'My husband,' she said, and pointed to where he sat in front of an easel in the shade of the black umbrella. 'I will get money from my husband.' She walked across the bruised grass, past the Stones which her husband had his back to. He was painting a view of the Mahwari Hills, delicately, taking infinite pains to achieve an illusion of distance.

He gave her his pocket book. When the man had been paid she put the wallet at her husband's feet and then picked up her own folding canvas stool and her parasol and sat, several feet away, holding the parasol open above her head. She closed her eyes. When she did this she saw the panic-stricken herd. She could smell the blood, the bruised grass, the smoky, bitter dust and the taper in whose light she sat motionless, like a goddess for whom incense was burning.

She sat like this for a long time. She lifted her head. Something extraordinary was happening to her. The heat moved over her face, burning the skin, exposing the beauty of the bone structure as the light from the flame moving over the face of a statue may reveal depths and subtleties beneath the surface of the stone. She thought: I too have been worshipped, and have received a blood sacrifice. A man has worshipped me with his body and with his soul and with his blood. I am blessed among women.

'How plain you've grown, Thelma,' her mother said. 'Not a bit like your father, or me. But you look as if you might have a sweet nature, and that's not like me or your father either, is it? How was he, by the way?'

'He met me in Bombay.'

'Well I know that, goose.'

'He sent his kind regards.'

'Is that all?'

'He said he hoped I would like Kashmir and that I would be happy.'

'Well I hope so too.' Her mother, applying make-up in front of the mirror, looked for a moment at the white-faced reflection of Thelma's eighteen year old face. 'But it is time,' she said, 'to think about marriage. That is what you've come back from England for. But happiness and marriage do not always go together, do they, child?'

'No, mother.'

'So perhaps your father took one look at you, thought marriage unlikely and happiness therefore possible. Anyway, you will be glad to have finished with rotten old school. I hated school. School is what I should call an unnatural place for a girl, if you see what I mean.'

She patted rouge delicately on to her sallow but still unwithered cheeks. The word 'blowsy' came treacherously into Thelma's mind. 'Were you popular?' her mother asked.

'No, mother.'

'Why not?'

Thelma sat down on the edge of the bed. She said, 'Because as you say, I'm plain, and because —'

'Because what?'

'It doesn't matter.'

'You were going to say because of the scandal about your mother and father, I suppose separation counts as a scandal still, but without divorce blame is impossible and real scandal avoided. And one has one's friends, one has one's sympathizers. You've learned one thing. You said it didn't matter, and you are quite right. That you are plain does matter. But less in India than in England or Europe. I have ear-marked half-a-dozen young men. I ask only one thing of you.'

'What, mother?'

'To accept with alacrity the first young man who makes a proposal, providing he is on my list and the proposal he makes is of marriage.'

'Yes, mother.'

'There may be other kinds of proposals. I don't want you to run away with the notion that your plainness is any kind of safeguard. In fact it's almost the reverse. Among men plain girls are commonly supposed to have fancy thoughts, and in the dark, you know, they think that we are all alike. Oh, dear. I've shocked you. Come here and be killed.'

Dutifully Thelma went to receive this token of her mother's affection.

'There are,' her mother said, 'exactly six weeks. By then the season in Kashmir is over and you will be relegated to the plains, to your Aunt Sarah in Marapore. In these matters your father's side of the family is less experienced than mine, and in Marapore you will find there are fewer young men, and those that there are will be minding their p's and q's and trying to please their superiors. So make the most of your chances here. It is what the young men come here for. There are scarcely enough unmarried girls to go round and the pretty ones are already spoken for. I am sorry, yes, Thelma, believe me I am sorry to speak so bluntly. But you want the truth, don't you? Would it be fair of me to let you imagine that your life will either be easy or even enjoyable? You should have been a boy if that's what you want. Your father wished for a boy. Of course I know you are fonder of him than you are of me. But that is because you know me better. Poor scrap.' She held her at arm's length. 'You have never forgiven me, have you, for the other men in my life? But you have forgiven your father for the other women in his. Do you know why?'

'Yes, mother. I know why.'

'Do you?'

'Because I never saw them.'

'Well.' Her mother looked at her, eyebrows raised. 'Common sense as well as a sweet nature. You will make a good wife. Yes. So. We shall see to it. A good wife to as good a husband as we can get for you. It won't be easy. Not only because you are plain but because your parents no longer live together. But your father is well off and holds an influential office, and your mother has a way with even young men still. How much do you know, child?'

'Know, mother?'

'About marriage. About the physical union.'

Thelma blushed.

Her mother said, 'I see. Good. Those fees were not wasted. In your mind you are already a woman of the world. My dear, only your heart is untouched. I find that sad. I do. Come. Kneel by me. There are things I must tell you. It would be wicked of me if I let you go into marriage with your heart in a state of innocence. It is the quickest way to lose it. And once you have lost your heart to a man, you are finished, kaput.'

Kneeling, as she was told, Thelma let her hands be taken by her mother. For a few moments she was aware of love. Beneath the powder and rouge she saw her mother's sorrow, and beneath the sorrow the same terrible instinct to be happy that she felt in herself, but in her own case the instinct was dark and secret, uninstructed, waiting to be shown, to be taught.

'The boy who is about to pluck up enough courage to come over and ask you for a dance,' her mother said, pencilling her own programme, 'is young Mark Scaithe. Do not look down at your lap, child, but at him. He was one of the three whom you met at the tennis, remember? No, of course you don't. You were shaking like a leaf and you are shaking like a leaf now. Use your fan. It gives a woman the same kind of courage men get from a chinstrap. If he asks you for a dance for heaven's sake don't write on your programme until he's gone or you're in control of your hands. Men are afraid of fear, illness and any excessive display of modesty, the latter I mean unless they are real scoundrels, and young Mr. Scaithe is not intelligent enough to be a real scoundrel. They say he went the pace in Calcutta but that was when he was fresh out. He's already sown most of his wild oats. He's tipped as A.D.C. to General Worth. His parents are in a modest way in Hampshire, but the General is a cousin of the father, and another cousin is the fourth Viscount whatsisname, so you would not be totally without connexions. He is twenty-three and looking for a wife who will not utterly disgrace him. He can't afford to be more particular than that, although, come to think of it, he is quite a handsome boy. Try, try, to look lively, child. He's coming towards us.'

'My Thelma was a success,' her mother said, kissing her goodnight. 'The supper waltz, the gavotte and the last waltz. Tomorrow your young Mr. Scaithe will call. On the day after that he will join us in the Nagin Bagh gardens. The following day you and he will ride. Tell me, child, is your heart still intact?'

'Yes, mother.'

'It's as well,' her mother said. 'It's all I ask. Keep your heart, my scrap,' and hugging Thelma, explained, 'Your father took mine. Keep yours safely. It's all I ask. Is it safe? Is your heart safe? Tell me. Truly now. Is it safe?'

'Is is safe, mother.'

It was safe, she thought. Somewhere it was safe. But where? It was at the picnic in the Nagin Bagh gardens that Thelma told herself she understood what she called the true position.

Apart from her mother and herself there was her mother's friend, Mrs. Donnelly; and Mr. Scaithe was accompanied by two men a few years older than himself, but younger than her mother and Mrs. Donnelly. They ate cold chicken and salad. The men, her mother and Mrs. Donnelly, drank claret. There was laughter. From under her parasol her mother held court. Once Thelma caught the Indian bearers who squatted some yards behind, grinning, watching in silence like monkeys. She noticed that Mr. Scaithe's friends were grinning in the same way. And things were plain to her; many things: her father's farewell kiss in Bombay, her Aunt Matilda's kiss in Rawalpindi, the silence of the older woman who travelled with her from Bombay through Rawalpindi to Kashmir; young Mr. Scaithe's laugh, the way he sometimes held on to her hand longer than was polite for a comparative stranger.

While they dozed she wandered past an ornamental pond, sat down on the grass and plucked the blades. She felt him approach. He had only pretended to be asleep. His shadow fell on her arm. He knelt. She looked up at him and then down and then up again, because he puzzled her. He did not really look like the sort of man who thought she was that sort of woman. But then she saw the vein that ran down the side of his neck and the beads of perspiration on his cheek. The collar of his shirt was open. Little ringlets of hair clustered at the base of his throat.

He said, 'Why are you unhappy?'

'What makes you think I'm unhappy?'

She went back to plucking blades of grass, thinking: I am plain, plain, but in the dark he would not care. My mother is what she is, and this he knows, but asks me why I am unhappy. I say: What makes you think that? He doesn't answer. He is watching, looking, wondering how it would be to kiss me, wondering how easy, how much trouble he need to go to before I let him do it. And still he does not reply.

'I asked you a question,' she said, angry at the thought that some look in her mother's eye had given him cause to think he might kiss her, and welcome.

'Did you?' he said. 'I'm sorry. I thought it was an answer to my question. Anyway, something else put it out of my head.'

She tried to say, Oh? What? But the words would not come. It was really a very childish conversation. She would not blame him if he got up and walked away. They were not children.

'Would you like to know what it was?' he said.

'I don't think I'd be interested.'

'How can you tell before you know?'

She went on plucking blades of grass.

'I was thinking,' he said, 'that you look very pretty in that dress.'

'He wants you to ride with him,' her mother said. 'He has asked you to ride. So, you will ride, unchaperoned. All that schooling. What did you learn? Nothing but medieval history? You think these are the Middle Ages? We live in the Twentieth Century. It is nineteen hundred and three and this is Kashmir. So. So. You will ride. And then you stand a chance of being Mrs. Scaithe. Oh, have some sense, child. You make me tremble. You do. Really you do. He is a man. Ah, well, yes, a boy still, a man all the same. Take my word. He will waken you in a way you do not suspect for all your funny little air of knowing what is to be known. Trust at least in my experience. Be grateful for it. Do you think after all these years I can't look at a man and tell, well, his potentiality? Physically he will make you happy. For a time. With men there is always that limitation. The better they are for you physically the more likely they are to be unfaithful. Now do you see? Now do you see why I tell you, plead with you, never to lose your heart to one?'

'I don't want to ride with Mr. Scaithe, mother.'

'Want? Want? Please be careful not to make me angry. You say you don't want to ride with Mr. Scaithe. Give me your reasons.'

'I don't think he is a man I can respect.'

Presently her mother took hold of her by the shoulders. 'Respect?' she said. 'What are you trying to say? He is on my list. Does that call for disrespect? Does that make him unrespectable?' She shook Thelma gently, persuasively. 'Does it? Is that what you mean? Is it a criticism?'

Thelma lowered her head. 'I meant only what I said, mother.'

'You have already been alone with him?'

'No!'

'Ah, then. What can you mean?'

'I don't know. I don't know.'

'Is he not quite handsome?'

'Yes.'

'And *gallant*?'

'Yes.'

'Full of good talk? Well connected? Amusing? Charming? Does he not cut a good figure?'

'Yes.'

'Then?'

Her mother's grip became an embrace. The severity of her mother's voice softened. 'Child. Goose. Poor scrap. He cannot help whatever it is you have seen in his eyes.' Her mother's fingers came under her chin, lifting it. Their eyes met. 'His eyes,' her mother said. 'Is it those? What they tell you? Ah, I grant you his eyes. They are expressive. Do not look into them too deeply. Never look deeply into a man's eyes if you are looking for something to respect in the way you mean. What you would respect is not to be seen in his eyes, but only in his bearing and his public conduct. So. He has asked you to ride. He has spoken to me first. He has been correct. And he is soon going down to the plains. Tonight I shall send him a note on your behalf, accepting.'

She set out with Mr. Scaithe at half-past three. He said that bearers had gone ahead of them about an hour's slow ride to prepare a picnic tea. He'd chosen quite a jolly spot, he said. He hoped she would like it. He hoped she liked the pony he had hired for her. Did it worry her having the syce following on foot? He always told his own syce to wait at the outskirts of the bazaar. If she'd give the word he'd tell this fellow the same.

It was extraordinary how far those fellows would run if you didn't stop them. It was kinder to stop them.

As they left the bazaar behind he turned round and shouted something to the syce.

It was a stunning sight, wasn't it, he said, the lakes, and the reflections in the lakes of the mountains? It was decent of her to agree to come riding. His leave was nearly up and he wanted to make every minute count. Her mother had been awfully decent to him as well. This was the first time he'd been in Kashmir. He hoped like anything to be able to come again one year. She was going to Marapore at the end of the month, he gathered. He wished he could stay on. He'd have volunteered like a shot, then, to act as escort. Whom was she going with? Mrs. Donnelly? It was a pity his own regiment was stationed such a long way from Marapore, otherwise they might have been able to see something of each other when she came down from the hills. His own station was in Madras Province. It was very hot there, but he liked it better than Calcutta. They say, her mother had said, that he went the pace in Calcutta.

The track led them through pines. Below them a stream tumbled over rocks. 'This way,' he said. She followed him along a fork from the main track. They reached a glade of emerald green grass. He dismounted and then came to help her dismount. She looked round the glade.

'The bearers aren't here,' she said.

'Oh, they're further on. But we stop here and rest and give them time to get tea ready.' He was smiling, holding her pony's bridle. One of his hands rested on the pony's neck, too close to her own hands.

'I'd rather not get down,' she said.

He stopped smiling.

'As you like,' he said presently. He returned to his own pony, mounted, and led off, back to the main track. Half-an-hour later they reached another glade. The grass sloped to the stream. A folding table and folding canvas chairs were set beneath the trees. A bearer squatted nearby watching a spirit-lamp kettle. Another bearer squatted by a pannier in which the food and crockery had been packed. Ponies were tethered in a copse. The bearers got to their feet and ran across the glade to help them dismount.

Mr. Scaithe stood by her.

'Shall we have tea?' he said. 'It seems to be just about ready.'

Thelma nodded. He spoke coldly. At the back of her mind was the realization that he had gone to a lot of trouble. If he had been a man she could respect, a man she could feel affection for, how enchanted she would have been; enchanted, moved, happy, sad. Was that what people meant by love? One of the bearers took her crop. Now she was defenceless. She walked with Mr. Scaithe towards the table. Walking, with the bearers watching her, she felt ashamed. The scene had been set not by Mr. Scaithe but by her mother with Mr. Scaithe's willing co-operation. She went on past the table towards the stream. She was aware of his hesitation, his brief absence, heard him say something to the bearers, sensed their going, sensed his approach. She sat down on the grass, and looked at the heel of one of her riding boots, smoothed the folds of her long skirt and felt the prick of tears. He sat beside her. After a while he said:

'I'm sorry you're not enjoying this afternoon.'

She envied him the ease with which he talked, found things to say. For her, talking had never been easy. She knew that this was connected with her plainness. If you were nice-looking people didn't listen much to what you said. If you were plain they listened hard, and waited for signs of intelligence, inner nobility, sincerity, beauty of spirit. Mr. Scaithe could say anything that came into his head, because the same thing went for men, and even if he was not exactly handsome at least he was not ugly. His arm, the one that she could see, was covered with fine blond hairs as far as the elbow where the shirt sleeve began. He was probably very strong.

'Why won't you even talk to me?' he asked.

He had spent a lot of money on the picnic. He was only a lieutenant. She despised him for the purpose to which he thought his money could be put.

'Please go away,' she said. He took her hand. She snatched it away.

'I know what you're thinking,' he said after a while. 'You're thinking I only asked you to ride with me because your mother suggested it. But I asked you because I wanted to ask you. I asked you because I like you. I like you very much.'

'Don't,' she said. 'Please don't tell lies.'

I am ugly, she thought, ugly, plain. How could he like me? He wants nothing from me, except what any man will take from any woman if he thinks it's easy. He looks at my mother and at Mrs. Donnelly and he despises them. He thinks it will be easy with me, to kiss me, to make love to me and then be gone, back to Madras. It is mother who is the innocent, not I. She sees a handsome face and she is lost, lost. In her heart she wishes it were she in this glade, by this stream, her hand that he had taken. It is knowing this that makes him despise us both, play with us both.

She felt an unexpected weight and warmth across her shoulders: his arm. She pulled away, got to her feet and walked quickly away along the bank of the stream. He did not follow. Reaching a secluded spot she knelt and dipped her handkerchief in the cold bright water and bathed her eyes. She knew he had seen the tears. She was ashamed of the tears, too. She knelt by the stream until she felt able to face him. She knew now that he would be cold and angry again. He would blame her mother and blame her too for letting him waste his time. He would have realized now that she was not a woman of that kind, that the scandal of her parents had not rubbed off on to her and made her careless of her chastity.

She stood up. She threw the wet handkerchief into the stream. She would not need it again. Now she felt strong enough to face him. She would not let him hurt her with his anger, his contempt or his indifference, the straight look with which he would try to tell her that if she had nothing to offer him but her plain face they might as well go home.

When she came back to the glade he was standing by the table. Seeing her he called to the bearers. He held a chair for her in readiness.

'I'd rather not have tea,' she said.

'Please. It's all ready. And they've brought it a long way.'

She sat in the chair. He still had his hands on it, standing behind her.

'Besides,' he said, 'there's some iced cake.'

When the bearers had brought the teapot and milk and sugar and the cakes he sent them away and began to serve her himself. She knew that it was she who should pour the tea, but she let him do it. He seemed to want to. While he did so he talked of things he had not spoken of before, of his home in Hampshire, of how he longed to see it again, of how long ago it seemed since he had been there, although it was only three years. He asked her where she had lived while she was at school in England. Briefly she answered him, gradually she looked from her lap, to the table, to his hands, his chest, his chin and finally his eyes. Do not look too deeply into his eyes, her mother had said, and she did not, could not, could not even look into them for longer than a second at a time, but it seemed to her that their expression had changed. He was a bit ashamed too, and that showed, but something else showed as well. Kindness. Gentleness. She ate a piece of the iced cake. He urged her to eat more. She shook her head but let him pour her another cup of tea. He had forgotten this time to offer her the sugar. She dared not remind him. She drank the bitter tea and remembered that he had said: I like you very much. She began to tremble. He turned to call something to the bearers. She looked at his profile, and a little shock of sweet astonishment caught her in the chest. Perhaps she was wrong to blame him much. Men, it was known, had difficulty controlling their natures. He had let his own nature and a misunderstanding, for which her mother was to blame, mislead him. But would he have allowed either to mislead him if there had not been, in his heart, some regard for her?

She turned away so that he should not catch her watching him.

The bearers came with more hot water for the teapot. She ate another piece of iced cake, forgetting that she had just refused one. After a while he said, 'I suppose we ought to be getting back.'

'Yes,' she said. 'It must be getting late.'

'I'll just go and make sure those fellows know what they have to do about packing this stuff up,' he said. He walked across the glade into the copse. When he had been gone for a few minutes she realized that he had given her the opportunity of undertaking a delicate mission, if need be. She blushed. She wandered down to the stream so that when he came back he would think she had taken advantage and not worry about having to put it more bluntly.

After a while she returned to the glade. He was standing smoking a cigarette. Directly he saw her he threw the cigarette down and ground it with the heel of his boot. Together they went over to the ponies.

Mr. Scaithe untethered them. He backed hers away from the overhanging branches and then stood as if to help her into the saddle, but suddenly he put his hands on her shoulders. She

137

looked up at him, startled. But there was nothing in his face of which to be afraid.

He said, 'Thank you for coming with me,' and then bent and kissed her on the forehead. Before she closed her eyes she saw the texture of his skin, the curious coarseness that came nevertheless tenderly upon her own; and the column of his neck that revealed the curling hair that must extend down over his chest. She felt the blood rising into her cheeks, and the violence of her own heartbeats.

His hands came off her shoulders and he stood back, as if regarding her. She could not look up. She turned. He helped her into the saddle. In herself she felt as heavy as lead, but he seemed to lift her as though she weighed nothing. She took the reins. Their hands touched. She glanced at him. He was looking at her seriously, but when their eyes met he smiled.

While he mounted his own pony she watched him. His physical presence was no longer distasteful to her. Slightly ahead of her he turned and began to talk, about riding, polo, going after big game in Bangalore. She studied his face because he was not looking at her fully. She answered in monosyllables although she found the things he talked about not uninteresting. She realized she had never really listened to him before. She was not really listening to him now, but she was watching his face and hearing his voice, and taking in something of what he told her. What people talked about was an indication of their characters. He will waken you in a way you do not suspect, her mother had said, for all your funny little air of knowing what is to be known.

'I have a letter,' her mother said. Thelma shaded her eyes from the morning sun that glared up from the garden into the dark of the verandah. 'A letter that suggests to me that in spite of everything, of all my care, my consideration and the time and effort I have spent, you have made a fool of yourself. And perhaps of me. You had better read it.'

Thelma read it. It was difficult at first to take it in. Mr. Scaithe had been called back to Madras. He had not even had time to call and say goodbye. He thanked her mother for her kindness and asked her to remember him to Thelma. Thelma handed the letter back: 'It is quite clear, mother,' she said, making light of her own misgivings. 'He is an officer. He is under orders.'

'Perhaps there is a mutiny in Madras,' her mother said.

'Have you heard of it? Has anyone? Yesterday you rode with him. You came back. You were silent. And yet I thought —'

'What did you think, Mother?'

'I thought you were happy.'

'I was happy, Mother.' And then: 'I am happy.'

'You poor child. Don't you know what this letter means? He leaves the impression —'

'Yes, Mother?'

'That he felt himself compromised. Driven.' Her mother looked at her. 'Have I misjudged you? Is it possible that beneath —? No.' Her mother sat down. She rang the handbell. The bearer came out. She ordered her breakfast. She ate her breakfast without speaking a word. When she had finished she said, 'I am sending you to your Aunt Sarah's, Thelma. By tonight it will be all over Srinagar. That you went out with Mr. Scaithe and that this morning he is gone back to Madras. Your chances here are ruined. I shan't cross-examine you. I can see it would be useless. Even now you sit there looking as you looked last night. It is not a look that becomes you in the circumstances, perhaps in any circumstances.'

He will write to me, Thelma thought. In Marapore I shall receive a letter. He is ashamed of his previous feelings. He will wait until I am out of my mother's care and back in my father's sister's household. He did not want to see me again here, with my mother, with Mrs. Donnelly. He did not want to laugh any more at my mother's smart conversation, or talk in private with his friends in the way they must have been talking.

'Where are you going?' her mother called.

'You said you were sending me away. I had better start packing.'

Her mother followed her. 'Child,' she called. 'Child.'

Thelma stopped. 'I am not a child.'

'So it has happened. In spite of my warning.'

'What has happened?'

'You have fallen in love. You have lost your heart.'

'No, Mother, I have not lost my heart.'

I have found it, she said to herself. I have begun to find it. It is he who helped me to begin to find it. I know now that it is not impossible for me to feel, to love, to think of someone, to see him in my mind, walking and sleeping.

'Do you think I don't know,' her mother was saying, 'do you

think I don't understand that look in a woman's face? Haven't I seen it many times in the past, in the mirror? Oh, you are a fool. You have made me angry.' She had followed Thelma into the bedroom. 'By falling in love you are giving up your one chance of happiness. It is his fault. You get it from him. He is already taking even you away from me.'

'How can he, Mother, when he is in Madras and I am to be in Marapore?'

Her mother stared at her, flushing slowly. 'I was speaking of your father,' she said, 'not of Mr. Scaithe,' and sat down on the bed, as if under the weight of a realization. For a while they watched each other.

'Father will never take me away from you,' Thelma said, 'nor will you ever take me away from Father. How could you. How could he? I have been nothing to either of you. Now that I'm grown up, and plain, you both feel responsibility. You both think, Poor Thelma! We've given her nothing, let's think of something to give her now, something we both prize, so that giving it to her will make us feel good. You would give me a husband, quickly, to have done with it, to pay your reckoning. Father would give me the respectability he's always managed to imply in his own relationship to the world, by lodging me with his spinster sister. But I don't want a husband or that kind of respectability, not from you Mother, not feel this responsibility so much. But if I were beautiful what hasn't been given to me in love. If I were beautiful you would not feel this responsibility so much. But if I were beautiful what compensation would that be for the years of separation, the years of waking, of crying in the dark?'

She looked in the dressing-table mirror.

'If I were beautiful,' she said, 'I should still look in the mirror and see what I see now. The emptiness, the horror of beauty that has never known love. You said that perhaps separation was a scandal, but that where there was no divorce there was no blame, one had one's friends, one had one's sympathizers. But what friends have I got, Mother, what sympathizers other than the people who pity me for who I am and for how I look? Look in the mirror, Mother. Look at me. There is your blame. There is your scandal. There is your disgrace.'

He will write to me, she thought.

'No, there is no letter,' her Aunt Sarah said, glancing up

140

from reading her own. 'Only these that you see. One of them is from your father. He sends his love and hopes you are better.'

'But *he* sends me nothing,' Thelma thought, going back to her room. For three months he has sent me nothing. Now I know he never will. Now I know the truth. On the banks of the stream where I wept he saw for the first time that I was a child. He tempted me with iced cake, he poured tea as an uncle might. He held me and kissed my forehead and felt nothing because I was a child to him. All the way home he talked in order to forget that he had ridden out that afternoon with a child he had thought a woman, a plain woman whose mother offered her in desperation and without too fine a sense of honour. And he was ashamed. And I was woken. For three months I have longed for him. He will never come to me. If he came he would see that I have become a woman, but he would not find me comely. I sit here in front of the mirror. I put on the sun-helmet to go out with Aunt Sarah. In this way I cover my head in an ancient gesture of despair. I am betrayed. Not by him. But by my awakening. I sense the secrets of my body. But I am without love.

She opened her eyes and saw her husband. She thought: He paints only the surface of the hills and what his eyes tell him he sees. He does not paint what is in his mind, nor does he paint what is in mine.

I need, Craddock thought, an illusion of distance, a perspective of these hills and of my history, because without the illusion, without the perspective, how can I justify my sitting here with my back to the Stones waiting for the moment when the lengthening shadow of Thelma's parasol will fall on the grass, near my foot, and it will be time to pack up and go home at the end of another afternoon with scarcely a word spoken between us? How has it happened that I am here, without occupation, without love, clinging tenaciously to life and to a woman whom I disgust with my gaunt body, my greying hair? Something monstrous must have attended my birth, something deformed, as dark, silent and vindictive as that African forest my parents died in, something which has never let me rest. It is in attendance now. It stifles my need to turn to Thelma and say: Come and help me with this, tell me where I have gone wrong. Yes, it has been a deformity, something inside or outside me that has made me crouch, has sent me stumping through the world as if one leg were shorter than the other. Only in this little game with canvas and easel has the monstrosity been kept quiet, but now even in this he has begun to show his venom. The hills he makes me paint are not beautiful like the Mahwari Hills. They are tortured, molten, full of purple lava and shadows and poisonous vegetation. Looking at my canvas I can smell the rankness. The colours are bitter, deadly. They consume the canvas in blue green and purple flames and in the flames I see the faces of those I have loved and those I have betrayed.

For three generations the men in the Craddock family had served the forces of the Crown, but his own father had gone as a missionary to Africa, taking his young wife with him, and it was there that he had been born and there his parents had been murdered, clubbed to death, their bodies burnt along with the hut, the church and the little school. The amah had hidden him. For three days, so it was said, she walked with the sick child on her back through the jungle to the safety of the Catholic nuns who cared for him until he could be sent to Mozambique and thence to Madras where he lived for four years in the household of his soldier grandfather, General Craddock. When the general retired he went back to England with him. In that same year, for the first time, he met his father's younger brother, hardly more than a boy still, who had entered the army like his uncles and father before him: young Uncle George, who felt himself disgraced by his elder brother's missionary life and desperate death, and deprived through both of the General's love, for the General had loved his elder renegade son more than ever he loved his dutiful younger son. Perhaps the passionate embracement of the family tradition by Uncle George was his way of saying to the General: Love me too. Look, I am following the flag you honoured, the flag my elder brother, your favourite son, turned his back on to preach the gospel to the niggers. Does it mean nothing to you that I should honour it, that I should follow it? Is your pride dead? Did my elder brother take your pride as well as your love? Are they both buried in Africa? Or are they centred now on this boy who bears on his cheeks the renegade look of his father, your prodigal son?

And there came a time, when Craddock was older, when his

Uncle said to him: You're not wanted. I'll see you're not. You should have stayed in Africa. Why don't you go back and lead those niggers into a nigger heaven?

Perhaps, Craddock thought, it had been a mistake not to go back. It was the one place in the world he had studiously kept away from. He had gone instead, when he was a man, to India in 1886, the year before the old General died and left him half the inheritance. He had gone, not as a soldier, but as a civil servant, stumping a district in the United Provinces, playing the rôle of a temporal God, righting wrongs, administering the white man's justice. He cared deeply for the land, for the people. So you're General Craddock's grandson, the older men said: old white men, old brown men: and for a time there was a sense of involvement, of belonging, of security almost of serenity; but this slowly evaporated in the heat of Indian summers, and he began to answer: Yes, but my father was a missionary and was murdered in Africa for interfering in what was nothing of his business. And he began to paint, and gained a reputation for eccentricity, for soundness even brilliance in his workaday duties, but for non-conformity that was put down to something of his bible-thumping father coming out in him, although in his possession no bible ever was, nor prayer-book, nor crucifix. On leave in England he went to see his Uncle George who had never forgiven him for anything, but least of all for inheriting half the General's money. George Craddock by then was a Colonel at the Horse Guards, forty-five years old. His wife had not been able to bear him a child for the first ten years of their marriage, and had died giving birth to Nigel, now aged ten. The boy had the look of his grandfather and even at that age some of the old man's mannerisms, his directness, and paid for it, paid too for his mother's sickliness and her death that had cost his father not only years of anxiety but the thick fist of children with which he had hoped to gain the General's respect; paid for them with beatings that he took without a murmur. Craddock told him tales of India that left him wide-eyed and thoughtful. My father, the boy said, does not want me to go to India, although he wants me to go into the army. Why? Grandfather was in India. Is that why?

Nigel was a wise child, a good child. Born a year or so before the General died he had warmed the old man's heart again, and this too was paid for with blows. He hurts me awfully, he said once to Craddock, then ate ice cream and described the splendour of his father's uniform, so that Craddock knew it was not only the uniform the boy admired, nor hatred that made his father treat him so badly. The wounds the father inflicted and the boy licked were the wounds of love.

'It is a splendid landscape you have painted,' old Lady Brague said. 'You should have been a professional, Mr. Deputy Commissioner.' Craddock smiled. 'You are before the times, Lady Brague. Not Mr. Deputy Commissioner yet.'

'Soon, soon. But in any case, a waste of talent. Any man can be a magistrate. Any man can rule a district. Few can paint. It has become suddenly airless.'

'A moment,' Craddock said. It had happened before in this house. He left Lady Brague's darkened drawing-room. Outside on the verandah the boy who pulled the rope that swung the punkah had dozed off. He stirred him with his foot. With his eyes still closed the boy resumed his task and Craddock went back in. She sat in the shadows of the lowered tattis, dressed in the fashion of forty years ago, the year of the Mutiny. She had borne Lord Brague twelve children, lost eight, and followed her husband the length and breadth of India, from the Himalayan snows to the tropical coast of the Carnatic. She was now very old, and alone in the world except for the grand-daughter people spoke of but few had seen, and whom Craddock, if truth were told, had come to see, driven by curiosity. The girl was the daughter of a union between old Lady Brague's favourite son and the illegitimate daughter of an Indian Prince, and was said to be beautiful.

'The boy had gone to sleep again, I suppose,' Lady Brague said. 'Ah, well. Let him sleep. He is only a child.' And she dozed off herself, upright in the chair, her bony yellow hands clasped in the silken folds of her crinoline skirt. For a while Craddock waited. She had dozed off on other occasions, only to waken and speak as if no time had elapsed between one remark and another. But today it seemed that her sleep was deeper. He tip-toed through the open doorway on to the verandah. There her voice reached him.

'Thank you for bringing your pictures, Mr. Craddock. They are better even than I have been told. Come again tomorrow. Then I will show you what you have really come so many times to see.'

'This is Leela, my grand-daughter,' Lady Brague said. The girl was sitting by the old woman's knee, on a foot stool. She wore a saree set with spangles. She rose and made namaste, and then curtsied to him.

'She knows who you are,' Lady Brague explained. 'She has heard all about you from me. We thought perhaps you might be kind enough to paint her portrait.'

'I couldn't do your grand-daughter justice, Lady Brague. I am not a portrait painter.'

'Get the boy,' she commanded. 'Tell him to raise the tattis. In this light you can hardly see her.'

He did as he was told, waited until the boy had raised two of the woven screens and the old woman called out, 'That is enough,' then went inside.

Presently he said, 'I shall try to paint her portrait, I shall try.'

'No, you are right,' she said, two weeks later, inspecting the canvas. 'You are not a portrait painter. But the painting was scarcely the object of the sittings, was it, Mr. Craddock? Tell me. Do you wish to ask me for her hand?'

'I wish this.'

'You would ruin your career? For what? For love? For infatuation? Or is it only pity you feel for Leela. Mr. Craddock? Perhaps you have become romantically attached, because she is beautiful, and day after day you have sat in this house, watching her, painting her. But is it pity you feel more than admiration? So lovely a young girl, with scarcely a word to say to you or for herself, imprisoned as you may have thought by this old woman in this house of ghosts? Roll up the tattis, is that what you have been thinking? Let there be light, let Leela go out into the world the old woman has protected her from? Ah, well. There is no love without compassion, no compassion without self-pity and no self-pity that hasn't sprung from deprivation and a terrible lust for possession. I am an old woman. I can't live for ever. You have a good face, a melancholy face, the face of a man to whom I could trust her without excessive fears for the future. If you desire her hand she is yours. I know her heart in this matter. She is ready to be your wife, but are you ready, Mr. Craddock, Mr. Deputy Commissioner that might have been, ready to be her husband? Whoever marries Leela risks everything, not only for himself, but for his children. The children of this union would have one fourth of Indian blood. There would be sections of our society closed to them. I need not tell you what you and Leela personally have at stake. And she has only a small dowry. Did you think perhaps there might be some money to compensate you?'

'I haven't thought about money. I have some private means.'

'It's as well. And you can paint.'

'Not for a living,' he said. 'And not portraits,' he added, smiling.

'No,' she said. 'But perhaps you had an eye on high office, Mr. Craddock?'

'No, I haven't had an eye on that.'

'On what then have you had your eye?'

He thought for a while. She did not speak, but waited with folded hands, upright in her chair.

'On justice,' he said at last.

At first he thought the old woman had dozed off. Her eyes were closed.

'Yes,' she said at last. 'That is a good answer. I shall write to the Lieutenant-Governor. He was Leela's father's greatest friend. As boys they played together in the garden there. When my son married Leela's mother, this man alone stood by him. So I shall write to him. At least I think you may be spared the necessity of resigning from the service. He will speak to the Commissioner, they will try to dissuade you but if you are obstinate they will let you marry old Brague's grand-daughter, half-caste though she is; but they will send you away from this district. For a time you will be an embarrassment. This too Leela understands, or understands as well as a girl who knows nothing of the world except the walls and garden of this house can understand anything. She knows that a lot depends on her, as well as on you. Have I been at fault, Mr. Craddock, in keeping her imprisoned so as not to expose her to the humiliations suffered by those whose only sin is a mixture of the blood? Am I at fault now, in exposing you to those humiliations? But time is short. It is always difficult to envisage one's own death. Even now my mind contradicts the evidence of my senses that my days are numbered. Is it possible, I ask myself, that for me India is coming to an end? After seventy years? I am not a woman to regret the past, to regret that it is over. Each day as it arrives is beautiful, Mr. Craddock. I have memories, but the hardest things to relinquish are expectations.'

Alone with Leela he said, 'Will you be my wife?' And she replied, 'I will be whatever you want me to be,' and knelt in front of him so that he experienced a sensation of being both mocked and worshipped, and wondered whether God too was alive to the ambiguity of such gestures. She had her mother's, not her father's bones. The creamy, only slightly tinted flesh was stretched fine, almost transparently over them. It seemed to Craddock that like so many Indian women she was built for burning. Dry and brittle in the body she would be gone in the first lick of the flame, all except her eyes through which so far she had seen nothing of the world; through which, now, looking up at him, she conveyed to him something of her great, untapped capacity for living. Through those eyes he was aware of a similar capacity in himself and of immense reserves of energy.

All my life, he thought, I have conserved, stored up against an occasion of expenditure on some act I could be proud of and thankful for. He made her rise and keeping hold of her small hands kissed them, as six months later, far away in the place of exile of their short marriage he kissed them as they were clenched, cold, sickly-sweet smelling, in the room where she lay dead of a cup of milk into which she had poured powdered glass, as if only the most agonizing end could adequately settle the reckoning of her brief encounter with the cruel world beyond the walls and garden of old Lady Brague's embattled, haunted bungalow. To die she had put on a simple cotton saree, made a pyre of the European clothes she had tried so hard to grace, and set light to them. The ashes, like her body, were cold, the bungalow deserted, the servants fled, the Mahwari Hills silent behind veils of mist that had melted on his eye-lids as he climbed the path calling her name and getting no answer, so that entering the darkened room he was already aware of the need to weep.

Watching him as he painted those same hills in colours which even from that distance she could see were no longer delicate but threatening, Thelma wondered whether in his life her husband had ever really experienced a sorrow as great as hers. Years ago, before she met him, she had known him through the stories told by his young cousin Nigel as a man whose ability might be reckoned in corresponding measurements of sadness, because of the early marriage to a girl Thelma had seen in her imagination as sinister, dark-skinned and dark-intentioned, muttering in an inner room to an idol whose neck was set about with fetid-smelling garlands.

'He risked everything for her,' Nigel said, and continued to woo her in that odd way talking seldom of himself but of the older man instead, as though he hoped to win her regard first of all as someone mindful of good, of sacrificial qualities he could be worthy of the name he was known by in India: Young Nigel, Bruce Craddock's cousin.

And in the end, in her dreams of Nigel dreams of the as yet unmet older man were intermingled, and she scarcely knew one from the other, imagined Bruce Craddock young like Nigel, looked at Nigel and suspected a worn maturity under the unused twenty-eight year old skin that had warmed, unexpectedly, towards her own. At last, entering gardens and drawing-rooms she carried with her that special air of a woman who was claimed, spoken for, no longer to be regarded simply as an impediment, a plain addition to ornate furnishings. Now she stood under ceiling fans and did not anticipate an imminent blowing away into marginal obscurity.

Her aunt Sarah grew quieter, even meticulous in the way she opened letters, and Thelma thought: She is afraid to disrupt, to obtrude, in case too awkward or too definite a movement could shatter the stillness and my chances, my sudden extraordinary expectations; she maintains a fine, well-judged equilibrium, and hopes by doing so to have me off her hands at last and into Nigel's, when she will be able to breathe freely and be heard in the house again, its undoubted chatelaine marching into a last ten years of certainty and ownership, such as nearly ten years ago I interrupted, turning up in disgrace from Kashmir, and asking each morning if in the mail there were any letters from Madras from young Mr. Scaithe.

'She died horribly,' Nigel said, still speaking of Leela Craddock. 'They say she went off her head, that she tried to burn herself to death, commit suttee, but it was her clothes she burned. She drank powdered glass in milk. Some people say she did it because she couldn't bear being looked down on, couldn't stand white people sneering at the colour of her skin. Some say it was because of that backwater Bruce and she were sent to, a place called Mahwar. Others say she did it because

148

once she was married to him and out in the real world she realized just how much he was risking for her, his whole career in fact. Of course I was only a boy at the time. When I first came out to India I was too shy to talk to him about it. Then when I stopped being shy and plucked up the courage to talk to him I found he couldn't or wouldn't talk about it. He's never married since, and never been back to Mahwar. It hit him hard. Since it happened he's worked like a black. Well, I mean. He's distinguished himself, hasn't he? He drives his staff, though. But they swear by him. If I'd been Civil instead of Army I'd have liked to be under him. But you'll see for yourself what kind of a man he is.' And then he said it. 'Shall I be able to tell him about us? I mean, will you marry me, Thel?'

Afterwards, sitting in front of her mirror, remembering his words: I've grown very fond of you: she saw from her reflection how over the years her plain features had not been hardened by bitterness but softened by slumber. I have been walking in my sleep, she told herself, preserving the image of that old awakening so that if it ever came to me again I should know it, and it would not be spoilt by ten years of waiting. Now it has come again or has not come. I have slept too long to know, and what I described to myself as love is described to me now by Nigel as fondness.

The thought was bleak, but there was comfort in it. The road from Mr. Scaithe had not led to Nigel but continued onwards, apart from him, and Nigel was another road. 'Mr. Craddock has asked me to marry him,' she informed her Aunt Sarah. The older woman hesitated, and then put one hand on her hand and after a moment said, 'I'm glad. I think he will make you happy. How pleased your poor father would have been.'

'And surprised,' Thelma said, and was at once sorry, because her aunt was embarrassed and perhaps ashamed, having herself been surprised, weeks ago, when Nigel Craddock's attentions had first become noticeable enough to cause public as well as private speculation.

The lengthening shadow of Thelma's parasol now came into his field of vision whenever he turned from his canvas to his palette.

By marriage, he thought, she became out of what are called my possessions. But what do I possess? The hills, which I paint, I will never possess. I do not even control the pigment.

Each movement of my hand, each stroke of the brush is arbitrary. Each beat of her heart is a brush-stroke. I cannot claim even to hear it, least of all to dictate it. I do not possess. I do not own. My roots are illusory. Notions of what is important to me come into bud like leaves. They unfold. Briefly they live, are viable. They grow brown and dry. They fall. I am subject to seasons of involvement and detachment, creativeness and fallowness, but unlike the seasons of the year these seasons are unpremeditated. They come and go without warning, without the merit of precision and formality. For a man there is no season of desire, no winter sleep, no spring quickening, no summer browsing or autumnal migration. In this way we are distinguished from birds and bulls and leopards. In the spirit we are always hungry for increase. What is inanimate in the world – trees, hills, mountains – they kill us with their tranquillity. At night the universe looks intolerable, unbearably indifferent. Nothing we can do will molest or change or halt it.

What was it that first turned me to Thelma? The look in her eyes when we met? The chemistry of our bodies? The way she had of holding her head erect as though she had learned long ago the lessons of humiliation and was now forewarned? My recognition that binding her and Nigel was nothing stronger than respect?

'She had a rotten time as a child,' Nigel said. 'Her parents were separated. The mother was a bit, well; you know. Fast. She's still alive. She lives up in Kashmir. The father's dead. Poor Thel has been stuck for years with that aunt of hers.'

'And you're in love with her,' Craddock said.

Nigel blushed. 'I've grown very fond —' he replied and Craddock remarked this shying away from the rounder, wholehearted word, and to his astonishment felt relieved, as if an impediment had suddenly been cleared away, leaving him free to explore that dark corner of his mind that had been briefly, curiously illuminated by his meeting with Thelma. In that dark there was impressed an image of Leela kneeling at his feet saying, 'I will be whatever you want me to be,' and the distant sound of old Lady Brague's voice saying: There is no love without compassion, no compassion without self-pity.

'Tell me about her,' Thelma said at their second meeting, 'about the Indian girl, about Leela.' In their conversations there was a rhythm that corresponded to the rhythm of dreams. Sometimes he felt they both knew what was to be said because the dream was a recurring dream. It ebbed and flowed like a tide, sometimes supporting them, sometimes leaving them stranded, apart, uniquely and irrevocably separate.

'She killed herself,' he said: 'Not because I made her unhappy. Not because she was afraid of ruining my chances of making a good career. Not even because in European clothes she looked wrong, looked like someone playing a charade. She killed herself because she felt she had betrayed her own people. But she had no people. That counted too. That weighed in the balance. Towards the end she created a fantasy that her parents were still alive, that they needed her to prove something creditable about their union. Don't ask me any more questions about Leela. She was incalculable.'

For some time Thelma said nothing. She sat in a wicker chair that kept her upright. A lozenge of reflected light from the garden moved across her cheeks, showing the gleam of gentle perspiration.

'No,' she said presently. 'You are wrong. No woman, no man, is incalculable. Before she met you she was asleep in what you call that old house, guarded by that old woman. You woke her in a way she did not understand and when she understood she realized you had woken her with pity, not with love, and she didn't have enough experience of the world to survive the shock.'

'You speak as if you did. Did survive.'

'I survived,' she said.

'And now you are to marry Nigel.'

'He is very fond of me,' she said, as if this were an explanation.

'Is fondness enough?'

'We are both the same age.'

'No,' he said. 'You are older. In many ways he is still a boy. For instance he is afraid to use the word love.'

'He uses the word he feels.'

'Fond.'

'Fond. If there is anyone in the world he loves I think it is you.'

'Which would make my treachery worse.'

'What treachery is that?'

'Asking you to be my wife instead of his.'

'Yes,' she said. 'It would make it worse. He would forget that he wooed me with images of a man older than himself,

151

images of a man he wants me to respect because that man is just and fearless, has known sorrow, is alone in the world, has been alone ever since he was born, but is not embittered and has none but the noblest aspirations. Are you that man, Mr. Craddock?'

'No.'

She smiled and said, 'I'm glad. Such a man would be difficult to live with.'

And then, without looking at him, she held out her hand. Taking it he was conscious of the capacity she had for the kind of gesture that betrayed a turbulence under the calm surface. He was fascinated and fractionally disturbed. With that gesture she lessened the impression he had gained of the strength of her self-control. No man, or woman, she had said, was incalculable, but at this moment she had seemed to be. He saw, for a second or two, the human paradox of her plain face and ripe body, the one apparently set in opposition to the expectations of the other, and wondered, even at the moment when he understood that her words and her gesture amounted to an acceptance of his proposal, a compounding of his treachery, to what extent she truly returned the love that had prompted it. He kissed the hand she offered him and looking up found her watching him as if astonished that it should be he, not Nigel, whose lips had touched her skin.

Presently he felt the faint pull of her arm and let her hand go. She stood up and walked into the shaded living-room, paused, stood near the threshold. Close behind her he heard her say, 'You will tell Nigel?' He said, 'Yes,' and put his hands on her shoulders, desiring her; let his hands move over her breasts with an increasingly persuasive pressure that marked the hardening of his blood; and in her response she betrayed a passion such as he had never succeeded in waking in Leela, but there was an awkwardness, an angularity about it that indicated innocence or, perhaps, a lingering childhood sense of shame. It increased the intensity of his longing. There were depths of undisturbed love in her that he would stir. Already he felt triumphant and went next day, in the same frame of mind, undeterred by the reminder of his forty-eight years in the mirror when he shaved, to join Nigel who had promised him some sport and had taken pains with the preparations.

In the hills above Marapore there was said to be a leopard that had been seen for several weeks; an old wise, cunning animal which Nigel thought, given the luck, one of them might bag. They would go first to a village whose headman had been a great hunter and was said now to be part mystic, part charlatan, but in any case still a man worth talking to, a good-luck symbol if no longer any authority on local jungle lore. They rode for a full morning to reach the camp Nigel had sent on ahead and early in the evening paid a visit to the old man who said, yes, they would find the leopard in the hills two miles to the south-west, and pointed.

'How can you be sure?' Craddock asked.

Because, the old man said, he had heard the leopard calling in the night, for two nights, last night and the night before, and always from the same place. He had tried to make some of the young men go after it, but they were afraid. Returning, Nigel grinned and said you had half to believe him, didn't you? It was what attracted him about this country, he explained, this odd mixture of the real and the unreal.

Craddock said, 'There is only real,' and chose that moment to tell him about Thelma.

After a while Nigel said 'I see,' and then nothing more until they were back in camp, facing each other across the square collapsible table in the dining-tent, their faces lit by the golden light of the hurricane lanterns.

'You are old enough to be her father,' he said.

'And to be yours,' Craddock reminded him. 'That is what makes it monstrous to you. You've looked on me as a father, not as a man, not as a potential rival. You have never looked at me square. Look at me square now. What do you see?'

'I see a man my father never trusted.'

'His distrust was unreasonable.'

'I used to think so.'

'It was founded on nothing but hysterical jealousy.'

Nigel looked down. He said, 'It touched you, then. I used to think you quite unmoved by it. It was one of the things I admired about you. The way he hated you, the way you didn't seem to care. I tried to imitate you. I tried not to care whenever it seemed he hated me too, hated grandfather, hated all of us.'

'That wasn't imitation. It was self-protection. You wanted to love him. You used me as the means by which you could.'

Nigel said, 'And now you're using me as means.'

'The means of what?'

'Of getting even with him. Getting even with all of us. You never had a family of your own. I'm surprised to find how much it rankled.'

'It doesn't. It never has,' Craddock said; but thought: Not in that sense. Not in a sense I knew. Not in a sense I know. But if I look back on my history isn't it a tale of emptiness I have tried to fill but never succeeded in filling? Even birds and beasts know the warmth of the nest, the comfort of the lair. But perhaps this is the beginning of corruption. Perhaps we should all emulate the turtle who buries her eggs in the sand and then goes back to the sea, leaving the eggs to hatch and the young to scrabble their own way into the air.

'There's one thing you're forgetting,' he said. 'Love isn't subject to the rules of loyalty and honour. You accuse me of disloyalty. Can you accuse me of not loving? You who only find it possible to use the word fond?'

'Love is more than a word,' Nigel said. 'It's a feeling.'

'Yes, it's a feeling. But fond is the wrong word to describe it.'

Nigel looked up. He said, 'Does it have to be described?'

In the morning they went after the leopard and found it where the old Indian had foreseen, in the hills two miles to the south-west, trapped in a thornbush, blinded by cataracts, lean and starving, baring its fangs and teeth at their intrusion, disputing a terrain it no longer had the power or even the wits to defend. From this sight Craddock turned away, leaving Nigel to despatch it and the boys to bear it home, limply at peace, suspended by its four paws from a pole.

'Take me to Mahwar,' Thelma said after her second miscarriage. They had been married for two years. It was the September of 1915.

'Not to Mahwar,' her husband said. He held her in his arms. She wept for the never-to-be-born child. 'Never to Mahwar,' he said. 'Mahwar is for dead people.'

She withdrew herself forcibly and lay with her eyes closed waiting for him to go, listening to the rain. Perspiring she fell asleep and woke later, alone, aching in every limb of the body her husband had brought to fever pitch for the embrace of a man whose body would give her corresponding joy, whose strong seed would seal the embryo safely in her womb, whose eyes she might look into during the long act of coition. She moved on the bed, like an animal, and slept again, woke this time to lamplight, and the sight of her husband sitting in the bedside chair, watching her.

She said, 'But we are dead. Take me to Mahwar.'

He repeated, 'Never to Mahwar.' He had the newspaper in his left hand. Lifting it he said, 'There's something I've got to show you.'

He left the newspaper with her, with Nigel's name there, in the list of men killed on active service. A week later she burned the newspaper in the bungalow compound, thinking: If I had married him, now I should be a widow.

The flames died. She stared at the ashes.

She thought: He should have touched me. He should have stood behind me and put his hands on my breasts. He should have pressed, as Bruce pressed, close to me, and let me feel the hardness of his sex, the physical eruption of his love. Only this eruption gives proof. Only this proof truly awakens. Now I need either joy, or sleep to endure a lifetime of lying with a man who touched me before I knew what touching was. How long is a lifetime? How many years? With every year I'm denied joy I shall grow ugly. With every year of ugliness he will desire me less. This will be my protection as well as my sorrow. He will enter me only from habit, to ease the pressures. Perhaps in time my own longing for relief will reconcile me to him and in sleep I shall dream he is Mark or Nigel.

She smiled, continued staring at the ashes.

'After all, it is not a world we are bound to,' she said aloud. 'We have great powers of possession. A lifetime is not too long. How long is a lifetime?'

The answer was ten years. Waiting for her at the end of them was Ned.

6

From those days spent wandering the ruins of Ampurias, days when piece by piece I fitted together the story of Bruce and Thelma in Mahwar, even finding in those ancient Greek and Roman remains an image of the field of the cave and the Stones of Darshansingh: so that at times, listening to the drone of the bees and the distant clamour of the surf, I fancied I could hear what Thelma heard: the sizzle of the spears and the thunder of the hooves of the running bulls. I would drive home along the straight Catalonian roads and find Myra alone on the terrace, staring through the dusk towards the sea, as if she too were waiting at the end of ten real, ten different years, for a man such as Ned, and had not moved from there since my departure in the morning.

I thought of saying. 'Tell me about him,' meaning the godling, but I didn't.

'In Figueras,' Myra said, answering my question: Where are Miguel and Domingo? This was at the end of the third of the four days I left her alone. Lola had prepared cold chicken and salad and left the food in the refrigerator. Presently we would eat. Each of these evenings was the same. We spoke casually of what we had seen and done, and then fell silent and let the sense of restraint between us grow.

The truth did not come to me suddenly. It came quietly, circumspectly, snuffling and whimpering, looking to be let in, reminding me it had looked to be let in many times before.

It was I and Myra who had turned up in disgrace. The Craddocks were pictures I had drawn on a mirror so that I should not have to face the truth directly. Facing it now I wondered what hunch-backed need made me portray Myra in the character of Thelma as ugly and unfulfilled, and myself as a man apparently devoid of feeling. Originally this had not been so. The Craddocks had turned up first in Playa de Faro, and on that occasion Thelma was beautiful, fascinating, the kind of woman even women turned to stare at; and that was Myra as she was, as she is; but I was not with her. She came with a man like John – John as he would have been if he hadn't climbed drunk into his car. That first arrival in Playa de Faro was my way of giving John and Myra back to each other, of making up to them for what I may have robbed them of by taking Myra for myself. No wonder this Bruce and this Thelma felt they had no future. No wonder words like 'date' and 'time' and 'soon' and 'later' were not, to use their own just outdated slang, okay words. It must have been my realization that this Bruce and Thelma had no place to go that made me leave them down there on the beach, looking up at the pretty white villa they were bound for but powerless to enter because Myra and I were already in occupation, had already entered (just as those other Craddocks had entered the Panther House) finding something arrived ahead of us: the shade of a wooden crate which if opened might have turned out to be empty of everything but hope, like Pandora's box after she had rashly raised the lid and let loose all those objects of desire that cause such havoc in the world.

Of course our name was Thornhill, not Craddock, and instead of a paint brush I worked with a pen to create illusions of distance, perspective of our history and of the hills in the seclusion of whose pines the villa stood (a little Mahwar of the Costa Brava). Myra, sitting with her head erect, protected by her invisible carapace, had no need of sun-helmet or parasol, although she used their counterpart of straw hat and sunglasses to preserve the fairness of her skin. But there were minor differences. The major difference between the Craddock's and ourselves was that our disgrace, in comparison with theirs, was muted, elusive. Like the scent of pines, the chanting of the cicadas, the low murmur of the sea it could either be consciously considered or, for a time, forgotten. But it was always there, an uninvited guest who sat with us, perhaps unrecognizable for what he was unless you happened to look closely and saw the curious thing that had happened to his eyes. He had been with us for a long time, but I could not think why. We had done nothing to deserve him, nothing outrageous. But then his presence, when you thought deeply about it, struck you as one intended to bring persistent nagging doubt, rather than a pain you were expected to feel keenly. Perhaps he had been with us ever since that moment in the garden of the house in Richmond when I told John that Myra had changed her mind, and he said, 'I see' and not much else, never as much for instance as young Nigel said to Craddock on the night in the tent when they faced each other in hurricane lamplight across the table and talked of using one person as a means of loving or hating another. And in the morning, for John and myself, there was no shikar, no walk into the hills, no blind leopard trapped in a thornbush waiting to be despatched and mercifully forgotten; but instead, breakfast, and a short while when Myra and John talked privately, and he told her he hoped she would be happy. It could be, certainly, that from then Myra and I were never truly alone, then we were first joined by the uninvited guest. Or it may have been later, at the time when we heard of John's accident. I don't remember what we said to each other on that occasion, which seems to prove that we said very little, believing that to speak would in all likelihood have been misinterpreted as special pleading in support of the contention that neither one of us was to blame. Yes, it could have been then, or earlier; it was impossible to tell. The conscience is an inefficient instrument of detection. Its edge grows blunt with use and you can lose the whole damn thing, like a panicky surgeon who, sewing up a wound he has made, leaves the knife inside and never notices it has gone.

I said to Myra, 'Do you feel it too?'

'Feel what?'

'The chill.'

She shook her head. Actually it was very warm. She asked me whether I had caught a cold. I said no. I only thought the temperature had dropped. The guest stood just beyond the pool of light that illuminated the terrace. It caught and lit the pearly blue ovals of his eyesockets. He sat sightless and patient in the shadows. The lights came on, down there in the bars and shops facing the playa, in the hotels and among the hills, marking the night positions of the villas that were filled, like ships, with transient populations. Somewhere among these lights and these shadows the godling moved. I watched Myra and judged that he also moved with her through the alternating light and dark of her thoughts, along narrow pineland tracks, over boulders to crests that rewarded climbers with sea and landscapes made for lovers; down hills, collecting delicate flowers that grew in the partial shade of spiky shrubs and stones; down steps and in through a now familiar doorway into the shuttered room.

She said, 'Do you feel like eating now?' and after I had said we might as well, rose, went inside and returned some minutes later carrying the food on a tray. She sat at one end of the table and I at the other. Tonight (this night of the several nights we were alone in the villa) she wore a dress that left most of her shoulders bare. She was a citadel waiting to be stormed. I suggested going down to the nightclub but she pleaded a headache, so I went alone after dinner to Rojas's bar and sat at one of the tables on the terrace, facing the sea, drinking brandy, looking up now and again to the villa, wondering where he was, what he was doing, whom he was with, whether he had one woman for the night and one for the day and, if he had, whether Myra knew and tried not to care.

Leaving Rojas's I walked about, hoping to see him. I had never seen him except on the beach in daytime. It seemed absurd; absurd too for a man like that to be on holiday alone, unless his instincts were entirely predatory, but if they were predatory, you would have thought, just once, of an evening, to see him standing at one of the bars, or sitting with a woman in the shadowy part of one of the pine-log terraces. I had a presentiment that on this particular night I should see him, drinking slowly and, between sips, sizing up his chances with a woman he had just taken note of. I willed this thing to happen, without knowing or even bothering to think what I should say to him. We would meet, and talk. The only object of such a talk was to be certain.

But he was nowhere; neither in the bars or the shops nor in the dining terraces of the hotels. I met Sarbosa. We went back to Rojas's for cognac. It occurred to me to say: Señor Sarbosa, in Playa de Faro there is a man. You have seen him. You know why I ask. You, Tonio and Carmen, you have all seen him talking to my wife under her umbrella. So. You understand the position. There can't be much that goes on in Playa de Faro that escapes you. If you have seen this man perhaps you know where he's staying, which road, which apartment.

But I did not say any of this to Sarbosa. We discussed the problems of controlling the traffic. He had an ambition to go elsewhere, to have men under him, to have done with the endless walking up and down in the heat. Presently he left and I sat alone, trying to make up my mind to what extent, if any, he had deliberately steered me away from a subject he guessed was on my mind because it was on his as well. At midnight I went up the road to the nightclub Faro, paid my hundred pesetas at the little box office that looked directly on to the narrow pavement and went in, stood by one of the pillars and watched the dancers and the people sitting at their tables. In the days when the nightclub was open to the stars Myra and I had danced here often, but now it had been roofed to eliminate a source of loss, the rain; and in this first year of the roof it had not rained at all. The club was dark and airless. I could not see the godling among the dancers or the watchers. I pushed my way to the Caballeros. He was not in there. I found a table in one corner away from the floor and ordered cognac. The waiter was an old friend. Later in the evening I might say to him as he bent low to take my order: There is a man. You know the one I mean. He swims with my wife every morning and sits with her on the playa.

I did not say this to him. Again I studied the faces of men in the crowd, sometimes hesitating because I thought I had discovered a resemblance close enough to deserve another glance. The godling was not in the nightclub. There was no point in staying. I stayed. It was safer to stay in a place where I should not find him and be tempted to question him.

That man Craddock: from the beginning he must have known about Ned and Thelma. He could have stopped it with a word, stopped Ned I mean. The boy admired him a lot. That made it worse for Ned, admiring the man he worked for and not being able to help himself making love to his wife. A word from Craddock would have stopped it. Why didn't he speak? Why didn't I speak? Only because I had no admiring Ned to speak to? What would a word to Myra do? Or a word to the godling? It would be easy enough to break habit, to go down to the beach at half-past eleven when he was still there, under the umbrella, and to say: Hello, we meet at last: then watch their faces and know the truth, even if I couldn't change what they felt for each other.

And then perhaps I should find that the affair was no affair; that I was deluded, had reached the stage of creating fantasies in my own life because for four years I had failed to produce them to my own satisfaction with words on paper. Perhaps the godling did not exist except as an optical illusion that faded at mid-day, came back briefly between three and five in the afternoon and faded away again in the evening, so that the man was nowhere to be found at night.

But he existed right enough; he swam and sat with Myra and made himself scarce ten minutes before I was due to join her; and she did not mention him, did not even look at him when he passed by, within a few feet of us. If he were only a tiresome boy, wouldn't she have pointed him out to me, made a joke of it? Or had she, instructed by her sense of vocation, so schooled herself that she would include a casual association with a young man on the beach in the list of things too trivial to mention to her husband, who to get the best out of himself needed privacy and time to think, especially just now when things weren't going well with his work?

And then I wondered: was she waiting for me to speak? Did she know I had seen them together? Had she intended it? Did she know about the shameful fieldglasses, know that like an old hack collecting newspaper cuttings I had taken to spying on lovers, husbands, wives, young men, young women, even children, storing them up as made-to-measure images against the imaginative bankruptcy of old age? Had she deliberately chosen the sandy cove because she knew it could just be seen from the window of my study? Was the whole affair carefully planned and timed as a succession of lures I was meant to respond to with increasing irritation, frustration and anger, like an old bull being put through the three acts of the corrida: the trial of the lances, of the banderillas, of the sword? If so, at what stage were the two of them expecting to judge me aplomado, ready for death? At the moment when lured out of my last querencia by uncontrollable jealousy I chose to face them? Was that the moment? La Hora de verdad? Did she then plan to say, 'Yes, it's true. Things are finished, Ed. Finished for us.'—?

My waiter bent over me so that I could hear him above the din of the orchestra. A girl called Dolores Izquierdo was to dance for us. If I liked he would move me to a better table. I let him move me. He brought me another cognac. The people around me were tourists, they were drinking champagne and having a good time.

The floor was cleared. The lights went out. A spotlight shone jerkily on a doorway at one side of the stage where the band were rolling their drums and holding a brazen introductory note. A solemn blue-suited guitarist had taken his seat on a chair down on the glass dance floor. He cradled his instrument and tuned soundlessly against the stronger announcement from the band, his left ear close to the strings.

Dolores Izquierdo. She came out of the doorway and

marched down the short path from the stage to the glass floor, one hand on her hip, the other held out waist high, palm inwards, loose from the wrist, fingers downwards, partially concealing the castanet. She had probably come up earlier in the day from Blanes or San Felíu, travelling by car with the guitarist, her red-frilled dress crammed into a cheap fibre suitcase that had seen more than one season's wear in nightclubs from Torremolinos to Estartit. The crumpled dress reached to just below her knees and then fell away to the floor in twin frilled cascades of red cotton where it trailed like the tail of a caterpillar. There was a rose tucked over her left ear. Her blueblack hair was parted in the middle, drawn tight across her scalp and wound at the back into a bun. She was small and angry and frowned at us in the approved manner. When she reached the middle of the floor she held her pose; and the guitarist, who was caught in the flickering spot that had followed her from the doorway, began a lyrical introduction.

Slowly she raised both hands above her head and one silkstockinged leg came out from the frilled skirt. When her hands reached their highest point they began the slow descent; the music quickened. The hands came down and round and were then behind her. Her chin was in, her chest out. There was a thump on the guitar. She jerked her head, then held it rigid. She began to walk forward with long, slow, deliberate paces and the guitarist took up a faster rhythm. Behind her back the castanets began to click. She circled the outer rim of the floor, looking severely over her left shoulder into our entertained but slightly incredulous faces, clicking the castanets, hoping for a quarrel. The spotlight showed the gleam of the greasepaint. When she had completed her round of the floor and reached her original position her hands had come up into an arch above her head. Her frown deepened. She could feel the onslaught of the first pain. The guitar quickened. The tremor of the pain flowed down her body, reached her ankles; she stamped to ease it, stamped again. Her eyes closed. The guitar stopped abruptly. The castanets hung silent from her tiny thumbs, like wooden fruits too heavy for the twig. She came towards us, beating with her heels. Then she was close enough for us to see the first sweat on her upper lip, the snag in her stockings, the scratched leather of her shoes. Poor dancer. Your ankles were not pretty.

Someone shouted Olé! A smile flickered on her lips. The

guitarist took up the rhythm again, and she answered it with the castanets. Now the frown had gone. Her eyes were open. They glittered down at us. The pace quickened. She was at it with feet and castanets, circling the floor, describing patterns across it, again and again, quicker and quicker mountingly brave, increasingly hurt, reaching every so often a fierce staccato climax and then beginning again, round and round, until all of a sudden we realized she was going, taking the dance and the music with her, away up the little pathway, a dancing gipsy, dancing back into the passionate darkness of Spain.

I left the club and took the long way home, back up the winding road, past the villas and a black huddle of two lovers who probably had no room to go to. Reaching home I entered my own room, undressed, entered Myra's, and rousing her from sleep, saying no word, not putting on the light, made desolate old man's love.

7

It was Saturday, September the eighth.

To see Ordóñez at the corrida twenty miles away in San Felíu it would cost five hundred pesetas for a seat at the barrera, sombra y sol y sombra, four hundred at the contrabarrera, three hundred and fifty, delantera, or three hundred in the first two files, tendido.

At five in the afternoon, tomorrow, Sunday: six bulls, six Bravos Toros, and Ordóñez, maxima figura, maximo triunfador en todos los ruedos del mundo. The posters had been up since Monday showing Ordóñez gold-jacketed and expressionless above a convolution of pink cape and black bull, gracefully transfiguring a moment on the journey to the grave occasion. It was forbidden to throw cushions at the toreros, but it wasn't forbidden to throw money or roses, to mix the scent of the roses with the blood of the bulls.

I had left Ampurias early, and driven faster than was safe on that road, back to Playa de Faro. I left the car in a garage that belonged to the newest block of apartments and asked the mechanic to check the oil, battery and pressures, and give it a wash-down. Then I walked to he playa, going past the posters that announced the corrida. It was only half-past four. The godling was not on the beach though. The kitchen boys were kicking a football, edging the game nearer and nearer to the prone round-bottomed bodies of two girls side by side. I passed the spot where until a few days ago when he found better things to do the godling made motionless love to the sand: his Poseidon-equipment nearby, in readiness for the five o'clock return to his kingdom.

Saturday: September the eighth. I had come back early to surprise them. I left the car in the garage so that the sound of it in the drive wouldn't act as a warning, went by way of the playa in order to reach the garden from the private steps in the hillside. Camino Particular, Prohibido el paso. I expected to find them on the terrace, even in her room – although staying there until half-past four would be cutting things fine. But there was no one on the terrace and the villa was empty. I went into the study. I felt cheated. I had been so sure that with Miguel and Domingo in Figueras and Lola dismissed early, she had taken to sleeping with him under our own roof.

I stood at the window looking down at the terrace and began to conjure a scene of the three of us sitting there drinking Cinzano Bianco out of tall glasses, discussing the price of seats for the corrida in San Felíu. In the six o'clock light we were caught in a glow like that which might follow a swirl of Ordóñez's cape: Myra whom a man from the consulate in Barcelona once mistook for my niece; the young man from the beach, whose name I did not know; and myself, an ageing animal at the hour of aperitif, observing these two others from the safety of his querencia. It was the godling who had raised the question of going to the bulls, but Myra was supporting him.

She said, 'We'd like to go. What about you, Ed?'

'Yes, what about it?' the young man wanted to know. He sat close to her, smiling like a young novillero at the beginning of the season in which he will take the alternativa. 'You could tell us what to look for.' In my absence in Ampurias he had been inside the house. He had seen the books in the study. The features of his face were not yet clearly defined. The smile alone was an indication of his ambitions.

'It's up to you,' Myra said. 'We're for it.'

'You're not for it,' I said. 'Neither are we. It's the bulls. They're for it.'

They wanted me at the corrida with them, not to tell them what to look for but to sit between them and feel myself crushed by them and by the weight of the last Pagan spectacle in the civilized world as, one by one, six bulls were done to death and dragged out by the mules while the crowd applauded. And afterwards, as we left the arena to the music of a paso doble coming over the tannoy, they would walk together a bit ahead of me. He would take her arm to protect her, usurping my place, making it clear from the way he held her, guided her, that they had intimate knowledge of each other, that he felt he had earned the right to make this intimacy public, having that afternoon dedicated a bull to her, and killed it, and been awarded the ears.

Looking away from the terrace whose actual emptiness came almost as a shock. I raised the fieldglasses. The kitchen boys had stopped playing football and were talking to the two girls. At first I thought one of the girls was Lesley, but I was wrong. I hadn't seen Lesley since the morning I watched her bending over the box in which there were the swimsuits going for a song. She was probably already back home, and days ago had knelt and hugged the dogs, pecked Aunt Evie on her cold dry cheek and then gone upstairs to conduct the ritual of brushing her teeth and washing her hair.

Lesley is for ever a child to me, one who was touched and woken before she knew what touching was, what waking meant. Like that, she is an embodiment not of her own innocence, but of everyone's, which is why she turns up in so many different disguises, not only as the memory of a girl I knew years ago in India, but also as Ned Pearson's wife, as Thelma Craddock with her mother in Kashmir, as an unknown girl standing on the beach at Playa de Faro, gazing at the sea; and also in that picture of Myra as a child, travelling as Thelma did between one parent and another, looking to be loved. Is that innocence, to look for love, knowing nothing of its wounds even though you have already suffered them?

I came away from the window, put the fieldglasses away and sat at the desk, chin in hand. Occasionally there were noises in the house, noises as of tiny creatures in occupation, the kind of creatures that fled the Panther House when the Craddocks arrived. Why didn't Craddock speak? A word would have put an end to Thelma's affair with Ned. Craddock must have been afraid of what Thelma would do if he tried to stop it. She was the only thing he had left. Work is no substitute for love. He wasn't really a man devoid of feeling, although there was a ramrod core in him that would sooner break than bend. To speak would have been to bend, after a fashion. It was easier for him than for most men not to speak. Even in those early days when he went to old Lady Brague's, hoping for a sight of Leela, the hardness of the core was already apparent. Could the same have been said of myself when I used to go to that curious museum of an apartment in Berlin hoping for a sight of Mitzi whom her aunt took such pains to keep hidden? Did the aunt ever say to me, 'On what then have you had your eye?' and did I say, 'On justice', or is that all part of the personal fable I have built out of a commonplace story of a young man who confused what he called love with what the world called pity, and was only looking for an occasion to act in a way he could be proud of and thankful for: in this case to save a pretty pale-faced girl whose mother was dead because she had committed the crime of mixing her blood and joining her flesh with a Jew whom no one could have saved? Yes, I think I did say that thing, 'On justice'. But I think I said it with more passion than Craddock. When young we use words glibly, haven't yet begun to question their meaning; but at least we feel what we may by them. When we begin to question what we mean we feel them less, and that is sad, but inevitable, and right. When Craddock said, 'On justice', he had given it careful thought and perhaps even as he said it he asked himself, 'But what is justice and what has justice anyway to do with my taking Leela out of this house into mine?' Perhaps I said this too, but there is a sense of Craddock never having been young, of having been born tall and gaunt in spirit, like one of the trees in the forest he was carried through as a child on the first leg of his journey to safety, to the nuns of Mozambique.

Craddock wasn't a picture I drew on a mirror to avoid having to face the truth. He was the man my hunchback made me see when I looked into it at my own reflection: the naked construction of bone under the dissembling flesh; the whole skeletal structure of the inner silence that would be left if layer by layer my pretensions to articulate compassion for human frailty were peeled away.

I got up from the desk and went back to the window. This time the shock was real. The terrace was no longer empty. Myra was sitting on the stone bench in the attitude of several evenings before. She had taken off the sunhat and had her head up like someone looking for the benefit of a movement of cooler air, or the late warmth of the setting sun. She was Thelma with her eyes closed, imagining the heat of a burning taper that had been lit in her honour. She sat like this for some time, not moving, her back straight and her hands resting on her lap, her legs crossed at the ankles. Even in repose her body was disciplined to conform to certain standards of conscious grace; but strip her of that grace and of her beauty and she was Thelma.

I called out to her. Startled, she looked round and up, and took off the sunglasses because the light was going and she could not properly see who it was. Without the glasses she was defenceless, beautiful; so defenceless, so beautiful, that I wanted to end at once with some perfect gesture the restraint that had grown up between us. Like Craddock in the Field of the Stones I wanted to say: Help me with this. Tell me where I've gone wrong.

'Hello,' she said. 'Have you just got back? I didn't hear the car?'

'I left it down at the garage. Stay where you are and I'll bring us both a drink.'

When I went on to the terrace, carrying the tray, she was standing by the balustrade, smoking a cigarette, her right elbow cupped in her left hand. Turning, she said, 'Well, Ed. You're back early. Did you have a good day?'

'Not bad. What about you?'

'Oh, I walked.'

'Where to?'

'Up by the rocks, down to one of those little bays.'

I handed her a drink. She was wearing old, scuffed shoes. Yes she had walked up by the rocks. They had walked up by the rocks together. 'And this morning I swam,' she said. She put a hand on her flat waist. 'It's beginning to have an effect. I think I've lost about a pound.'

'Yes, it must be the walking. Are you going to Ampurias again tomorrow?'

'No, I've finished with Ampurias for the time being.'

She sat on the stone bench, and I on one of the iron chairs.

'It's done you good,' she said. 'You're looking better. Where will you go tomorrow?'

'I'm not sure. It depends on the car.'

She asked what was wrong with it. I told her it had given trouble on the way home but could probably be fixed easily enough. There wasn't any reason why she should doubt me, everything we were saying seemed to have to be filtered first through the fine mesh of the other's suspended judgment. We were talking like actors feeling our way into lines we had learned but not yet understood.

'Who is he?' I asked, suddenly.

We were not living in a book. In life there had to be a confrontation. The realization made me tremble.

'What?'

'I said, who is he?'

'He?'

Trying to keep my voice level I explained. 'The man. The boy. The young man on the beach. The one you swim with and who sits under your umbrella and passes us without looking

168

when we're drinking champagne.'

Having said it there was more to say. I did not say it. Ridiculously, absurdly, I began to cry. She came over, as if to comfort me. She even put a hand on my hunched shoulders. All I could say was, 'Damn you. Damn you, Myra.' And after a while, after saying twice or three times, 'Ed, don't. Don't,' and getting no response, she went into the house.

And that was my proof. She shouldn't have gone into the house. She should have made further pretence of not understanding, of being astonished that I should have misinterpreted those casual meetings on the beach. She should have been concerned by my taking it to heart. She should have done more than stand near me and touch me and ask me not to cry. She should have seen that I only wanted her to tell me it wasn't true, that there had never been anything between them.

'Is it true,' I asked Tonio Rojas that night, 'true about the horses?'

Pinned to the shelves behind the bar there was one of the bullfight posters. Rojas was polishing glasses. He saw where I was looking. He said, 'The horses at the corrida?'

'Yes, is it true?'

'Someone once told me that the horses were operated on so that they couldn't scream if the horn found them as it sometimes did in spite of the protection of the padding, I explained to Rojas. Someone else said that the padding was no protection anyway (Hemingway probably), but it stopped the customers having to put up with the sight of a horse going round the ring with its entrails hanging out.

Rojas seemed deliberately to misunderstand me. He said, 'The horses are blindfold so that they don't see the bull. One eye is covered, so. And it is always on this side, the blindfold side, that the picador must take the charge of the bull. The horses are protected on this side, and the leg of the picador, that also has strong protection.'

'But is it true that something is done to the horses so that you don't hear them scream?'

'Scream? What is this, scream?'

'Cry out.'

'You must not worry about the horses. These horses are very old. They would anyway be killet.' Killet was Tonio's word for killed. 'I have good tickets. See for yourself, tomorrow.' Jok-

169

ingly, he was always suggesting I should go.

I took my glass of cognac into the arcade. There were people shopping, turning the picture postcard stands, looking at the paper-backs, the espadrilles and the souvenirs. The shops and bars would be open until long past midnight. There was another bullfight poster outside Rojas's with a printed sticker tacked across it saying 'Tickets'. On Wednesdays an agent came up from San Felíu and left a batch of tickets with Tonio. On Sundays at mid-day he came again and took away the money Tonio had collected and the tickets he hadn't been able to sell. I had watched the ritual a score of times. The tickets were numbered, and noted on a list. The check was made carefully, in a business-like way, over cognac and cigars. The unsold tickets were taken back to San Felíu and put on sale outside the plaza. The agent went from one resort to another. He was an aficionado and a friend of the toreros. I had never thought to ask him whether it was true about the horses.

But if it wasn't true about the horses perhaps it was true about Craddock: that the amah who carried him through the jungle to safety first cut his vocal chords so that he couldn't cry out and give them away to their pursuers. And this would explain why since then he never let any sound of pain escape him. And perhaps it explained why he hit Thelma when she sat on the packing crate crying out for Ned to come and take her away; hit her because that was the only way he had of relieving his feelings.

I ate at the Hotel Playa de Faro, out on its pine log and bamboo terrace at a table from which I could see the lights of the Villa Vora la Mar. 'Is that it?' Thelma said. 'But then it must be. It's how I imagined it, how I hoped it would be.' And stood there with Bruce smiling a smile that nothing could destroy, because this Thelma, this Bruce, were romantic figments, at most impossible projections of John and Myra into a future that was never theirs. Piece by piece their harlequin luggage was taken up the hill. Case by case they took possession. If you looked long enough you could just make them out, arm in arm, silhouetted against the light in one of the upstairs rooms, looking down at the little bay that had been scooped out of the shoreline by a white horse from Poseidon's stables, just as two dark-eyed children had looked down in wonder, from just about that spot, at the shape of the hoof and the distant apparition, far out on the horizon, its wet mane gleaming in the sun; centuries ago; long before the advent of a civilization that brought strange gods from across the sea, and altars for the sacrificial killing of bulls, and left their stone relics in Ampurias.

And long before that there had been no bay. The blue-green sea scourged an unbroken line of terracotta coloured rock. Immense trees stood on the hills with their thick branches heaving in the wind, jerking the long bell ropes of the lianas that chained them to the ground. In the deep indigo shadows of the trees fleshy plants clothed the hill-sides, stirred by the movement of the ropes and the wild currents of air. Sometimes the sun was obscured by boiling clouds from which rain lashed down and forks of lightning struck, lighting the eyes of serpents coiled watchfully under rocks and in the shallows of the sea. And when the storm of creation had died the serpents emerged and wound their way into the dense carpet of leaf and stalk. Strange birds flew above the trees and the plants were stirred now not by the wind but by the movements of animals.

This was the scene of an arrival too. They came from over the hill after a long cold journey and sat warming themselves against a rock; and after a while, not speaking, began to throw stones into the sea, remembering Eden.

8

Regard him then: a tall man of sixty clothed en fête in blue Terylene trousers and crimson shantung silk shirt, with bare feet tucked into canvas espadrilles. This Sunday morning he has swum as usual in the warm deserted sea, frog-legging it in slow spurts in the direction of the cork-bark floats that mark the position of the lobster pots, passing them, heading for the cove where his wife is in the habit of sitting with her lover, floating on his back after every dozen strokes or so to get his breath which has grown shorter every year, like his expectation of life.

Reaching the cove he is glad to sit, his long thin legs thrust out, his sagging trunk supported on stiffened but trembling arms. The salt water has cauterized his eyes and nostrils. He is cold. The cove is in shadow, the sun not yet up above the north eastern promontory of rock. Across the bay the villa is almost hidden by the configuration of the pines which give no clear hint in the complex tracery of their branches of the gap which makes one place visible from the other. To distinguish it concentration and prior knowledge are necessary.

He shifts his weight and hurts his hip on a stone which he brushes away and then picks up. Round and smooth, cold at first, it warms in his hands. He pushes it into a patch of wet sand. There are other stones within reach. He selects one and pushes that into the sand too, alongside the first. He adds a third. Presently he has formed the letter M: and so continues, reaching for stones, pushing them into the sand until he has written 'Myra'. The stones are different sizes, shapes and colours and the patch of sand, dotted with these stones, is almost obscured. A swimmer lying here might never notice that the stones spelled out a name. For a moment he is tempted to obliterate them, but remembers the horses who cry out soundlessly when the horn finds them, so leaves them there, making their mute appeal, and re-enters the sea for the long swim home.

He has greeted Lola, sister of the dolorous widow of Figueras. Her twin nephews will be back some time this afternoon. He remembers it is Sunday; the day of the bulls. He takes coffee upstairs to his room, showers and puts on the blue trousers, crimson shirt and canvas espadrilles, goes into the study and stands at the window from which, without the glasses, it is difficult to make out the cove.

Regard him then for a moment as I do, objectively, on what is the last day of his life. It is nearly eight o'clock in the morning. He has less than twelve hours. At a few minutes past seven this evening he will get into his car. The car will reach its destination, but the man who gets out of it will not be the man who is standing at the window wishing he had the courage to open a door, cross a few feet of floor space, open another door and say to Myra: 'Now we can talk. Now you must tell me the truth. I apologize for my weakness last night. I promise not to make another scene. I promise not to stand in your way if you think your future happiness lies in being with this other man. But I must know. You must tell me: if it's too soon for you to think of him clearly in terms of your future happiness, then tell me so. I promise not to say or do anything that will make you feel an immediate decision one way or the other is imperative. I'll be patient. I can be patient. I want to be patient. I don't say this to you because I'm indifferent to the final answer. I say it because I love you and it looks as if not standing in your way but being patient may be the last proof I can give you that I care for you and care what happens to you. If what I'm saying seems cold I beg you to remember my behaviour on the terrace last night. Then you will have a picture of two extremes of behaviour, but the man in each case is the same man, human, fallible, muddle-headed, jealous, puzzled and committed in the last resort to stand by a principle he's always tried to stand by, the principle of every human being's right to say and do what he thinks and feels is right for him and to accept it as a duty not to resist other people doing and saying what they think and feel is right for them. He sees the paradox in this, and beyond the paradox to the bitter moral lesson: that the principle may turn out impossible to stand by if he's not prepared to sacrifice his own rights and his own needs when they conflict with someone else's. As mine with yours, Myra. If you were prepared to sacrifice as well, then perhaps we should approach a state of what the world might call perfect love. But what would that perfect love be, Myra, if you gave this young man up and stayed with me? Would you love me again because you had given him up? Would I hold you in my arms and be happy because I had not won you back but only received you back? We know the answers. If you love this man and think you can only find happiness by going to him, the sacrifice must be mine. It is a question of weighing different passions in the scales; your love for this man, my pain at losing you, my hatred and envy of him. My passions would be more colourful than yours, but they would be negative, self-destructive. The scale would tip in your favour, Myra. Which is why, when you are ready to tell me, you must tell.'

But he lacks the courage – or is it the conviction? After a lifetime spent observing, and commenting on human behaviour he seems to find it difficult to understand his own. He keeps thinking of the horses in the plaza de toros. The horses stumble round the ring, bleeding into the protective mattresses, their visible eyes rolling, their teeth bared, trying to scream. In the old days, before the horses were protected, they were often killed outright. When they were killed they were covered with sacking and left to lie until the bull was killed too. There might be two or three dead horses in the ring by the time the trial of the lances was over. They say it was fairer to the bull to let the horses be killed. It made him feel he was winning.

At nine Myra came out on to the terrace carrying her beach bag and the furled umbrella. I came away from the window, sat at the desk. There were letters from the past few days that I hadn't answered. I answered them now. A little after ten Lola tapped on the door. She had brought my coffee because the señora had said I was working and probably hadn't noticed the time. I asked her to tell the señora I would work until mid-day and then meet her as usual at Rojas's bar.

At ten to eleven, taking the fieldglasses, I went back to the window. Myra had left the terrace. Lifting the glasses I focused them and watched the silent moving pictures performed for me by the sunbathers on the playa and the shoppers in the arcade. I panned the beach, searching out Myra's umbrella, and found it in its usual place, with Myra under it oiling her arms. She oiled herself both before and after swimming. Moving the glasses from the beach across the water to the lobster pots I picked out the godling, lying on his back, sculling gently with his hands, waiting for her in accordance with the rules laid down for the curious ritual of their morning assignation. Seeing him like this I thought it likely that she had yet to tell him I knew about their meetings. Last night she had had an opportunity while I was drinking at Rojas's and eating at the hotel. She could have left the villa for an hour or two without my knowing, but the light was on in her room when I got back and at the time I had the impression she had been in her room ever since she left me alone on the terrace. In any case, their meeting today would be especially interesting to watch.

Moving the fieldglasses I caught her just as she was walking into the water. She stood ankle deep, adjusting her swimming cap, and then went in up to her waist, leaned and let the sea take her weight. She swam a slow elegant crawl. I moved the glasses ahead of her. He had seen her and was treading water. When she was about ten yards away he dived under. She reached the pots and looked round, wondering where he had gone. He surfaced behind her, swam a few strokes and put his hands over her eyes. She turned, laughing, and he carried her under the water and there, no doubt, in the safety of his kingdom, kissed her.

Even knowing her affair was discovered she could laugh, let herself be taken under and embraced. She laughed, I thought, because this morning the burden of secrecy had been lifted from her shoulders. For her, the sea that she used to gaze at was no longer an immense waste but a friendly element to which she now committed herself with joy. Emerging, they turned and swam indolently towards the cove and were lost to sight for a while in that stretch of water between the cove and the lobster pots which was hidden by the pine trees on my side of the bay. They seemed to be a long time re-appearing, so long in fact that I thought they had found another place, one that would not be visible to a man standing at a window watching them through powerful lenses. I scanned other parts of the sea and shore and then, finding the cove again, was in time to see him helping her gain its shelter, holding her hand to steady her through the gap in the rocks. They sat down close together. He helped her take off her swimming cap and then lay back resting on one elbow, watching her. He was at ease, untroubled. She had not told him yet. She was still sitting up, close, I thought, to the place where her name was written in the sand with pebbles, but she hadn't seen it. She was looking out to sea, probably wondering how to break it to him that their affair had never been a secret. He said something to her; it could have been: 'What's wrong?' She answered him. I think she told him then. He sat up. Her head was lowered but she seemed to be talking. When she had finished talking they were both silent for a while, but then he turned and looked in the direction of the villa and spoke to her. She looked in the direction of the villa too. For a few seconds they stared across the bay, but their faces did not look like the faces of people who knew they were being watched. Of the two of them he was the more suspicious, the more troubled by the thought that they could be seen. He continued looking in my direction while Myra turned her attention back to him. Perhaps it was something she had said that finally made him turn to her, dismiss the idea of being watched as relatively unimportant; something like, 'So what are we going to do? He actually cried. That was unfair, wasn't it? Even he realized it was unfair. It made him lose his temper. He said, "Damn you," and that means it's all over between him and me, doesn't it? So what are you going to do?'

What indeed? The key to the future seemed to be with him. Who was he? I knew nothing about him, not even his name or nationality, so how could I judge what kind of a man he was? There were questions whose relevance I had been aware of but only now admitted as vital: where did he come from? How soon would he go back there? What was he doing alone in a place like Playa de Faro? Had he come here with a friend, sharing the expense of an apartment from which they could sally forth separately down to the playa to see what might be in it for them, to meet later and compare notes and come to an understanding about the times of day each of them could rely on having the apartment to himself? Poor Myra? What kind of a man had she become infatuated with? Would he say to her: 'I thought you knew the score, I thought it was clear. I mean, look, I've got a living to earn. In a day or two I've got to go back and start earning it again. I can't swan around the Med. renting nice white villas, just as the mood takes me. I wish I could. If I could, fine, there's nobody in the world I'd rather have along than you, Myra. But to me Playa de Faro isn't life. Life is a one-man flat, doing a nine to five job trying to earn a bit more money than I need to spend.'

He was saying something to her now. Presently she looked away from him. He took one of her hands as if to persuade her to understand the reasonableness of his point of view. She let her hand stay in his but would not look at him. At one

176

point she shook her head and then bent it, freed herself and covered her head with both hands in that gesture of despair I had so often imagined her offering up, if only to her own reflection in a mirror. For a few seconds he stared at her, astonished at the effect his cool appraisal of the reality of their situation had had on her, but then he put his arm round her shoulder, and she responded. They clung to each other like young lovers who had been cruelly sentenced to separation and had stolen a final hour together. They kissed passionately, courageously. And so I guessed the truth.

It was Myra who had tried to make the cool appraisal. She had not said: 'So what are we going to do?' She had said, 'He knows. So it's over. He's not a young man. I can't desert him. I made vows. They are vows I've got to keep. I came here this morning to tell you, and to say goodbye.'

But she had reckoned without him. He was not prepared to have goodbye said. He was not going to let her go without a fight. I felt the first dull prick of admiration for him. He was again the godling. I remembered that when I first began to notice them together I had thought: He looks intelligent. It was only when I began to suspect them of sleeping together, first in his apartment and then in the villa, that the image of him changed. Now it had reverted to its original form and I knew that Myra would never be attracted by a man of straw, by one whose feelings were shallow or whose dignity as a human being did not complement her own.

And surely in that sense she had of her dignity lay my security as well as my danger? I had nothing to do now but keep silent, make myself scarce, withdraw from the arena. I was dealing with Myra Thornhill, not with Thelma Craddock. For me, Myra would never reveal the crack in her armour. If I struck her she would keep her head erect. And this man, the godling of Playa de Faro, was no Ned Pearson. He would never stand himself against one of the white walls in one of the narrow lanes and shoot himself rather than live with the disgrace. For the godling there was no disgrace in loving Myra. And to Myra, in front of the man who was probably the first fully to have awoken her to what she thought of as the meaning of love, there was no disgrace in covering her head in that ancient gesture of despair, because the gesture itself was a measure of her human dignity. What is that dignity after all if it is not a way of holding yourself, preserving yourself, in a world where you feel yourself utterly alone? And in that sandy cove, clasped in his arms for what she thought must be the last time, she allowed herself, as I had allowed myself the evening before, the luxury of revealing the crack in the armour to the one person who held out promise of containing that loneliness by circumscribing it with his own.

But she would not let him contain it, ever again. She was still trying to tell him goodbye. She broke away from him and stood up, walked to the water and stumbled. He stood up too and was in time to save her from falling. He held her by the shoulders, and then releasing one of them used that hand to lift her face up by her chin to make her look at him. He released her other shoulder, held her face in both his hands. I think she had her eyes closed, But her lips seemed to be moving. Perhaps she was begging him to let her go and not to follow her but to say goodbye now, in this place where they had first learnt to love each other.

He let her free. For a moment they stood close, but without touching, then she waded into the shallows, putting her swimming cap on, pausing when she was up to her waist until the cap was fastened. Before she plunged in she looked back at him. I imagined that she said: Goodbye; that he called to her, that she said, No, don't follow. You promised. Don't make it any harder.

He stood watching her, waiting for her to reach a point where her determination would crack and she would make the kind of sign that would send him swimming strongly after her. But she swam away. Presently he sat on his haunches, and gathered stones at the water's edge, inspected each one before flipping it into the sea. He had stopped watching her progress to the lobster pots. The rocks that jutted on each side of the cove probably already hid her from view.

Now she had reached the lobster pots. She went on to her back. She was Ophelia drifting on the current. When she was rested she swam for the beach. The godling had lost interest in the stones. He got to his feet and ran in, dived under the surface and re-appeared several yards ahead of his point of entry. He shook his head to rid his eyes of water, faced the horizon and opened his shoulders to punish the sea.

She came ashore, trudged up the slope to her umbrella, took off her cap and then knelt, straightened her towel and lay on it full length. face down, as swimmers do. She lay like this for a long time. She had forgotten to oil herself. Eventually the heat of the sun on the backs of her legs reminded her. She turned over and searched in the beach bag. Having found the oil she sat up, put on the sunglasses and the tall-crowned sunhat and opened the bottle. While she oiled she seemed deliberately to keep her attention from wandering back to the water. She put her wrist-watch on. I looked at mine. It was twenty minutes to twelve. She smoked a cigarette. A beach ball tumbled against her arm. It startled her. The child it belonged to came to reclaim it. She smiled and pushed the ball towards him. She looked at her watch again, stubbed the cigarette in the sand, rose and collected her things together, towel, beach bag and umbrella. With these, at a few minutes to twelve, she walked up the playa towards the tables on the sand below Rojas's bar, to keep the mid-day appointment.

I swung the fieldglasses back across the bay to see whether in that now dazzling water I could distinguish the godling's head, but the sea in the direction he had been swimming was empty of all but a couple of pedal-rafts. Moving the glasses slowly I quartered every section of what I could see of the bay through the gaps in the pines. His absence was ominous. I did not think he could yet have swum so far out as to be invisible. The sea was calm. He was not the kind of man, surely, who would take his loss so much to heart as to swim until he was exhausted and unable to get back. He must have swum ashore; and this is what was ominous. Somewhere down there on the playa he was waiting. Of this I was convinced. I swung the glasses back to the beach. He was not there. But I was not far wrong. I found him swimming close in to the shore, pausing, treading water, watching the tables below Rojas's terrace where Myra now sat talking to Carmen who had brought the ice-bucket of champagne.

Why? To see if Myra had spoken the truth when she said, if she said, that I was not in Ampurias today and expected to meet her as usual at twelve? Or to watch for my arrival and time his own so that he could emerge, dripping, stride up and say: I expect you want to talk to me? Or was he watching simply to be nearby if, when I joined her, it looked to him as if she needed his support, his protection?

It had gone twelve. Already I was late. Carmen had poured Myra a glass of champagne. I said to myself: I must go now, it must be faced now. But I stood on, at the window, watching her, but mostly watching him. Now he had begun to swim for the shore. He had decided on a course of action. I had to wait to see what it was. He came out on a part of the beach above the tables where Myra sat, where she could not see him. He had left his towel and cigarettes there. He dried himself quickly and then, carrying the towel and the cigarettes, walked towards Rojas's. There was a moment of hesitation. I thought: He admits he's beaten, he knows it's no good, now he'll go up into the arcade and get away from the beach as unobtrusively as he can.

But he continued towards the table. He stood a few feet behind her, Perhaps he spoke, or she may have sensed his presence. She turned round in her chair. He came and stood beside her. She looked away from him. She stubbed the cigarette in the ashtray Carmen had placed on the table. Perhaps her hand trembled while she stubbed the cigarette. Please go, she was saying, please go before he comes; go now before he sees you; I know what I've got to tell him.

He knelt by her chair. He put a hand on its arm. He said: You must tell him the truth, that we're in love. that we can't live without each other.

She turned further away, looking towards the pinelog and bamboo terrace as if the man who knelt by her chair was a stranger who had unaccountably sat too close to her. Perhaps behind the dark glasses, she wept. She said, almost whispering it: No, I'll tell him it was partly true, there was a man, a young man, he was lonely; we met once when we were both swimming near the lobster pots, and often after that we met, but there was nothing between us; he was a young man alone on holiday, now he's gone, that's all there was to it. Please go.

He looked down at the sand. He dug his fingers into it. Knowing that his eyes weren't on her she could not resist turning her head until she could see his profile. He said: No, I'm staying here, it's wrong to run away, we've got to face it and make him face it.

It's no use, she said. It's over. Why don't you understand? I'm not free to love you in the way I want to love you.

You could be free, he said, if you made him face it; you could make him free you.

He looked up at her.

If you wanted to be free, he said.

He would not be able to see behind those dark glasses. When she was wearing them her mouth alone had to suffice as an indication of what she was thinking and feeling.

But you see I don't, she said. I don't want to be free.

He bent his head. When he had dug his fingers in the sand he must have scooped a handful up. He held it in his clenched fist and now let it flow out slowly as if his fist were one end of an hour glass. When the sand was all gone he straightened up.

There's no more to be said, then?

No, nothing more. Please go before he comes.

Did they say goodbye? It would have been unlike him, I thought, just to have left without another word. When he had gone (trudging up the playa, making for the narrow lanes behind the hotels and bars, letting himself be taken back into that anonymous complex of pavements and steps and doorways) she sat for a minute or two absolutely motionless until some thought, some resolution, broke the spell. She moved, looked towards the sea, considering again its immense wastes, its extraordinary untapped fertility; then lit another cigarette, glanced at her watch and poured herself another glass of champagne.

I should have gone down then, but I didn't. I put the field-glasses away and went to find Lola. I told her I had to go out and asked her to tell the señora I would be back some time that evening. Leaving the villa I took the long way down, but I avoided the beach and went instead to the garage, collected the car and paid the mechanic what I owed. Then I drove out of Playa de Faro, leaving Myra sitting on at our table with the bottle of champagne, waiting for me as if nothing had happened that needed an explanation more badly than my accusation of the night before. I had put the fieldglasses down and left the villa because the sight of her sitting there had suddenly become unbearable. Such grace, such beauty, such composure; at all costs they had to be preserved. She had worked out which side her private bread was better buttered on, and sent him packing; and I had nothing more to fear from her liaison with him. There was no need to pity him. He would soon find someone else. She had enjoyed her affair. I had enjoyed my jealousy. We were all well satisfied. Throw out the humbug and ten seconds from now who would care?

In Palafrugell I queued up for Super at the petrol pump in the square. Twin glass cylinders, each holding a litre, alternately filled and emptied as the girl in charge of the pump worked the handle up and down. I drove on towards Palamos and in that place parked the car and walked along the broad, straight promenade and up to the quay where they land and sort the fish for marketing, but there was nothing much going on at that time of day. I left the quay and found a bar and drank wine until it was two o'clock and time for lunch. The waiter directed me to an hotel. I sat at a table in the roofed-over terrace, ate paëlla and drank a bottle of Rocabardi. The people at the table next to me were rich middle-class Germans. They had survived. Spain had survived. I and Myra, I supposed, would survive too, survive to go on turning up wherever my restless search for some kind of tranquillity directed me. Beneath that equable behaviour-image of Myra's there was probably a corresponding agitation. It was a flight with no hounds of heaven in pursuit, a running through the dark after a will-o-the-wisp whose light had never been lit, a journey from one house of cards to another, through fields of stones and petrified gardens ringing to soundless carillons, along tracks that bordered but never cross the frontier between the two kingdoms.

I sat on after lunch with coffee and brandy, smoking one of the Spanish cigarettes I had had to buy because I had run out of Chesterfields. Poor Spain; brave Spain; with its back to the wall of Europe and its face scorched by the ovenbreath of Africa. It was the one place in the world I had been that least lent itself to the comfort of the bereaved. In Spain the funeral is always over. Inspiring sorrow she rejects mourning. Contemplation of the mysteries is always cut short by the reality of the hummocky grave and the flowers wilting in the heat, stirred by the wind from the mountains.

I should have paid my bill and gone back to her. I know it, I know it. We needed each other. In any other country I swear this is what I would have done, even if, arriving, facing her, no explanation for my failure to join her that morning had been offered or demanded; and even if, going back, I had expected nothing beyond a resumption of that incompatible silence in which we explored our apparent need of each other's company. But there I was, in Palamos, confronted by the uncompromising image of Spain which carried tourists on its back as a herd of bulls might carry birds to peck and relish the delectable fleas. So I paid my bill and drove south, away from Myra, away from Playa de Faro. The time was four o'clock. After a while I became conscious of the fact that there were far more cars on the road than usual. I passed several, impatient of delay, but came at last to the back of a procession of them there was no getting ahead of. We trundled along in each other's wakes, closing up, getting slower and slower. At one point we came to a halt. A traffic policeman was standing in the road. I leaned out of the window and asked him what the matter was. He said, 'Toros.' It should have been obvious, but since that morning I had forgotten the day of the week; and I had never driven to San Felíu before on a Sunday afternoon. The traffic began to move, taking me with it, through the town, always in the same direction, the one that must lead to the plaza de toros. There were more police. They waved us on impatiently. There were several intersections where I could have turned off, but I didn't. Spain was called the tune. It was easier to dance than to resist.

We turned into a square and then into a narrow lane, waved on all the time by the men in uniforms like the one Sarbosa wore. The lane was taking us up a hill, away from the centre of the town. There were people walking on either side of the slowly moving line of cars. Among them were peddlers. Already there was the sound of canned music: a paso doble. I looked at my watch. It was ten to five. Forgetting that I had never intended to come, that indeed I came to Spain always especially not to see the bulls, I began to fret at the delay. I have always hated to be kept waiting, hated to be late, to miss anything. I must have waited hours of my life arriving early and sitting in half-empty halls and auditoriums, sweating with impatience.

Now I could see the high white wall of the plaza. It was surrounded by another, lower wall, and then by fields and empty spaces. There were flags flying, and Civil Guards stationed at the entrance, gripping the slings of their rifle, watching us with those flat unemotional eyes. The line of cars and the lines of pedestrians diverged. We were being directed into a broad field hedged by trees, already crammed with motor cars. There was a place for me somewhere in the chaotic centre. It would take hours to get out. I paid an attendant five pesetas. It was already five o'clock. I had no ticket. At the gates in the outer wall that surrounded the plaza I asked an attendant where they could be bought. He sent me back along the lane about fifty yards. There were several Spaniards buying tickets at a window in the white wall marked 'Sol'. The other window was marked 'Sombra'. Both windows were shaded by trees. There was no one at the window marked 'Sombra'. It seemed to be closed. The tickets at the other booth were going for a hundred pesetas. For that price you would sit far back, high up, facing the sun. From there you would not see the gradations of pain in the eyes of the bull or hear the talk of the peóns behind the barrier, or the words of love that are sometimes said to be spoken by the matador who is winning to the bull who is losing. I turned away without buying a ticket.

A man said, 'Señor,' and touched my sleeve. He wore a broad-brimmed hat and squinted up at me from under it. In the plaza there was a burst of applause. They were still playing the paso doble. A few stragglers were running through the gateway to get into their places before the paseo ended. The ticket tout was short, dwarfish. He was leaning against the wall between the two windows. The ticket he showed me was for the second file, Tendido, sombra y sol y sombra. It was marked 300 pesetas. He asked three fifty. I shook my head and began to walk away. He called after me, once, twice. I stopped and looked round. As I did so I caught him in the act of looking back to see if the Civil Guards were watching him. He wore a crumpled white suit. The sun shone on the tight smooth surface of the cloth where it was stretched across the hump between his twisted shoulders. He came up to me. He smiled. It was a gentle smile; one, almost, of recognition.

'For you,' my hunchback whispered, 'Three hundred and twenty-five.'

And that is how it came about that I went to the corrida in San Felíu, alone, and was late, and missed the paseo, filled the absent picture in for myself from what I knew of the bearing of matadors when they enter the arena abreast to music, their arms wrapped and stiff from wounds they have already received.

9

When I climbed up into the brightness of the arena the paseo was finished. Men were smoothing the sand where it had been churned by the toreros and the horses. The paso doble was still coming over the tannoy. The plaza was packed. A young boy led me along the curve of the narrow aisle between the contra-barrera and the delantera, and up the steps to the second file of the tendido. The ring was composed of tier upon tier of solid concrete benches. I stumbled over feet and knees to reach the tiny space the boy pointed out to me. Stencilled on it in black paint between two black lines defining the area permitted the occupant was a number which corresponded to the number on the ticket. I sat down between two men. Our shoulders touched. My knees were in danger of pressing into the shoulder blades of the man in front. I signalled to an urchin who had cushions for hire. One was passed to me hand over hand. In the same way my money reached the urchin.

In the ring the sand-smoothers had been joined by two men bearing placards on poles. The placards announced in four languages that it was forbidden to throw objects, especially cushions, on pain of arrest and prosecution by the police. There was some ironical applause. On the other side of the ring were the closed wooden gates of the toril, through which the bull would make its salida. To the left was another set of gates marked 'Arrastre'. Through these the dead bull would be dragged by the mules. Further still to the left were the main gates through which the paseo had entered and exited. In the archway behind the gates you could see some of the toreros in their suits of lights, and men in civilian clothes. Through these gates the picadors would enter when the trumpet announced the start of the climax to the first act, the trial of the lances.

I took my dark glasses. Colour leapt into the arena. The barrera was painted a brownish red, to neutralize the shock of the bloodstains. Draped over the barrera, near one of the burladeros, were three or four of the pink capes that were used by the peóns and the matadors in the initial stages of the first acts and by the peóns at any time if the matadors got into trouble and had to have the bull taken from them. In the folds of the pink silk you could see the yellow of the linings. This part of the ring was in shadow, and in this gentler light the colours of the capes were hard and vivid. The shadow line described an arc across the sand, leaving three-quarters of it bright golden yellow, and the other quarter a dull grey ochre. As the sun went down the area of bright yellow would contract until it had disappeared altogether, and the spectators on the opposite side of the ring would be able, tier by tier, to take off their hats and sunglasses. For the moment they sweated in the sun's direct rays. Here and there among the browns, reds and greens of summer clothes a white shirt dazzled. Behind the uppermost tier of all, all around the high outer wall of the plaza, there were advertisements for the ubiquitous Pepsi-Cola, the wines of Jerez and the Gran Licor Estomacal. On this same top level, but in the shade, behind and a little to the left of where I was sitting, was the enclosure of the president, the presiding judge of the afternoon's corrida. He was probably a local official, and it could be that he knew little and cared less about the bulls. But among his retinue one man would be his official adviser, an ex-torero who would tell him what was happening, what to deprecate, what to applaud, what signal to give with what coloured handkerchief. The sweepers and the placard bearers had gone and we were waiting for his signal now, as were the men who stood by the gates of the toril. The music stopped. There was a blast on the trumpet. The crowd fell silent.

First they opened the gate in the barrera. It was the width of the callejón. The gate in the wall behind was of equal width. When both were opened at opposing angles of ninety degrees the callejón was sealed off and the two doors formed a passage. I could see through the passage into the tunnel that led down to the toril, in whose semi-darkness the first bull of the day must now be standing, staring at the rectangle of daylight that had unsealed the place where it had been kept prisoner since the sorting and pairing at midday.

For a while nothing happened. Each of the peóns from the first matador's cuadrilla had collected a cape and taken up a position in the callejón, near one of the burladeros, the stout wooden fences that shield the gaps in the barrera and through which a man but not a bull can squeeze his body. They were ready, separately, to step into the ring. But the bull had to enter first. This one seemed disinclined to. A man in the crowd shouted, 'Hey, hey! Toro!' and one of the ring servants at the entrance to the toril leaned over and slapped the gate with the palm of his hand. A murmur of amusement spread through the crowd, and then the bull came out, strong and fast, levantado, and was one-third of the way across the ring before its impetus slackened and it slowed to a trot, looking round to see what there might be in the offing that was ready to dispute the terrain it found itself surprisingly in possession of. The murmur of amusement became an exclamatory, guttural sigh of welcome, and was then drowned by the applause always accorded to the bull who comes out well.

One of the peóns entered the ring, trailing the cape, pink side uppermost, across the sand to catch the bull's attention. The bull saw the curious apparition and charged. The man ran for the barrera and disappeared behind the burladero, taking the cape with him, leaving the bull apparent master of the situation. The bull hoofed the sand and tossed its head. The spectators sighed again: a mark of their approval, of identification with this snorting, black, defiant complex of brain, bone and muscle. The second peón emerged, holding the cape in front of him, and stood poised on the edge of the shadow line. The bull had wheeled round and had begun to trot towards the centre of the ring, turning his head from side to side, pleased with himself for having despatched the strange piece of coloured cloth. But here was another. He veered in its direction, still trotting; the cloth began to move; he got his head down and went for it. At what should have been the point of impact there was, suddenly, nothing. Hooking with his horns he tossed air. The impetus of his charge carried him forward; and there, ahead of him, was a third cloth. This was the one he would get. The cloth was skulking against a section of the barrier that he realized now penned him in. It could not get away. He grunted with satisfaction, anticipating the violence of the meeting and the despatch, hunched his huge shoulders and hurled himself into the attack. The strength of the cloth was astonishing. A wave of shock surged through his horns and into his body. The cloth was like wood. He butted again. It was wood. The cloth was not there. It had unaccountably escaped.

Snorting, puzzled, he turned away from the burladero behind which the peón had retreated. From the file behind me an Englishman yelled, 'Windy!' meaning the peón, and added to his neighbour, 'Boy, that's a big wild fellow,' meaning, in all likelihood, himself.

But the bull wasn't big. Perhaps it barely tipped the scale at the minimum legal weight; and the peón was not windy. He was trying to perform strictly according to the instructions of his matador who was watching from behind the barrera and alone had the honour of passing the bull with the cape. The matador was signalling now to the peón, who had begun to come out again from behind the burladero, telling him to get back and stay back. The bull had moved closer to the centre of the ring. It was panting a bit from the force of its collision with the wood. It should not have been run quite so close to the barrera. The peón had made an error of judgment. The matador gathered up his cape and stepped out. The bull was faced away from him, looking about for the first sign of further invasion. If it was a very intelligent bull it might already have begun to see beyond the phenomena of the capes to the lesser phenomena of the man-creatures who were attached to them. As the corrida progressed the danger of its transferring its attention from cloth to man would increase.

The senior matador is the first to come out. Perhaps, being a man of experience, the bull's first three charges had told him all he needed to know. Was it Ordóñez? The star attraction is not necessarily or even likely to be the senior man, the man who has fought longest as a full matador. This man did not look like Ordóñez. But then, what did Ordóñez look like? I tried to recapture the image I must have had of Ordóñez from the photographs in some of the books in my study, but was unable to. If the matador now entering the ring was not Ordóñez, the next one was bound to be, because the third matador to fight is always the junior man, and Ordóñez could not be as young as that.

The bull was going away from this particular matador, having failed to catch a glimpse of the cape from the corner of its roving eye. The matador signalled. A peón stepped out. The bull saw him and was after him. The peón retreated, running the bull into a position from which it could see both lures, the peón's and the matador's. It slowed, halted, lowered its head and scooped sand with its hoof, considering the problem of two enemies instead of one. But the peón was now at the tablas, close to one of the burladeros. Capes so close to the wood had a habit of disappearing and the other cape was spread wider and was out in the open, altogether a worthier opponent. Without seeming to have paused for longer than it took to recover from a momentary confusion the bull charged.

He must have felt himself within an ace of beating the cape this time. This cape did not move erratically, nor did it suddenly disappear. He had it on his horns, but yet not quite. He could sense it, smell it, feel it, but he could not hook it. It was as though he tossed it without touching it. It flew round in the air, extending and displaying itself as it veered off and away to his right – not quickly but too quickly and at too sharp an angle for him to twist the length of his own body round to keep track of it. But this time he knew where it had gone. He turned and there it was, in the same place on the sand as before, and he was after it again, getting his head down but keeping the cape firmly in his eye to judge the split second when by jerking his head he could not fail to impale it or send it heavenwards.

But the cloth seemed to be judging too, beating him to it, sending itself up and round a bare inch ahead of his horns, turning itself from the substance to the shadow of what he was intent on punishing. And for the second time he felt and smelt it, was aware of it curling away so close to him it touched his flank in gentle mockery. He swung back as sharply as he could, his unevenly distributed weight creating a pressure on his back and shoulders, and there it was again, spread in the same attitude. He charged, and it escaped him for the third time. He turned and charged again, and again it fluttered just beyond the real reach of his horns. That time he sensed the presence of a power in the cape that came from a source other than itself. He turned back, hurled himself at it, determined to be rid of it before the power got stronger, and then the cape spun up and slowly round, taking him with it in a curve that strained every muscle in his body, and was gone entirely, leaving him stopped short, at a loss, his eyes in the shock of the sudden disappearance fixed on nothing that made sense to him.

The crowd shouted their approval, and the matador walked away, having executed a series of rather flashy verónicas, and ended with the media verónica that had swung the bull to a full breathless stop.

The bull was alone in the ring in the place the matador had left it. It did not react to the sound of the trumpets. In the archway behind the gates of the main entrance you could see the two picadors already mounted, looking like twin versions of Sancho Panza in their broad-brimmed round-crowned hats. They carried their long lances at an angle that inclined a few degrees from the perpendicular. As the gates opened inwards the three peóns came back into the ring to take the bull further away and give the picadors time to get into position.

The crowd jeered and cat-called. It is part of the ritual of the corrida to insult the picadors. As they came out of the gateway, each led by a ring-servant, they parted company, one going left and the other right. The picadors must do their work close to the barrera: between the boards and the outer of the two white circular lines that are marked on the sand. The picador who turns right is especially vulnerable at the moment of entry because he rides with the unprotected and unblindfolded side of the horse towards the ring. At a point below the president's box the picador who had turned to the right was halted and then led round to face in the other direction, where he waited, looking cumbersome and top-heavy. The ring servant now stood between the horse and the tablas, still holding the bridle. On the other side of the ring, facing into the sun, the second picador was similarly positioned. The gates were closed. The matador came out to join his peóns.

The bull had recovered. But the capes had lost a lot of the power to excite him. Puzzled, he attacked them more from habit than from conviction. And there was a new, bewildering aspect to them. Where before there had been one, at most two, there were three, four, fluttering, curling, leaping, leading him from one place of failure to another. In the back of his mind there was an awareness of the odds growing against him, of an invasion of his territory more subtly outrageous than the appearance of the first capes had led him to expect. The leaping coloured cloth-images were mixed with man-images, and the images were part of a complicated pattern of confusing shapes, scents and sounds. Reaching the end of a short running attack that ended like all his attacks, abortively, he halted, stood his ground. At the same instant, from that spot, he saw the horse and was no longer puzzled. The enemy was revealed. Scarcely believing that the luck had come to him at last, that he had solved the mystery of the cloths, he stood for a moment in the place of revelation and then began to move forward, out of it, head up, judging the angle of his attack on this insolent creature that had finally lost the power to disguise itself. One of the pink cloths manifested itself, proof that the cloths and the horses were part of the same rhythm of combat. Snorting, he allowed himself the luxury of chasing the cloth. The cloth was retreating in the direction of the horse and then, evading the half-hearted hook he made at it, was gone, and the horse alone stood there, four square to him, splendidly vulnerable. He lowered his head and rushed at it, bracing himself for the force and joy of the bloody collision.

He felt a prick, and then a pain. He had his horns into something, and pushed. Pushing, the pain flowed from his tossing muscle down into his shoulders and along his spine. The horse had horns. In some extraordinary way he had overlooked the horns of the horse. Instead of locking horns he had got his own horns into the horse's belly, and the horse had got one of its horns into his shoulder. It was the horn-piercing of his shoulder that stopped him getting his own horns further, satisfactorily, in. The flesh his horns had entered did not have the feeling of real flesh. It felt more like the flesh of the pink cloth creatures and lacked heat. The pain in his shoulder sharpened. He disengaged. Momentarily his vision was impaired. When it cleared the horse was still there. He moved in again, and felt a second stab in his shoulder. The stab had weight behind it, a weight that was trying to push him away from the horse. He could feel the horse giving way, moving backwards from the pressure of his own forward thrust. As he pushed the pain got worse. Blood was flowing down his flanks. The pain, and the weight behind the pain, were weakening him. He was being turned away from the horse. Again he disengaged. As he did so he saw one of the pink capes. He moved in to attack it. It was so close he couldn't miss. But he did miss. The pain in his shoulder increased when he hooked. The cloth had gone, but there was another one that moved ahead of him, swung out of reach and then appeared again, flowing and twisting. As it curled away he saw, right in front of him, another horse. Bellowing, he charged it. Again he was stopped by the weight and the stab. He pulled away and rushed in again in an attempt to reach the belly of the horse before he could be stopped by the sharp, punishing weapon the horse seemed to be able to conjure out of nothing. This time the pain came further back. He pressed in, jerking his head, hoping for the hot gush of the horse's blood. The horse was giving ground, but he was losing contact, and he needed respite from the pain. The coloured capes were hovering. The capes did not wound him but they were still the clue to the situation. The capes were cunning. Having no armour of their own they led him to the strange horses that would not bleed but carried weapons that stabbed him where it hurt and weakened. The capes had to be got rid of. Panting, he renewed his attack on them.

He did not hear the trumpet that announced the end of the trial of the lances, or the applause of the crowd acknowledging the bravery of a bull that had taken two pics from the first picador and two from the second and was now being run by the peóns so that the horses could leave the arena. He followed the capes until they were all gone and he stood alone again in an empty ring. In the sudden weakness following cessation of combat his bowels emptied. He tried to raise his head, but the pain in his neck and shoulders kept it low. He was trying to think back to the moment when he had seen the first horse. He turned, moved to the place in the ring in which the revelation of the meaning of the capes had come to him, and stood there. In this place he felt his confidence returning. Here he would stand. From here he would defy further invasion.

It was at this moment he heard a sound and, looking up, saw one of the man-creatures, alone in the ring, connected neither to horse nor to cape. He considered this new phenomenon. The man-creature was standing still, straight ahead of him, and not far away. It was the man-creature that had made the sound. Now it made it again. It sounded like a challenge. Suddenly the creature stamped its foot, lifted its outstretched arms a bit higher and challenged him again. He lowered his head, braced himself and went for the man. Directly he moved the man-creature moved. He followed it round, judging the point of interception. The man was now directly in front of him. He jerked his head down in the first motion of hooking, and at that instant saw the man's feet move away and felt two stinging pricks in the torn muscle. He tossed his head. Something light but tenacious was clinging, swaying, biting into his shoulder, and would not be shaken off. He wheeled round. The man-creature had gone but parts of it had been left behind in him like thorns. And now there was another man running across his front, shouting. He charged, and again at what should have been the moment of impact the creature escaped him, stinging him in the shoulder. He reared and bucked, trying to get rid of the painful maddening barbs. He was aware of one going, falling away, but there were still three. The pain of them spread, reheating the pain of the deeper wounds sustained in the battle with the horses. And still there was a third man, standing like the first, insolently stamping its foot and raising its arms. If he could get his horns into the man-creature the pain in his shoulders would be eased. He hurled himself at it, and again the man began to run. Again he nearly cut the man off and again missed and was bitten by the stinging thorns. When he jerked his head and neck the pain spread like fire. He could feel the thorns hanging down, bouncing against his body, just out of reach.

He stood still. His head felt heavy. The pain was less when he stood still. He realized, dimly, that he had come back to the place where the meaning of the cloths had first been revealed. Now there was the hint of another revelation. Was it after all the man-creatures, who were attached to the cloths and to the horses, who were the real enemy? There had been the cloths, and the horses; finally the men without cloths and without horses, running just ahead of him, escaping him, stinging him in the shoulder. The cloths had gone, the horses had gone. The man-creatures had not gone. He could see them, many of them, watching him from behind the wooden barrier, and one of them had come into the arena. It had its back to him. He watched it warily. For the moment it did not appear to challenge his claim to the territory of the ring. It did not even appear to have noticed him. It had strayed from the herd on the other side of the barrier. It seemed to be making an appeal to them, standing there, facing them, ignoring him. If it had been closer he would have attacked. It would be dangerous to let any of the man-creatures close to the place of revelation.

The man-creature had turned round now and was facing him, coming towards him. It was attached to something, but he could not see what it was until suddenly it opened. It was smaller and darker in colour than the other cloths, nearly as dark as the colour of blood. Forgetting the man-creature he stared at it. As he did so it moved, tempting him, at the same time betraying its animal origin and then his frustration and sense of failure were forgotten too. There were his anger, the pain of his wounds and the proximity of the red cloth-creature. These urged him forward, out of his querencia. To impale or toss the cloth-creature would be an agony. This he knew even as he charged it, but the temptation and the need exerted a stronger influence on him than the anticipation of pain. The force of his hooking shot fire through his body. Why? Why? What horned animal had he truly encountered? Why did he hurt? Why did he bleed? Clothes, horses, men – what were they to him? What was he to them?

The cloth had fluttered away. Dazed by the punishment he inflicted on himself by charging and impaling nothing but air he wheeled, charged and tossed again only to see the cloth turn, unhurt, and lead him round in what he now began to understand to be the slow movements of a dance of death: a travesty of the locked-horn conflict of an old bull with a young that had challenged his right to rule and procreate and leave his mark on the herd; the herd which he himself knew only instinctively, atavistically in the coursing of his blood and in the labyrinthine corridors of his racial memory. The cloth-creature leapt and danced, low and away to his right, high and away over his painfully jerked up head, and became translated into a red heart-beat of longing and regret for the wide grass-lands and the scented winds of the ganadería he knew he would never see again. Dazed, at the end of the tether of desire, he broke off from the unreal conflict and stood, head down, aplomado, watching the red cloth which had become very still as if it too had worn itself out. Slowly it recovered, rising from the sand. And in that instant, seeing that it had not recovered at all, but was raised from the sand by the man, he understood his tragic mistake. Still watching the cloth he was aware of the man coming in at him fast. He tried to raise his horns, but failed. Attached to the man there was a long shining barb. It entered between his shoulder blades. Sharp and cold, he felt it penetrate. There had been the cloths and the horses and the men. In the last moment he knew that only the men had counted. They were surrounding him now whirling the capes. Obediently he followed the capes round, working the steel of the sword wider into his body. He sat on his haunches. He felt cold and sick. Blood was coming out of his mouth and nostrils. He could no longer see the men, or the capes.

The time was nineteen minutes after five.

The matador walked round the ring, smiling at the crowd, acknowledging the applause with an outstretched arm, but he had made a bad kill, sidestepping at the last moment to avoid going in over the horns. His work in the faena had been unin-spired and hurried. From the beginning of it the bull had been mesmerized by the muleta and he could therefore have given the crowd a better show for their money, excited them with an adorno: thrown the muleta and sword away and knelt in front of it, leaned in and touched its forehead. He should have stopped the trial of the lances when the bull had taken two pics. Two would have been enough for this animal, even though three is supposed to be the minimum number. Four had been too many and what was worse the fourth had been too far back. The picador had come close to ruining the bull with the fourth pic.

The mules, harnessed to a spar and a chain, and run in by men and boys to the cracking of whips, were now halted by the body of the bull. The chains were fastened round its neck. The whips cracked and the mules strained forward and round, dragging the body behind them. It left a long broad scar on the sand. Its exit was marked by further applause. The paso doble was coming over the tannoy again. As the matador left the arena men came in to smooth the sand and clean up the excreta, and the two men came back with the placards that gave warning of the consequences of throwing cushions. Along the aisle between the contrabarrera and the delantera a man walked carrying a tray of soft drinks. Another man was holding up pairs of banderillas, cellophane wrapped and going at fifty pesetas the pair. A third offered booklets explaining the corrida in English, French and German. Below, in the callejón, they were sorting out capes, muletas and swords. In the callejón near the main exit a man who might be Ordóñez waited alone.

The ring was empty again. The aviso sounded. The gates leading into the toril were re-opened, sealing off the callejón and forming a passage for the second bull, which came out almost at once, looking fast and heavy. It sped round the ring, feinting at invisible enemies, and scarcely seemed to notice when these imaginary enemies became real in the shape of the peóns. It went automatically for the capes, but showed a tendency to let them go rather than attempt to follow them through. The peóns began to work it in pairs, closer and closer. While they were still working it the matador came into the ring and stood just beyond the shadow line, holding his cape in the way St. Verónica is said to have held the cloth to Christ, to wipe his brow, on the road to Calvary.

I asked my right-hand neighbour, 'Is it Ordóñez?' Ordóñez

was said to be the foremost exponent of the verónica pass.

'Sí, sí. Ordóñez.'

The man in front of him turned round and said that it was not Ordóñez. The first matador had been Ordóñez. My neighbour did not argue but smiled at me and shook his head.

The matador who was or was not Ordóñez was waiting for the peóns to bring the bull to him. He stood quiet and still. Perhaps the attitude was familiar after all to the man in front who turned round again and begged our pardon. The error was his. This man was Ordóñez. My neighbour nodded. He said that on his good days there was no living matador better with the cape than Ordóñez. From the way he was standing waiting it looked like one of his good days, although you never could tell. And the bull was a bad bull. Even Belmonte and Manolete would have made nothing of this bull. Yes, it was a bad bull and it was the bad bulls who were dangerous. But because there was nothing even a good matador could do with a bad bull the matador would probably get nothing but jeers from the crowd.

The bull had gone away from the peóns. Their attempts to bring him to Ordóñez had so far failed. Some of the spectators were already laughing. The bull was standing near the gates of the toril, watching the peóns. Clearly Ordóñez had chosen to fight the poorest of his two bulls first. But his second bull would be the fifth of the day and there was a saying that the fifth bull is always the best. Meanwhile here was this ridiculous creature: 400 kilos of black stupidity that seemed to have no idea what was expected of him and would obviously have trotted back to the toril if the gates had not been closed again directly it had come in. It was up to Ordóñez to teach him. The lesson was about to begin because he had waved the peóns out of the ring.

A vulgar performer would have waited until he and the bull were alone, then folded his arms perhaps, or struck a pose whose purpose was mockery. But Ordóñez, as his peóns took refuge in the callejón, walked closer to the bull, holding the cape rather awkwardly as if to say: 'Well, yes, it is difficult, at the beginning of every fight we are all ignorant of each other's capacity, and all a bit clumsy. There is a lot to learn and not much time to learn it. This is the first step. Here it is, the cape. Yes, that is the way of it. Your eyes on the cape, so.'

When the bull charged Ordóñez was not well positioned. His arms were too high and his balance looked precarious. It made

196

the bull look better. Perhaps this was the intention. What use was dignity if it was not complemented? The crowd expelled breath, experiencing the sensation of being caught off guard, nearly knocked over by the blundering animal that had already turned and was charging again as if suddenly excited by close contact with the cape into a coherent plan of action. This time Ordóñez passed it with a suave natural that turned the bull into a position from which, turning himself, he faced it at an angle of forty-five degrees and from there cited and passed it with what looked like a superb verónica cargando la suerte, which was repeated from the other side, and then again from the original side, so that for three distinct movements bull and man seemed to flow together. With each pass the crowd roared. At the end of the third cargando la suerte Ordóñez lifted one hand high and dropped the other low and as the bull came in spun round in a graceful chicuelina and so came to the remate, the finishing pass. He began to swirl the cape round, let go with his left hand which he put behind him so that he could grasp and gather the cape as it swung up to meet him. The bull, coming in, was turned and fixed, the cape gone. Ordóñez walked away. He had done the seemingly impossible. He had made the bull look good. The applause was for both of them.

The comedy began again with the horses.

But I do not want to write about the horses, or about the corrida in detail, not in the way of saying, this happened, then that, then this, making up out of my head what I've forgotten, just for the sake of creating an illusion of continuous action. And anyway, what does it matter now? All those bulls are dead. When one was dragged out another was sent in. Perhaps it was the same bull.

Some of the toreros may be dead too. I remember one of them, a peón who had probably fought more than twenty years ago as a novillero and never quite made the grade. No change of expression ever showed on his sunken, parchment face. He had seen men and bulls come and go. He was beyond cynicism. He gave to his job in the cuadrilla what he was asked to give, but each year he would be asked to give less; his suit of lights would become him less, the pink clocked-stockings show a few more wrinkles at the calves and ankles. There he was, a thin-shanked man in fancy dress and dancing pumps, performing for the bull, the matador and the crowd. Yes, he could be dead by now, of accidental or natural causes. When I think of the cuadrillas and of the way the peóns ran the bulls it is always this man's face I see, over and over again, the same face under the several identical comic black hats with ear-like protuberances on each side of them. He was not asked to place banderillas. Remembering that, it is difficult to conjure the faces of the peóns who actually placed them. Apart from this one man's face it is difficult to conjure the faces of any of the toreros who fought in the ring that afternoon. From one of those books I keep having to refer to in a probably failing attempt to get some of the jargon right (someone will probably point out that no matador could execute three verónicas cargando la suerte and follow them up with a chicuelina and a rebolera without twisting himself into a plait) even Ordóñez's face, staring up at me, comes as a surprise. In the ring there is a curious anonymity about bull-fighters that matches the anonymity of the bulls, and is somehow necessary to the spirit of the corrida. You end with a stylized representation of man and bull such as artists paint for the colourful posters. The posters portray what the corrida should be, not what it is. And that, in general, is what you are supposed to remember. The fight that has just finished is less important than the fight that is about to begin, and next week's corrida will be better than this week's. Next week the perfect bull will meet the perfect matador, and then the corrida will be brave and beautiful and even the women will weep.

When Ordóñez walked away from his first bull I applauded, but my neighbour shook his head and said, 'No, he is faking. The bull is a bad bull and he is trying to make it look brave.'

'I know,' I said. 'That's why I clap.'

He shrugged his shoulders. He didn't understand what I meant. He may have been right and I wrong. If in the pairing and the sorting you drew a bad bull perhaps you should play it for what it is worth and not for what it might be, even if in doing so the bull, being bad, makes you look clumsy and you have to stand there listening to the cat-calls. And perhaps Ordóñez had really faked it up, had made the bull look good with the cape for his own sake, and not for the bull's sake or the sake of the corrida, as I had thought. When the horses came on, the bull took only one pic and jibbed at taking more. In taking the one it managed to knock the horse over but it didn't like that. Knocking the horse over didn't make it feel good. The pain of the lance and the noise and confusion of the horse and the picador coming a cropper frightened it. The peóns gathered it into the folds of the capes and led it away, but it would not charge the second horse. The spectators laughed uncomfortably. The bull was being sensible as well as clumsy. Out of the ring it might be a nice bull to know. In the ring it was an embarrassment.

'Black banderillas,' my neighbour said, making a forecast. But Ordóñez did not appeal to the president for black banderillas. 'The bull is a coward,' my neighbour complained, 'but he is still trying to make it look brave. It does not deserve ordinary banderillas. He is faking. So let him fake. In the faena he will regret it. The bull's head is too high. He will make a mess of the faena. The kill will be terrible.'

The faena was dull but not a mess; but the kill was as prophesied, terrible; clumsy and bloody. He went in with the estoque when you could see the bull wasn't properly fixed on the muleta. Perhaps he did regret the ordinary banderillas. But I think he just wanted to get it over, put the clumsy creature out of its misery. At the last moment, to avoid the horns, he had to sidestep. The sword seemed to bounce on solid bone. At once the peóns surrounded the shocked, confused beast and caped it away while Ordóñez walked to the barrera and took a new sword.

This one went in for no more than half its length. It had to be hooked out eventually with the tip of another sword, but the bull was now dying on its feet. Ordóñez called for the descabello, the long straight sword with a cross piece four and a half inches from the point, whose target is the cervical vertebrae. He thrust it in. The bull trembled and died. Ordóñez scarcely acknowledged the applause. He knew it was mostly inspired by relief that the farce was over. He had used his skill to make the bull look good, he had risked his life to avoid branding it a coward. His efforts had been for nothing. He did not need to be told. He did not want to be flattered. You could see it from the way he walked out of the ring. I liked him for that.

I suppose the honours went that day to the third and youngest matador. Whereas I've forgotten the colours of the satin of the first matador's and Ordóñez's suits of lights, I remember clearly that the third man's was pink with silver encrustations. He struck you at once as a man who was conscious, perhaps over-conscious, of the need to develop a style. He had probably worked at it hard in front of a mirror. As he grew older, you felt, there would be a danger of self-parody, but on this particular day the tendency to self-dramatization coupled with his youth and skill with the muleta suggested only freshness, vigour and youthful poetry, and the crowd responded. He was lucky with his bulls, too, which had corresponding qualities of freshness, strength, courage and minimal intelligence. So fixed on the muleta was his first bull that he got down on his knees at one point, and, with his back to it, discarded the cloth and the sword in the first and only adorno of the day. He muffed the first sword thrust but the crowd forgave him not only because his second attempt was hasta el puño (clean to the hilt) but also because having all the time in the world to go into the kill he made a graceful job doing it. Even my companion clapped him; but then my companion was an aficionado; he had the future of the corrida to think of as well as the great days to remember, and he was all for encouraging a promising youth, even one from South America whose alternativa had probably not yet been confirmed in Madrid.

'Was he good?' I asked.

At once he pulled down his mouth but nodded his head, and so achieved that expression of grudging praise accorded to anything that has appealed to the emotions and has hastily to be denied by the intellect.

'Well was he?' I said.

He looked at me, surprised that I should insist on a less equivocal answer. 'He will learn,' he said at last. 'He feels it with his back and legs and arms, but not yet here, and here.' He tapped his head and his heart. 'Until he does that he will not convey what he wants to convey to the bull.'

I smiled. I don't think he saw because he was looking again at the happy young matador, and clapping his hands. Scratch a lover of the bulls and ten to one you find a man with that romantic notion of the corrida as a love affair between articulate man and inarticulate animal, a love affair whose object is to persuade the bull to surrender willingly, and whose consummation is death for the brute-beast. Scratch deeper and ten to one again you'll get the whiff of that old pagan fear of animals as creatures sometimes to be worshipped, sometimes to be destroyed. Bull god. Bull sacrifice. The need to propitiate has always been coupled with the need to slay. And the idea of the perfect sacrifice has always been that it should be a willing one. Before you put the bull to the sword it is necessary to instil in it the desire for death. In this way you are forgiven and the bull is ennobled, acceptable to the gods. The spectators are purged by pity and terror. If you can't stomach that explanation there is a less esoteric interpretation of the corrida which holds that it symbolizes man's eternal conflict with authority. Against the bull's brute strength comparatively puny man pits his wits and skill. Sometimes he loses out, but another man is always ready to take his place.

Or you could say that the corrida is a celebration of the dimensions of courage, of the stature man can achieve when he spices his civilized intelligence with primitive blood-lust. In this concept the corrida portrays man's desire for recognition as the supreme creation. Or again you could call the corrida an acceptable public display of sexual prowess whose symbols are the testicles of the bull and the cojones of the matador and whose prize is the woman in the lace mantilla behind the wooden barrera who has vowed never to sleep with a bull so long as there is a well-hung man ready to leap into the arena to dispute the propriety of such a coition. And you could find, if you wanted to, perverse or transvestist undertones. There are people who say the man and the bull are conjoined in an act of unnatural love. There are others who see the matador as a woman dressed like a man for purposes best known to herself. Or you could say that the corrida is just an entertainment, but if you say that you may be left wondering what is entertaining about the public slaughter of six bulls which will be too tough to be eaten except by the poor or the unsuspecting tourists in the cheaper pensions.

And there is another thing about the corrida, whether it is seen as a pagan spectacle, a celebration of Man, a drama of endless tyranny and eternal rebellion, a masque of love, a comedy of sexual deviation or of woman's wiles, or a simple entertainment whose only prohibition is sickness at the sight of blood; and this other thing is that there are always at least three fights going on at any one time in the plaza when a corrida is in progress: the fight the bull puts up, the fight the torero tries to conduct and the fight the spectators think they see.

What did I see? A succession of slightly varying images? dramatic representations of my own endless struggle to transmute the raw perpetual motion of life into the perfect immobility of art? As an art the corrida, to be sure, is a series of tableaux. Its purpose is statuesque. Its apparently rapid movement is no more than the sum total of isolated moments of tranquillity seen one after the other in rapid succession like the frames of a motion-picture. To say of a torero as he draws near to the end of the faena that he is tranquilo is to praise him. In the end, too, the bull is tranquilo, motionless, translated by death into a symbol of the vanity of men who seek that tranquillity without having themselves to die. Is that what we mean by tragedy? That a man can snatch at an illusory moment of peace through the death of a creature he thinks threatens it? But peace itself is an illusion, if by peace we mean something more durable than temporary respite from the prick of ambition, and the soaring and sinking fever of passion. Perhaps it is only in art that this more durable peace is to be found; not in the creation of it – no, not there – but in contemplation of what has been created, endless Edens, shapely worlds formed out of the terrible void and the deep blue darkness of endless frightening space; the carved stone, the painted canvas, the living word, the sound of music, the poster announcing the splendours of next week's corrida.

Yes, I could have seen in all that stylized tuppence-coloured ritual a reflection of my own penny-plain attempts to hold, on the page, moments of truth about less obvious but just as bloody human affairs. Or, as the psychologists would say, I could have identified with one, or several of the performers: with the bull, for example, say Ordóñez's first bull, the one that wanted out; or with his second that seemed to know no difference between out and in, was a dead loss as a fifth bull, and took up a querencia on the spot where the first bull had died, as if to compensate for its failure in a previous incarnation, as if indeed possessed of the spirit of that first clumsy creature who had seen the point at last and wasn't going to be had again, but was, because again it recognized too late the relationship between the cloth and the man.

In each of the skilful parts that amounted to the bloody whole I might have seen plays within plays such as made a King and Queen squirm in their chairs one night in the rotten state of Denmark. Well, John never stood in front of me aplomado; he was never chained by the neck and dragged out of an arena, and Myra never sat at the barrera applauding, but with a little free rein to the imagination it wouldn't have been difficult to see a connexion between what happened that day in the garden of the house in Richmond and what was happening in the plaza de toros in San Felíu de Guixols; or between what was happening in the plaza and what had been happening in Playa de Faro in the last days, or years before in Berlin, or earlier than that in the place I call the Mahwari Hills. It would not have been difficult to have seen in the pattern of the corrida the whole pattern of a single human life. When you think of the empty ring and of the young bull coming out into it, you can build up out of that image if you're so inclined an allegorical fantasy in which the bull is a young man (well an orphan say, from China, or Africa, somewhere where they bury their eggs) and the arena is that little bit of the big wide world God tells him he can have for himself if he works hard at it and is able to teach every other marauding bastard to keep his hands off it. So he works hard (like that man Thompson worked hard on the farm and later in the junkyard) and tries to keep the marauding bastards out. It's surprising how many of them there are. Is the world so over-populated, the young man wonders, that there are this number of men who don't have a circle of sand of their own? Each time he sees one of the marauders off he feels pride. Each time one of them gets in a blow under the belt, he pities himself and calls it sorrow. Pride and sorrow are self-inflicted wounds. They make him bleed, and that is the beginning of the end. To staunch the wounds he feels he needs what he thinks of as the balm of love (as Thompson felt the need for it, thinking of Mary Dee that night alone in the truck), someone to believe in him, someone to believe in. Together they could despatch the marauders from the arena, run up the flag and say, 'It's ours,' which is two people's way of saying in unison. 'It's mine.' The end comes quickly enough. He is taken out, his heels dragging in the sand.

Another thing: it could have struck me then that only years of pre- and post-palaeolithic experience could have taught men to select the bull to act out the part of their adversary. Speed, strength, size, great powers of endurance, little wisdom, an inborn tendency fatally to misjudge: what better attributes could men ask of a creature they were willing to face to test and prove their own? And if this had struck me that afternoon perhaps as the gates of the toril were opened for the fourth or the fifth time I should have seen in my imagination the brave salida not of a bull but of my old friend, panthera pardus fusca. What a leap into the arena that would have been. Perhaps only my own tired ageing peón would have come out from behind the burladeros, his eyes having grown so used to bulls a pig could have entered and he would not have seen the difference. His ears, no longer even bothering to distinguish between applause and cat-calls, would fail to interpret the cries of horror and the shouts of warning. So out he would go, trailing his cape; a fine pink and yellow robe for the spitted leopard or the black panther. You can picture the beast crouching, snarling at the capes, ripping them to shreds, then launching himself at the men and the horses, leaving them broken and bloody, leaping into the stands, scattering the screaming women and the yelling men until some of the trembling lads of the Civil Guard remember their rifles, take aim and let loose a fusillade that sends the enraged beast tumbling dead down the empty tiers of seats into the callejón.

Yes, that would be a corrida to remember, a sight to see. At the end of such an affair, with the ring cleared and swept and the spectators coming gingerly back to their places (which after all they've paid good money to occupy) you would not be surprised to see walking into the arena to confront the new bull that comes out a tiny figure in a suit of lights of black silk and jet encrustations, who moves on thin legs that look too weak and crooked for the weight of his pigeon chest and humped back, a little Quasimodo of the Plaza de Toros, who capes the bull with surprising agility, and astonishing success considering that the cape is black on both sides and not distinguishable from his own body. Cape, bull and man cohere together like some great broken-winged bat struggling to get up off the sand. The sight is fascinating, grotesque, but difficult to take seriously because the little man looks so funny. When the trumpets announce the picadors a ripple of laughter spreads through the crowd because the picadors are hunchbacks too. Their lances are as big as tree trunks in their dwarfish arms. Incredibly the first picador stops the bull with the point of the pica, but the second is knocked flying. The roar of delight drowns the screams of the horse.

Now it is time for the banderillas, and it is impossible to stop laughing. The matador is going to place the banderillas himself and the thought has already occurred to the people in the stands that the hump on the matador's back looks the same as the hump on the shoulders of the bull where the banderillas are supposed to be lodged. When the matador cites the bull he stamps his foot. Down in the barrera seats a pretty woman goes into a paroxysm. People have to hold their sides because they are beginning to hurt. The matador places the first pair al cuarteo, the second pair poder a poder and the third al quiebro. He is so short in relation to the bull that when he holds the sticks high to get them into the big shoulders he looks like a little boy reaching up to steal the jam from the shelf.

When he comes out for the faena he dedicates the bull to the crowd in the traditional manner, by taking his hat off, sweeping the hand that holds it in a gracious gesture round the arena and then throwing it on the ground. Even the president has to wipe his eyes with one of the coloured handkerchiefs. The matador unfurls the muleta. That is black too. The sword is so big he has difficulty hiding it behind the cloth. He executes a series of naturals, so slow and grave and beautiful that several of the women go into hysterics and one of the old aficionados is sick over the barrera into the callejón. After the naturals he produces, like a dwarf magician producing rabbits out of an enormous hat, an abanico, an afarolado, a pase por alto, a cambiado por alto con la izquierda, a pase de castigo, a chicharrina, a derechazo, a pase de las flores, a ki-kiri-kí, a locomotina, a pase militar, a molinete, a pedrisina, a pase en redondo, a rodillazo, a trincherazo, a vitamina and a vitolina : a dazzling display of virtuoso muleta passes that only the most knowledgeable notice come in alphabetical order, as if the executant had learned them by heart and can only do them in the order he had learned them. The howl of laughter is now continuous. The matador, sighting down the blade at the dazed, languishing bull, goes into the kill a volapié, thrusts the sword hasta el puña and the bull drops like a stone. The matador falls to his knees. He seems to have exhausted himself as well. The spectators are too weak to clap. They just sit there holding their sides and bellies. Some of the stronger ones begin to point. The comedy isn't over yet. The matador is holding the bull's head. He seems to be trying to lift it up as if he's just remembered another pass he'd like to try with the cloth before he calls it a day. Only the men who come in with the mules see that the little man is crying. As the bull is chained and dragged out, the hunchback is still clinging to it.

So regard him again, an anonymous face in the crowd, a man of sixty years sitting hot and uncomfortable in the second file of the tendido, wearing a crimson shirt loose outside the waist band of blue Terylene trousers. The fourth bull of the day has just come out and the senior matador is there at the tablas, preparing to make his second and, it is to be hoped, more effective appearance. Most of the spectators are applauding the bull, but the man in the crimson shirt sits motionless, as if the plaza is empty and he is alone, waiting for the corrida to begin, or sitting on long after it is over, solitary among the litter, watching bits of paper blow across the sand, waiting for next Sunday, hoping to witness, just once, a meeting of man and bull that will provoke in him a reaction far different from the one that makes him sit there apparently incapable of movement.

The senior matador is at work with the cape. He seems to be doing well. At the end of each pass the crowd yells its approval. The matador walking away after the remate, smiles, because even in a provincial arena like this, full of tourists whose ideas about the corrida are of no importance whatsoever, the sound of applause is not to be despised. The bulls are the bulls wherever you fight them. This bull is not unworthy of him. Although he has passed the peak of his popularity he has forgotten more about the bulls than some of the flashy youngsters will ever learn; seniority is seniority, and for a moment there, passing the bull's horns within a few inches of his belly, he felt sandungo, muy hacho; as sandungo as he used to feel in the days when he passed the horns with barely an inch to spare and was carried in triumph from the ring, saliendo en hombros. And who can blame him, in his losing battle with his waistline, for inclining almost imperceptibly away from the punishing tip of the weapon whose marks he will bear on his thighs for the rest of his life, even if he is lucky and skilled enough not to get more, and will never again make the cold sick journey through the callejón to the infirmary that smells of ether and is haunted by the ghosts of men who never came out of it alive?

Watching the matador, the man in the crimson shirt seems to shrug. He lights a cigarette. If you challenged him now he would admit that he has this terrible facility for looking at a man, making judgments about what he is thinking and feeling, and then continuing to look, with an eye open for the expression or gesture that alters the whole picture. If you asked him why he goes to such trouble he would say that in this way he builds up pictures of the mystery of human behaviour, and that he does this not in the hope of solving the mystery but for the purpose of celebrating it, of isolating for the purposes of recognition, not of cure, the virus of the disease of our passions. For instance (he might say) look at the senior matador now, down there in the callejón. The smile he wore in the ring as he walked away from the bull is quite gone. In the split second or two when we stopped looking at him something happened. Someone made a joke that he took as an insult; somebody failed to congratulate him; he caught a sarcastic smile on the lips of the young torero in the pink suit of lights and assumed it was meant for him; the bota was not immediately handed to him by one of the mozos when he held out his hand for it; passing through the burladero he stopped feeling sandungo and was suddenly afraid at the prospect of passing through it again in a few minutes' time; a face in the crowd reminded him of someone he dislikes; after the brief excitement of the work with the cape he remembered that his wife is ill, that there are debts piling up that will mean fighting for one season longer than is wise at his age. One or several of these or similar explanations account for the angry look on his face, but whichever one it is, he feels at the moment the terrible injustice of a world that reserves its loudest applause for the young man who fought the third bull. He hates the bulls and the crowd and all young sandungos toreros. He also hates this old peón, yes, this one with the sallow face who waits nearby to see whether the matador will change his mind and ask him to place a pair of the sticks but without caring one way or the other because sticks are just sticks and in his time he has placed both well and badly every kind of stick you can mention.

But before the sticks there are the horses, aren't there? And here they come, bearing on their backs the stout squat men whose hands have grown as big as hams with holding and jabbing the long lances. Well, what a life, to be a picador; to sit there astride your bony horse, the one you suspect the vet only passed as fit after a nod and a wink from the dealer had sealed the bargain in promised pesetas; to sit there, waiting for the gates to open so that you have to go in and face the howls of derision. What kind of a skin do you grow for that? You would have to develop inner compensatory armour, such as being kind to children and sending money to your old mother down in Seville. Perhaps for you, as the bull comes at you, the bull and the jeering crowd are one and the same, so that you thrust with a will and watch with a certain cold pleasure the point of the pica dig out of the bunched morillo muscle a fine pink meaty crater from which the blood gushes, gilding the sweating black hide. You question that word gild? But it is the right word. It may be a trick of the light but at certain angles the blood that streams down the bulls shoulders has a metallic look, like thick veins of copper-gold in black rock.

You ask (the man in the crimson shirt says) why, with this fourth bull, I sit here and scarcely move, except to shrug or light a cigarette, and why I have applauded nothing since that moment with the second bull when it struck me that Ordóñez attempted an act of charity. Presumably that name given to those passes with the cape, the verónica, is meant as a reminder of what is involved. A man stumbling up a hill under the weight of a cross must be in a muck-sweat. To step forward and wipe his forehead is, of course, an act of charity, you might say an act of love if you could be sure what you meant by that; but above all it is a gesture that helps the man with the cross regain and preserve for a few more steps, before the sweat breaks out again, the sense of composure and the sense of dignity which are supposed to be the distinguishing marks of the larger mammals. I suppose you could make out a case to prove that the corrida may be interpreted not only in all those other ways already mentioned but in terms of the betrayal and the crucifixion: a curious blend of Christian and pagan ritual that leaves you uncertain at the end whether man has killed God and been forgiven or whether man has slain a bull to propitiate God. But then you could probably make out a case to prove that the corrida means anything you want it to mean.

Which is why I have been asking myself: What does it mean to me? What do I read into it? What do I see? In what way, bearing in mind certain things that have happened to me recently in a place called Playa de Faro, does it affect me?

Well of course in the first place there is the blood, isn't there, and the suffering of the animal. The intention I formed to come to Spain but never to go to the corrida was entirely due to a distaste I felt for the idea of an animal actually being baited and killed in the course of a public entertainment. Even before I began to read seriously about the bulls I was aware of the corrida's claim to be recognized as an art, but it seemed as an art to defeat its means by its end as would, say, Rubens's picture of the rape of the Sabines if the action weren't arrested and you had to sit there watching from behind one of the columns. Any piece of sculpture would be monstrous if it moved, and the end of Hedda Gabler unbearable if the actress actually shot herself. I mean monstrous and unbearable in terms of art, not in terms of life because we are, God knows, inured to death by violence, so long as the show is free and we come upon it accidentally and not by design. But here in the corrida is an art that defies the principle of simulation and so is unique. You ask me why in the end I've come to see it. Would you believe me if I said I was here by chance? I'm no longer sure I believe that myself. I think I always intended to come. If it had not been today it would have been some other day. My curiosity has always been stronger than my good intentions.

So now it has been satisfied. When I look in the mirror tomorrow, shaving, the lines from my nostrils to the corners of my mouth will be a fraction deeper and that residual optimism of youth will lie that much deeper embedded. When I watched the first pica thrust I thought: Well, can I really watch this? Isn't it now time to go, even at the risk of being hissed by the Spaniards? Oughtn't I to put back on my expensive Mediterranean sunglasses, gather up the pack of Chesterfields and my lighter, say Excuse me, and push through the line of reluctantly moved feet and knees and impatiently jerked shoulders, down the steps and along the aisle and down those other steps into the subterranean gloom of the complex of pillars that stop the concrete tiers from collapsing in a fine rumble of débris and a cloud of dust; and so back out into the late sunshine to find and extricate my car from that chaotic park, and drive down to a sea-front bar for a drink before going home to my wife, Myra, who will be sitting there alone on the terrace in rather special need, tonight, of someone to talk to because she is alone and although the boys will be back from Figueras and both admire her to the full capacities of their warm but somewhat disparate natures, there is a limit to what she will permit herself by way of intimacy with them?

But I haven't yet got up to go. Obviously I shall stay to the end. Of course, I have always had a strong stomach. Only bad food or too much bad liquor will make me retch. When I found my first wife Mitzi dead of coal gas poisoning I turned off the taps, opened all the windows and rang for the ambulance and didn't even have a brandy until an hour or two afterwards. When the pic first went in, an Englishman a few seats away, a couple of rows down, that one there, covered his eyes. He is a bit younger than I, but perhaps he suffers from dyspepsia, and of course it is Sunday, so most of the tourists will have had paëlla for lunch and are due to have steak to-night, and you can understand the effect of an association of ideas.

But if you come to the corrida you should have prepared yourself for the sight of blood. The pica wounds are a bit deeper than you anticipated, but then the bull is a large animal and although the second bull, Ordóñez's first, hung back from taking another pic-ing after being bitten once, that could be counted more as a sign of its intelligence than as a sign of agony, because the first bull scarcely seemed to notice, did it? It just went on, plugging away, trying to get its horns into the horse and had to be turned away by the capes. So really the first trial of the lances was over before you could think clearly whether or not you wanted to go to all that trouble of collecting your things and running the gauntlet of obstructing bodies, hisses and insults that would hurt your pride and upset your equilibrium. And once the first trial of lances was over you remembered that the next stage was that of the banderillas, and well you know what they say —

– they say that the banderillas irritate and annoy more than they hurt. The idea is that the barbs, holding just beneath the skin, inhibit the contractile movement of the morillo muscle, which is the muscle that comes up behind the bull's neck when it is angry, when it is sandungo, the muscle in which there is already at least one of those pink meaty craters. But apart from that they say that the act of the banderillas is supposed to have a greater aesthetic appeal than any of the other acts of the corrida, unless in the faena the matador brings off some especially poetic effect of humility that convoys his compassion for the animal he is destroying. And there certainly is,

210

with the banderillas, an interesting juxtaposition of form and colour as man and bull converge: the man with his arms raised high, getting up on to his toes, dressed in a glittering suit that fits his body like a glove and gives it no protection whatsoever; the bull, usually black, and just as graceful in its own way, with its horned head low and its big back curved in an arc like a tautened bow ready to let fly; and the banderillas, decorated with frills of red and yellow paper, poised between man and bull. This is the Harlequinade of the plaza de toros, the comic interlude between two melodramatic acts. Its purpose is as merry and mischievous as a scherzo. Of course when it is over and you are left with nothing to look at except the bull with six of the coloured paper darts hanging down its sides you remember that the mischief was deadly, and intended not only to give visual pleasure but to put the finishing touches to the job of bringing the animal to the requisite state of leadenness.

And remembering this you also remember that the work in the last act, with the small red cloth, the muleta, which is hung from a stick to keep it always partially open, is that by which a matador is finally judged. The horns are lower, more dangerous; the cloth in comparison with the cape is an insignificant lure. The bull is more likely to go for the man when he has only the muleta. The slightest wind may move the cloth in such a way that the bull, following the deviation, will get his horns into the torero; by mistake, yes, but that is no comfort to the torero.

So after the banderillas you decide anyway to wait for the faena. You tell yourself that there will be opportunity enough to leave the plaza between the dead exit of the first bull and the lively entrance of the second, and the faena is the faena, the high product of the art. There will be blood, but there may also be poetry. Well, you remember the first faena, that of the senior matador with his first bull? Was it better or worse than the one he is conducting now with his second bull, the fourth bull of the day? You note how they start up the music to accompany it? It reminds me a bit of that old music they used to play at the movies when the girl was sent out in the snow, or when she ran after the truck that was taking her lover to the wars, or of the quicker music that accompanied sword fights, endless chases through streets, prairies, valleys and mountains. When one art fails the thing is to bring in another to help it out, make it look as if it's succeeding; attack your audience on two fronts.

No, this second faena of the senior matador is no worse, no better than the first. The brave music doesn't disguise the fact that between this man and this bull there is a dissimilitude of purpose. The bull is aplomado, not with a desire for death but because it has worked itself to a standstill, fighting for its life. The kill is better, though. Look, he is going in over the horns. And the estoque is in up to the hilt. Everyone is applauding. They are glad to have the opportunity to applaud this older man. It makes them feel good. They remember his performances of ten years ago. The matador feels good too. He is smiling again. He loves the bulls, he loves the crowd, every one of his peóns, his two picadors, and all young toreros, even those in pink suits. He has forgotten his debts, his ailing wife, and the incident of the bota. The president is making a signal. The senior matador will get both ears and the tail as well, for old times' sake and for the sake of today. And I sit on, neither applauding nor deprecating, and again you ask why, and I tell you—

—I tell you why. I sit on because when I consider everything that is going on, quite dispassionately; when I stop trying to identify with the characters or trying to project myself emotionally into the action, when I acknowledge that I am simply sitting here, over-hot, pretty uncomfortable, but perfectly safe, quite unmolested, I realize I don't care. I don't care about the blood, or about the size of the pica wounds. It doesn't bother me to see the bull come in full of life and to know that in fifteen or twenty minutes it will be dragged out dead. I don't care whether the bull feels the pica badly or hardly at all, whether the banderillas sting it, hurt it or merely irritate it. It does not bother me when the sword won't go in properly, and I am therefore not relieved to see it go in deep and true. The bull's blood is its blood and its excreta is its excreta, its life its life, its death its death. The same goes for the toreros, young, middling or old; slim-, medium- or thick-waisted; on form or off; grave, grinning or only cautiously cheerful; brave or cowardly; in debt, rich or making ends meet. I don't care about them. Their lives do not impinge on my own life and their deaths would not be any affair of mine. In the crowded plaza de toros, I sit alone, with a full belly and an empty heart: a two-legged animal with opposed thumbs and a tragic inherit-

212

ance of speech; waiting for the personal revelation of what he really means when he says, as he has said so often, so glibly, for nearly sixty years: I love, I care, let justice be done, teach us to forgive; hoping that once, today, through the medium of this art that is unique because it defies the law of life arrested by artifice, there will be a glimpse of the reality behind the illusion that man can care for someone other than himself.

But there has not been any such glimpse other perhaps than in those few minutes with the cape when Ordóñez artfully or humanely disguised the shortcomings of his first bull as if it mattered to him that the crowd should stop laughing at it and start remembering that it was a creature like any other creature, entitled to pity if unable to inspire envy or admiration or any other kind of fellow-feeling.

And it isn't a case, you know, of there being just one man, that is to say myself, who does not care about the bulls or about the toreros. We are all members of the same disgraced species. The man in that seat down there who covered his eyes when the first pic went in covered them for his own sake, not for the bull's. This old aficionado sitting next to me claps his hands or keeps them still in accordance with some scale of values that is important to him because through it he can arrogate to himself a sense of personal judgment of an art that may one day achieve the standard he sets for it. And he sets the standard at a level no lower than that from which he will feel himself elevated by demonstrable proof and public recognition of his wisdom and sensibility. When he criticizes Ordóñez he criticizes Ordóñez. When he claps the young matador in the pink suit he applauds himself.

Is there a cruel action in the world that any of us will resist if we don't perceive in it, however distantly, a threat to ourselves or to our self-respect? Is there a cause in the world we will support unless by supporting it we feel ourselves individually uplifted? Do we really care a damn about the murder of a million Jews in Europe or about the lone buck nigger lynched in Alabama? I mean care for *them*, care for *him*? No. We don't. We don't. We will only line ourselves up in good causes to the limit of expenditure of the time and energy we think necessary for the preservation of our own peace of mind; beyond that there is the pride of martyrdom, or the enviable inner stillness of the saint.

Ordóñez's turn now; his second bull; the fifth of the day.

Only the men in the ring and the knowledgeable men and women in the plaza can assess in terms of danger, difficulty and beauty, the difference between this bull and the four that have preceded it. But their knowledge can't extend beyond the boundaries of their personalities. Add to that sum of knowledge the sum of the less knowing spectators' impressions and you have a thousand corridas contained in the space of a single plaza; a thousand corridas, a thousand cushions, a thousand roses; four thousand pics, six thousand banderillas, one thousand faenas, one thousand moments of truth, one thousand deaths. And so to the sixth, the last bull: the second and last entrance this day of the young torero who, like the little black hunchback, dedicates to the crowd and walks bareheaded to the wounded beast as if to say:

Toro, Toro, now it is between us two; you in your querencia, I in mine. Come, come, follow the cloth. You are not alone. We all follow the cloth, we are all deluded. Too late you will find the cloth was nothing, that there was no enemy at all other than your pride, your greed, your self-esteem. There is a sword behind the cloth, but that is nothing either, until you have fought yourself to a standstill and found that the cloth was nothing. Then you will see the sword. But not before.

Now it is over. The last bull has been dragged out. The paso doble is coming over the tannoy. I gather up my pack of Chesterfields and my lighter, and stand, move, going with the crowd, making for the car park, leaving behind the tiers of concrete seats, the red barrera and the yellow sand from which this week's blood has already been erased so that next week's can come fresh and clean. In the park, the car engine fires at a touch: a little monument to man's creative genius. The sun is down. Against the violet sky the white walls of the plaza are also a monument.

Perhaps it was under the sand of a plaza de toros that they buried the body of the poet Lorca which it is said was never found.

It is five weeks since I went to the corrida. The playa is almost empty. The sun still blazes from an almost cloudless sky, but at night there is the low grumble of thunder, far off. I get up at six, and swim in the warm deserted sea, and work until ten when I join Myra on the terrace. We drink coffee and go through the mail. When I go back to the study she goes down to the beach. She swims alone. At midday we meet at Señor Rojas's and drink champagne. She asks me how things have gone and I say something non-committal. The tourists have nearly all gone from Playa de Faro, and so sometimes Tonio and Carmen sit with us. We agree what a wonderful season it has been and discuss the weather which is said to be breaking up. There is a danger of floods after such a dry summer.

At two o'clock Myra and I walk back across the playa for the lunch which Lola has cooked and Miguel and Domingo will serve. The sand is already smoother. There are only a few people left to mark it with footprints. We eat under the almond trees and then go to our separate rooms to sleep until five, the hour of the bulls. We shower and change and go down to the terrace and sit, waiting for the dark.

At night the hills seem to be very quiet. Music no longer drifts up from the bars and the hotels and the apartments. You can hear the surf on the rocks below. We sit alone, the three of us: myself, Myra and the uninvited guest. He sits close to her, not bothering any longer with me because I have recognized him. She does not see him but sometimes a gesture of hers, a sideways look, a hand brought up to rub her bare arm as if the evening had turned chilly, betrays her knowledge of his presence. He sits with her on the stone bench. In the moonlight he casts a long shadow. You can see on the flagged terrace the nature of his deformity.

I want to say to her: 'He has been with us a long time, and he will be with us a long time yet. You'd better get used to him. Once you admit he's there it isn't too difficult to learn to live with him. Of course there will be times when you will look at me and think: But I do love Ed; just as there are times when I look at you and think: But I have always loved Myra, I still love her, now I must let her see it, now I must prove it to her. And at those times you will find that the stranger goes away, back into the shadows, where he watches us from behind the pearly blue scales that cover his eyes. After a bit he will come back though, and you'll find yourself thinking: I thought I loved the godling too, I thought I sent him away for Ed's sake, but I sent him away for mine, because this life with Ed is the life I've got used to and I wasn't ready to give it up.

'And so we sit here, Myra, each having made our choice. But there is a sense, isn't there, of opportunity? I once wrote about a man called Biddle who was a missionary like my father and had strange dreams that drove him mad. One day the dreams went and he said, "Thank God, now I can have a bit of peace." But he was wrong. He should have said: Now I can begin to make discoveries.'

10

Returning on their ponies down the track to Darshansingh, she let her husband go a few paces ahead of her and remembered that it was here she had seen the young man on the pony that walked sideways and that she had seen him before that, watching her in the bazaar and riding past the field with the temple in it where her husband painted and she sat on her folding stool, hiding her face from the world under the parasol and the wide brim of the old-fashioned sun-helmet, thinking the thoughts that were more dangerous than the heat and dazzle of the sun.

'He sees me and pities me,' she thought, 'married to that old man. He follows us. He would like to speak. He hopes to find me alone so that he can say: Why are you unhappy? And I should tell him: No, I am not unhappy. When we first came to the hills, to the Panther House, I was unhappy, but this is no longer so. Today I remembered that I was worshipped, and that the man who worshipped me died for me. I used to think he died for shame, but he died because death is the price the world demands for love. This world, this world we move in as my husband is moving in it there, ahead of me, astride his pony, this world has become old and bitter and does not want us to love. The penalties it exacts are harsh, as harsh as the temptations it offers us to incur the penalties are strong, irresistible. The stronger the temptation the harsher the penalty for succumbing to it.'

It was on horseback she first met Ned Pearson who had come to the station to work with her husband. She had just returned from the hills, from the Vale of Kashmir, from a visit to her ailing, ageing, rouged and painted mother. Her confrontation with Ned was on a track such as this, but early in the morning. Seeing her coming he had reined in to give her room. He wore no hat. His hair was the colour of thirsty wheat. He said, 'Mrs. Craddock?' and then, when she looked startled, had said, 'I'm sorry, I should have explained, I'm Ned Pearson.' He rode back with her. He helped her to dismount. His wife was not at the station yet, she was with her parents in Murree. Her name was Lesley.

Thelma said, 'I came through Murree on the way back. You must dine with us. Tomorrow.' In these small matters of her recognizable duties she was meticulous. He thanked her. She went into breakfast. She sat at one end of the long table. Her husband sat at the other.

'I met your young Mr. Pearson,' she told him. He had said the night before that he was pleased with his new assistant.

He asked her how she had met him, then said, 'We'd better have him in one evening,' and went back to the draft minutes that were propped in front of him on the reading stand, alternately buttering toast and turning the pages.

When the two of them were alone she saw the table as an enchanted lake. You could throw pebbles on to its smooth surface but the pebbles would bounce. There would be a sound but no ripple. But when there were other people from the station gathered round it the surface became liquid, misty. Tongues emerged from it like serpents, and coiled unintelligibly, spitting forked words and barbed thoughts. She is dull, they were thinking, dull and plain, and he is dull too, dull and dry, but they are, God help us, above us in the way the world reckons who is above and who is below.

When the guests took their leave she stood there in her strangely hopeless dresses, the repository of their dislike or fear or simple lack of affection for *him*. You could feel from the pressure of their cold hands and the naked revelation of their eyes, the questions: Do they make love? What wouldn't we give to be flies on the wall and watch them beasting under the mosquito net shroud that drapes their marriage bed?

Under that shroud she would lie, listening to him snoring and muttering incantations in his dreams which were the dreams of an old dry man who felt passion only for his work and the slow grinding waste and dryness of his days. He did not snore as her Ned had snored, murmuring his love and warming his hand upon the mound of Venus during the two days they robbed the world of, living naked, starved, savage for love and the infinite variety of means by which they found their hungers satisfied and sharpened: lingam to yoni, yoni to lingam; the congress of the crows.

They rode past the hotel and down through the bazaar. There were men in the bazaar who looked at her and looked away again. She thought: I ride past them and they see only the ugliness, the thin breasts, the penitential shadow of the solar topee. They see only what is there to be seen. They do not see the burning arrows I fire at them, the flames leaping, the hordes of bulls sweeping down to destroy their paper street, their paper houses. They don't understand the miracle of a stone woman riding a stone horse through their destroyed town, leaning in immortal sleep against the stone breast of her lover whose hands they are that are holding the stone reins over mine.

Beyond the bazaar the road curved and then entered a long straight stretch that led to the Dak bungalow. They went past the field with the temple in it and again she remembered the young man whose pony had walked sideways. When they rounded the bend there was a car parked in the unwalled compound of the Dak bungalow. A man and a woman were standing by it, and a young girl and a young man; the same young man who had watched her, the young man she had been thinking of. He would not speak yet because he was not alone, neither was she. Perhaps tomorrow they would meet, and be alone, and he would speak to her then, saying, 'Why are you unhappy?'

There was a movement among the people who stood by the car. The woman and the girl were going. The older man was bending down, wrestling with a picnic basket in the back of the car. But the young man stood upright by the bonnet, watching her. She turned her head away slightly, so that she was looking at the twitching right ear of her pony. As she rode past the car she felt the weight of the young man's gaze. It pressed on her, entered her and was absorbed into the stone.

Now he is in me, she thought. He rides on with me, down the winding road, through the jungle where there are to be seen the langurs and the parrots, and through the opening and along the path of the garden of the Panther House. The long ropes of the lianas stand motionless. Even the sound of the great bells they swung centuries ago is petrified. This evening there is no wind. The tendrils on the verandah are still. The house too is under sentence of silence, the seat of my desire and of my deprivation and of his curiosity.

At dinner her husband said, 'You saw what happened?'

'Happened?'

'At the Dak bungalow.'

'I saw nothing.'

'Perhaps it's as well.'

He pushed back his chair and got up, stood for a moment watching her. Then he went, leaving her alone at the end of the long table. The Panther House was lighted by oil lamps. Insects flew round the globe of the one that was suspended above the table. On the walls there were fly-blown prints of tiger and leopard, and old rusty weapons that had been collected by the man who once lived there and wrote in his diary about the mist on the Mahwari Hills: a sabre, spears, a primitive bow and two crossed arrows. The boy came in to remove the plates. When he leaned over her she smelt the musky odour of his dark flesh. Sometimes he watched her from behind doors. He was afraid of her husband, and afraid of her, but he was afraid of her in a different, subtler way.

She went on to the verandah. Her husband was sitting in a cane chair in the pale light that came from the porch. He was staring into the dark garden.

'What was it that happened at the Dak bungalow?' she asked.

'There were some people there we used to know. I remember their faces. I can't remember their names. But they remembered ours. The woman and daughter cut us dead.'

She said, 'Does it matter? That life is finished.'

'It was the only one we had.'

'Not we. You. It was never mine,' she said. 'You could have saved it for yourself. You could have divorced me.'

He shut his eyes.

'Yes,' he said presently. 'But then I would have been alone. I didn't want to be alone. Perhaps you don't understand that. You're younger than I. And what would have been the point? You would have been alone too. He shot himself rather than face me. He couldn't have cared much for you really, could he?'

'He cared.'

'But he shot himself. He cared only for himself.'

'He cared for me.'

She left him. She went into her room and sat on the bed. She said, 'It isn't true. He did care. He did,' and struck herself on the thighs with her fists and cried again, 'He did! He did! And so did I!' over and over until she was exhausted and leaned back, seeking the comfort of the pillow.

Sleeping she dreamed herself naked, clasped in Ned's arms, feeling the warmth of his cheek against her loins; until, looking down, she saw that it was her husband who clung to her, begging for forgiveness. In each of her hands there was an arrow. She raised them high above her head and stabbed down, pinning them into his bare hunched shoulders. The blood flowed. He cried out, but no sound came.

She woke in terror and was aware of silence. There was no sound tonight of the panther. The panther had gone. Before she slept again she thought: It is I the panther has claimed, I she has taken. Her soul has entered mine. In this way I am reborn. The passion of the panther has become my passion. I long for a child. What I was, and what Ned was, has passed from this dimension of space and time to another. I stand naked in the field of the Stones of Darshansingh, running my hands through Ned's burnished hair, leaning over him as he kneels, naked too, pressing his cheek against my thigh, moaning, finding me with his lips and tongue. I let him draw me down on to the bruised grass. He enters the wound he has opened. With my hands I feel his back burning in the sun. And like this we are turned suddenly to stone, because here a union, an awful wholeness has been achieved between man and nature; and so we lie for ever in carved cohabitation, in the dark and in the light, in the rains, through all the seasons of the year, immortally joined and lying as still as if we were dead so that the birds light on my nipples and on my toes, on his neck, his heels and his marble buttocks. They fly away from us flapping their wings, cooling us in the heat when we have no moisture to sweat. Centuries pass. My cheeks and hands and the long curved column of his back are lichened over. Thunder bounces away from us. The flash of lightning reveals his face, petrified in its expression of ecstasy. The dew settles and we lick these tears of heaven with our parched stone tongues. The heat of the summer scorches our stone bones and the frosts of winter fracture our stone flesh. But we are joined as no man and woman were ever joined before, and only the crack of doom can destroy us.

FINE WORKS OF FICTION AND NON-FICTION AVAILABLE FROM CARROLL & GRAF

☐ Lewis, Norman/THE MAN IN THE MIDDLE $3.50
☐ Martin, David/FINAL HARBOR $4.95
☐ O'Hara, John/FROM THE TERRACE $4.95
☐ O'Hara, John/HOPE OF HEAVEN $3.95
☐ O'Hara, John/TEN NORTH FREDERICK $4.50
☐ Proffitt, Nicholas/GARDENS OF STONE $3.95
☐ Purdy, James/CABOT WRIGHT BEGINS $4.50
☐ Rechy, John/BODIES AND SOULS $4.50
☐ Scott, Paul/THE LOVE PAVILION $4.50
☐ Scott, Paul/MARK OF THE WARRIOR $3.95
☐ Short, Luke/MARSHAL OF VENGEANCE $2.95
☐ Smith, Joseph/THE DAY THE MUSIC DIED $4.95
☐ Wharton, William/SCUMBLER $3.95

Available at fine bookstores everywhere or use this coupon for ordering:

Carroll & Graf Publishers, Inc., 260 Fifth Avenue, N.Y., N.Y. 10001

Please send me the books I have checked above. I am enclosing $_____ (please add $1.75 per title to cover postage and handling.) Send check or money order—no cash or C.O.D.'s please. N.Y residents please add 8¼% sales tax.

Mr/Mrs/Miss _____

Address _____

City _____ State/Zip _____

Please allow four to six weeks for delivery.